THE ATENISTI

AIDAN K. MORRISSEY

The Atenisti

Published by The Conrad Press Ltd. in the United Kingdom 2022

Tel: +44(0)1227 472 874

www.theconradpress.com

info@theconradpress.com

ISBN 978-1-914913-93-8

Typesetting and Cover Design by: Charlotte Mouncey, www.bookstyle.co.uk

The Conrad Press logo was designed by Maria Priestley.

Printed and bound in Great Britain by Clays Ltd, Elcograf S.p.A.

'Your rays, embrace the world,
To the limits of all that you have made…
You are distant, yet your rays are upon the whole land.
You are in all men's faces yet your ways are secret from them

(From 'Hymn to the Aten' accredited to
Pharaoh Akhenaten, Egypt c. 1350 BCE).

This novel is dedicated to all and anyone,
irrespective of age, colour, creed, race or
sexual orientation who has ever suffered
physical or mental abuse of any nature.

CHAPTER 1

London, Sunday morning 8 a.m.

I was about to leave. Their presence in the doorway opposite paused my movement. The same two guys as in the bar last night and now they're here.

Coincidence?

No. I don't believe in coincidence.

'Bloody amateurs,' I said, too loudly.

The clattering of china cups on saucers and Sunday morning conversations came to a momentary stop. Heads turned towards me, a dozen sets of eyes stared disapprovingly. Despite my protestation to the contrary, those men, being in that spot, at this time, was not the behaviour of amateurs. Who are they? How are they here? What mistakes had I made?

'Never enter a building unless an escape route has been identified,' Giacomo had taught me. *Via di fuga* the Italians call it, a very useful concept. This particular West End café, famous for its septuagenarian, coffee-connoisseur owner, and efficient baristas, was already well known to me. Whenever in London I made a point of coming here. Almost a ritual, one which would have to change if it was putting me in danger.

Handing the cashier a ten-pound note and a 'keep the change,' I walked to the white-tiled bathroom, opened the window and climbed out.

I would need to move again. My work in London was finished, so that wasn't problematic. They couldn't possibly know who I really am. Only Chiara and Giacomo know that; even I have to forget the truth sometimes.

There was no need to retrace my steps to the hotel.

'Always leave expecting not to return,' more of Giacomo's wise words. I never disobeyed one of his lessons. He disobeyed once and it got him killed.

I had been looking forward to a few days' isolation at the cottage in the Northumbrian Hills, but that would have to wait. I had almost everything I needed in my back pack and wallet. I could collect my new documents from the locker at Heathrow, Italian passport and ID card, Gianfranco Rossi. It had been a while since I used that name.

Arriving at Milan Malpensa airport was a formality. A cursory check of my ID card by a surly *poliziotto* and a wave of his hand ushering me towards baggage reclaim. No bags for me to collect, I walked straight out of the exit and took the bus to the *Stazione Centrale*. A taxi would have been quicker, but taxi drivers like to talk; bus drivers, and I, don't.

One hundred and twenty-five euros bought me a business-class seat on the three o'clock express. Four hundred and seventy-nine kilometres in under three hours; how the trains have changed since my childhood. I arrived in Rome in time for dinner at my favourite restaurant with a view of the Coliseum.

'*Buonasera Signor Matteo,*' Carlo, the *Maitre D,* said as I entered, using the name I always used when in Rome.

'*Buonasera Carlo,*' I replied. '*Il mio solito tavolo, per favore.*'

He did as I asked and showed me to my usual table.

Time to think and decide on the next job. It wasn't the act

of killing that excited me. That part was easy. They all deserved to die. It was the meticulous planning I enjoyed. Choosing the target. Once inside their head the most appropriate method of disposal usually came to me instantly.

More complex, and therefore more interesting, was choosing who would get the blame for the killing. A clear suspect would deflect the police from looking for me. One thing I had discovered which united the world, is how the police don't look beyond the obvious when they're led to a suspect with motive, no alibi and impeccable incriminating evidence. From Düsseldorf to Dublin, Milan to Mumbai, Seattle to Sao Paulo, the Police everywhere are overworked and susceptible to not searching beyond the obvious. If they started to, there was usually a friend, high up in the department, who would discourage unwanted curiosity.

I didn't like to dwell on past jobs, but London was a distraction. The kill had been quick and clean, the evidence on the computer easy to install, so how had those guys turned up? I needed to put them out of my head, move onto the next project.

I picked up the first of the newspapers I'd bought at the station. It was the *Corriere della Sera*. I didn't have to look far to find the diversion I sought. The headlines were enough.

BAMBINA DI 10 ANNI VIOLENTATA E ASSASSINATA

A ten-year-old girl, raped and murdered.

Outside the window, the Coliseum tourists were milling around in their hundreds. Mopeds and small motorcycles, the favoured transport of young Romans, weaved intricately and dangerously between cars, ignoring traffic lights and pedestrians.

The restaurant's triple glazing protected me from the cacophony of horns and shouting, but the general mayhem, gesticulations and internationally offensive hand and arm signals were all clearly visible. The Eternal City's monumental ruin with huge columns and violent history held a fascination for me. Gladiatorial sacrifice for the entertainment of the populus.

'Let the games begin,' I said, and toasted myself with the glass of Brunello Carlo had placed in front of me without my asking. Carlo knew exactly what I liked to eat and drink and that was more than almost anyone else alive would ever get to know.

All of the papers led with the same story. Kiki Jachenholz, the daughter of a holidaying German lawyer, had gone missing while out sightseeing with her parents in the *Piazza del Duomo* in Milan. Three days later, yesterday, her body had been found at the bottom of a hill beside the *via Cristoforo Colombo*, on the road from Bellagio to Como. Early reports suggested she may have been thrown from a car travelling along that road. No-one had seen or heard anything.

That of course was a lie.

The murdering, rapist scum had seen and heard everything. Did the bastard act alone? I asked myself. Most killings of this type are by men acting in secret and without help – most maybe but by no means all. The number I preferred to deal with generally was two; one to die uncomfortably, and the other to give all the appearance of committing suicide due to remorse or, more frequently, fear of capture. More times than not, a suicide note pointing the Police in the right direction would be left. That was neat and tidy.

Giacomo had always liked neat and tidy, he would not have liked his own crime scene photos. There is nothing neat about having your face chewed off and throat ripped out by dogs.

The meal was wonderful, *ossobuco alla romana*, a simple veal dish cooked with celery, carrots and peas, just enough tomato sauce to permit a *scarpetta* – the traditional Italian way of using bread to wipe up the sauce on the plate. The plate cleaned, using the bread slipper, the bill arrived, cash was exchanged, Carlo gratefully accepted his usual hefty tip.

'*Molto gentile, come sempre, Signor Matteo,*' he said, deftly folding the crisp fifty euro note and sliding it into a pocket.

In Rome cash opens doors better than any key. The small apartment I used in Rome, a welcoming ten minutes' walk away awaited me.

I studied the newspapers and watched the news. Each small detail lodged in the file inside my head. I booted up the computer and gained entry to the Police system. I'm not a hacker and wouldn't have a clue how to break through even the simplest of firewalls, but I had the access codes, updated regularly and informed to me through a well-established system. Being a member of *The Atenisti* had its advantages, a group formed several decades ago by Giacomo.

Like many things about the Atenisti, its precise date of formation was a mystery, even to me. Perhaps there were others like me, other groups; I neither knew nor cared. I would carry out my work for as long as I was able, or motivated, and then die or simply disappear and live out my days in one of the forty-two properties in seventeen countries to which I had access.

Giacomo, a former soldier and diplomat with a passion for Egyptology, was meticulous. Fascinated by the Amarna period of the Eighteenth Pharaonic Dynasty, he had created this group, the name inspired by the ancient worshippers of the sun disk and financed by a multibillion-dollar inheritance.

The fourteen Atenisti, each one representing one of the sun's rays in the hieroglyphics of the period, bought three properties where they believed they would be most useful. The Aten's rays covered the world, so did the Atenisti. I bought the cottage in Northumberland as a safe haven, this apartment in Rome and the lakeside 1960s style boathouse on the Lecco side of Lake Como. That's where I would be heading tomorrow, across the lake from where the girl's body had been found.

The police information soon gave me what I was looking for; the current list of known predatory paedophiles in the area of the kidnap, rape and murder. My own list was not always up to date. The police intelligence gathering over the last three days was exceptional. Scrolling through pages of details, the words I dreaded ended the report; ten letters divided equally into two words,

Snuff movie.

The bastards had filmed the rape and murder, no doubt to sell for large sums on the dark web. Impressively a copy was already on the police files. They must have agents permanently scanning the dark web for such things. Even knowing it to be essential that I watch this film, my hand refused to move the cursor to the icon.

This kind of homemade movie was often an efficient, some-times the only, means of gaining clues to the identity of the perverted perpetrators. I was repulsed at the thought of this one. A young girl's life taken away, a family irreparably and permanently damaged, with anyone forced to watch the film, traumatised, often for life.

Some years ago, I attended a conference organized by the Forensic Anthropology Society of Europe and heard a prosecutor explain how, having watched one such film involving the rape of a three-year-old girl, he could no longer allow his granddaughter to sit on his lap as it brought back such vivid and horrific memories. Why should decent people have to change their lives because of the actions of the detritus of society?

One of my motivations, in doing what I do, is to limit the number of people who are obliged to watch this most despicable of all pornography. I avoid the need for a trial. With no trial, the judge and, in those countries where they exist, juries, would not have to be subjected to the trauma of seeing the life changing images. Victims' families don't need to give evidence and hear the details of the last hours and minutes of their precious children.

Not all my work involves paedophiles, although nowadays it seems a larger proportion of my time is spent on crimes such as this. Normally I am called on to deal with kidnappers or commercially motivated assassins, crimes driven by greed or jealousy, not perversion.

Times change, as do criminals. I agree with the Interpol assessments and remain convinced there exist wealthy, well-run organizations behind the buying and distribution of this sewage. Sick, rich individuals with the wealth to pay others to do what they fantasize about, but wouldn't risk doing themselves.

I couldn't bring myself to watch the film, so kept busy with Interpol, searching for any recently added Green Notices and comparing these to the information gleaned from the Milan police files. My Italian Police accreditation allowed me access to information beyond the reach of public access sites and even the best of hackers.

My accreditation was of a real person, with sufficient rank to allow searching for such information, without suspicion. If he was ever questioned about his searches he would explain that it was part of an ongoing investigation. Giacomo had developed a complex web of like-minded people who believed that the Justice system could only do a certain amount and that there were times when drastic action was required.

Vigilantes the press would call us, and the courts would not treat us kindly if we were ever caught. People like me were never caught. Assassinated, eliminated or liquidated maybe, as had happened in the end to Giacomo, but never caught. One day I would find his killers and exact my own kind of retribution. Not yet. The time didn't feel right and Giacomo taught me to rely on my instincts.

All the research I could face for tonight done, I unpacked from London and repacked for Lombardy, double-checked the train timetable for tomorrow and climbed into bed. I carried out the nightly ritual check of the Beretta M9 I kept under my pillow. Criticised by some as being too big, I loved the ease of disassembly and cleaning it provided. Satisfied it would work if the need arose, I lay back and fell asleep.

Waking without an alarm, showering, shaving and dressing took minutes. Two stops on the *metropolitana* line B, quiet at this time, brought me to the *Termini* railway station. A *cappuccino*, *brioche* and a freshly squeezed grapefruit *spremuta* at the Station Café, I boarded the 06:30 FrecciaRossa train to Milan.

I sank into the leather, electrically-operated, reclinable seat, in the 'silent' area of business class that my freshly purchased 240 Euro Business Area *Silenzio* travel ticket entitled me to. I settled back for the promised two hours and fifty-nine minutes of the journey.

The train arrived precisely on time at 09:29. I boarded the first available train to Lecco and, almost immediately after arriving, I jumped aboard my final train for that day for the eleven-minute trip to my destination.

I disembarked at the small town that was famous for the manufacturing of a brand of motor cycle. Giacomo informed me that this was where the wind tunnel had been invented. I think that Francis Herbert Wenham would take issue with that statement, however it does boast the world's only wind tunnel for testing motorcycle aerodynamics.

I mused about this as I walked from the station. The factory was to my left around a corner, out of my sight. Crossing the street, the newsstand, with its coloured magazines pegged out like washing on a Neapolitan balcony, drew me in.

'*Ciao Emilio,*' I said, to the man who had owned this stall as long as I could remember and who had, so he told everyone repeatedly, never taken a day off sick. He handed me the local paper and very little change without my asking in exchange for a five euro note.

Passing the *Carabinieri* station, in less than five minutes I was at the Lake shore. Turning right, passed the football pitch, the abandoned velvet factory, and the pier, locals used for sunbathing, I continued down the road to the white building with green shutters and flat roof that was my home and main base in Italy.

As I entered, mustiness hit me. It was wonderful living on

the lake but damp was always a problem and, with its low odour-detection threshold, it didn't require many airborne particles to create a strong, unpleasant smell. Shutters and windows flung open, letting fresh air and the gentle westerly breeze, ever present on the lake at this hour, sweep the high humidity outside, dissipated the obnoxious odour quickly.

Thirteen steps brought me down to the garage where my locally-manufactured touring motorbike, named after an American west-coast State, rested under a camouflage green tarpaulin. It wasn't that I needed to conceal my two wheeled treasure, but the heavy-duty cover came as part of my equipment for a jungle warfare exercise and my first encounter with the redoubtable Gurkhas.

Satisfied all was in excellent working order I collected a bunch of keys from a hook on the wall, took the ramp down to the boathouse. As I approached, the doors responded to the remote control in my hand and rolled upwards. The recently-serviced Japanese outboard motor on my boat hummed into life at the first attempt. The boat, specially adapted to enable me to transport my motorbike to most marinas in the area, made living and travelling around the lake even more fun than it was for tourists. Content the engine wouldn't stop in the middle of the lake today, wasting valuable time, I prepared for departure.

At best, I had forty-eight hours to identify and deal with my target, or targets, before the police net would close in on them.

I already had an idea who I was looking for, and the Police would either know that too, or it wouldn't take them long to figure it out. As of last night, the Interpol Green Notice had not yet been linked with the Police report but it surely would be soon. A Belgian national, recently returned from Cambodia, where a child-trafficking arrest warrant had been issued a few hours after he had successfully left the country and landed in Switzerland, was who, my gut said, I needed to find. Interpol had been informed of his arrival too late and they had lost all trace of him shortly after he landed in Zurich.

He had hired a car at the airport under a false name. This had been found abandoned at a Swiss Service Station on the A2 near Bellinzona. The rest area was undergoing renovation and the CCTV cameras were conveniently temporarily out of action. I don't believe in convenience in such circumstances.

Bellinzona, the capital of the Ticino canton and famous for its three medieval castles, is only an hour and a half from Milan. The abandoned car was found three days before the girl was abducted.

The Interpol report said he spoke fluent German, so could feasibly have convinced the girl to go with him. Her lifeless and mutilated body had been found the day before yesterday and she had not been dead long, so he had no more than two days head start. Two days; so much can be achieved in forty-eight hours. Theoretically, he could already be back in Belgium, or anywhere else in the world.

He would know the Police would start looking for him, to eliminate him from their enquiries if nothing else, so he needed to keep a low profile. This meant avoiding airports or other places with heavy security cameras. I know this part of Italy well, the various ways into Switzerland, the local trattorias and hotels.

I could never think like a paedophile, but I could think like a fugitive and that was where I had an advantage over the Police. They would assume he had moved as far away from the area as possible, I believed he would stay. His Interpol profile showed photos of him with and without facial hair. I would know him if I saw him.

I donned my leathers and darkened glass-visored helmet, loaded my black machine on board and set off across the lake. I headed diagonally across the water to a small marina attached to a restaurant. I didn't go into Bellagio as it was always full of water taxis and tourist boats. I tied the blue hawser to a freshly painted green cleat on the small pier, set the ramp and disembarked together with the bike, parked it, and entered the restaurant. I wanted to get an idea of the place the body had been found and from here I didn't need to go into the crowded tourism mecca.

The restaurant owners were not around and I was served by a young, efficient and definitely unsmiling waitress I had never seen before. Perhaps she was in a hurry to finish her shift and leave, there was no extraneous talk. It was late for lunch, almost at the end of service; the restaurant was sparsely occupied. A few local women taking their time over coffee and glasses of red wine.

The *Menu di Lavoro*, the daily cheap but filling lunchtime specials which included pasta, a main course, today it was local fish, a glass of wine and coffee for less than the price of a gin and tonic in the tourist areas of Rome, was thrust at me in silence. I imagined the sound of foot tapping as the waitress hovered with pad and pen. I ordered the *penne all'arrabbiata* and a glass of red wine, it was wonderful and spicy. Food was one of the best things about living in Italy.

I finished my lunch before the ladies had finished their coffees and chat, so it wouldn't be me who faced the rising ire of the waitress.

I drove along the high road towards Como. A Police road block was the clearest of all signals I had found the place I wanted to see. Two uniformed officers, standing beside a blue car with *Polizia Locale* emblazoned on its sides, questioned everyone who passed. These were the local police, not the *carabinieri* who would be leading the investigation. I stopped, showed them my Italian ID card and my press accreditation in the same name. They made it clear that journalists were not welcome so I didn't linger. I had seen all I needed to whilst waiting for my interview.

On the opposite bank of the lake, the dark-green railings and open shutters of my house stood out against the white walls. I followed the road towards Como, then headed for Lecco and took the Lakeside road through Malgrate back to the restaurant and my waiting boat.

Once home, I walked to the local budget supermarket and bought rice. Tonight I was going to make *risotto alla Milanese*. I wanted to use the remnants of the saffron I'd bought in a market in India. I needed something heavy on my stomach if I was going to watch that film.

CHAPTER 2

Lago di Como, Tuesday morning: 6 a.m.

Sickened by what I had seen, I didn't sleep well.

Images from the thirty-minute film I forced myself to watch twice, made me shudder as they replayed repeatedly in my mind. The first run through had been at normal speed, but with no sound. The sound would have been too much to bear.

I imagined Kiki's pleas for the agony to stop; not understanding what was happening to her. I didn't need to hear the real thing. It had been particularly sadistic and horrifying. The second run through was in slow motion and at times frame by frame. I ignored what was happening and concentrated on the man in the film.

As always his face didn't appear, but other parts of his body, his hands, fingers, torso and at one point an ear drifted in and out of view.

One thing was obvious.

The camera was being held by a second monster. Each was as guilty as the other and both would pay my price. The lens zoomed in and out to get all of the disgusting and gory details. Courts require strong evidence, my threshold was slightly lower, although I also needed to be certain.

I had ways of obtaining the truth which modern police interrogation couldn't achieve. I didn't subscribe to torture, at least in the physical sense, but putting pressure on someone with the threat of violence was not the same thing. At least in my opinion.

I had learned a lot about the rapist. I couldn't yet say for certain the same man was the murderer, that might have been the cameraman. In a sense it didn't matter, other than deciding on the order and manner of their deaths.

My tourer motorcycle had large paniers; thirty-five litres each according to the specifications. I packed into them what I needed for two days and set off on the hunt. Kiki's innocent face with its distinctive features was now burned into my mind. I was even more convinced that the Belgian was the guy I needed to eliminate.

The Interpol Green Notice listed several names for him, Luc Peeters, Peter Maes, Martin Pauwel and Paul Pieters, which immediately struck me as having a pattern and connection. There were three standard name derivatives. Peter, Martin and Paul. Somewhere in those three names was his real one. Not that his actual name mattered but the search for him was made that little bit easier by his lack of imagination.

My names are chosen at random from names on grave headstones. Perhaps, because of my work, I find peace in cemeteries, particularly those in England and America. Vast green fields where everyone is sleeping. Many as beautiful as parks but without the crowds. People who visit cemeteries are normally private people. Going to respect their dead, through love, guilt or duty, they lay their flowers, think their thoughts, sometimes speak a few words and then leave. Occasionally a smile at other visitors and a *Good morning* but generally no attempt at long conversation.

I quickly checked for any updates on the Interpol Notices, there was a new name which immediately caught my eye:

FERGUSON Edward
Age today. 40
Nationality. United Kingdom

To the side was a space for a photograph. There was only a faceless grey outline and above, was written, *No photo available.*

This had never happened to me before. This was me; this was the name I had used in London. There is no such thing as coincidence. I moved the mouse to the entry. The name turned red, a blue circle with a white *i* appeared with the word *Details* beside it. Another page opened.

Again, the name appeared on the top of the screen with the faceless grey icon at the side. *Wanted by the judicial authorities of the United Kingdom,* was written underneath. There followed a more detailed description of the person they were looking for. This added nothing; the details of date and place of birth, languages spoken and nationality were all wrong but roughly matched the details of that alias. The physical description was vague.

Then came the charge: *Details as provided by the judicial authority.* I read the entry out loud.

'Murder, unlawful handling of firearms or essential components thereof or ammunition, perverting the course of justice.'

The final words on the page were, *This extract of the Red Notice has been approved for public dissemination.* I would need to access the Red Notice at some point. This is where information *To seek the location and arrest of a person wanted by a judicial jurisdiction or an international tribunal with a view to his/her extradition* was detailed and open only to certain police and judicial authorities.

Everything was so vague, perhaps I shouldn't worry. I couldn't use that alias again and the documents, relating to it, would need to be destroyed the next time I was in England. I didn't use that name either entering or leaving the country, so there would be no photographic trace of that person at the airports. I had obeyed Giacomo's instructions and had found a small anonymous hotel, outside the city, without security cameras, in an area of CCTV black spots. I was more curious than concerned, at least I tried to convince myself of that. The issue was neither immediate nor logically dangerous. It could wait; I couldn't allow distraction and had to concentrate on the work which I had undertaken.

The first stop in my search would be Bellagio. It was a cliché to say, find a needle in a haystack, however, it was a cliché for a reason. Where is the best place to hide? Unless you have access to a property in the middle of nowhere then always head for a crowd.

At this time of year Bellagio is full of tourists; one or two Belgians, or whatever they may be, would go unnoticed in the small town at the end of the promontory. Known to the Italians as the Pearl on Lake Como, this one-time fishing village had become a destination of the stars. No trip to Northern Italy would ever be complete without a visit here.

The lake's beauty is unsurpassed, which is why it has become the home of the rich and infamous. Not the town of Bellagio itself, that's too small and the properties surrounding it are never available on the market. Most are owned by institutions.

I was told by Giacomo that there were only eleven lakeside properties in the area of Bellagio that were in private hands. He owned one of those, or rather his family did. When he was alive, I was a frequent visitor. It was his presence here that led me to buy my house on the opposite side of the Lake. With binoculars it was possible to see each other's house and this had proved useful on a number of occasions.

I climbed the green metal steps to my rooftop terrace. No matter how many times I stood here I never tired of, or failed to marvel at, the magnificent views. The cloudless sky and bright sunshine created a blue hue on the rippling water. Small waves lapped the shore below creating a rhythmic, soothing sound. Beyond the houses the peaks and rocky slopes of La Grigna created a dramatic backdrop. Still capped with snow, even at this time of late spring, *my mountain* dominated the skyline. The tiny dot of refuge *Elisa* was visible, bringing back memories of walks and climbs, alone or with friends in my youth.

I reluctantly drew my gaze away and looked back across the lake. The traffic was already heavy. That narrow road linking Lecco with Bellagio was bad enough when it was quiet, even on a motorbike. Overtaking opportunities were minimal, particularly when hordes of cyclists decided to have an impromptu road race.

I didn't want to take my boat as I wasn't sure I would come back the same way and didn't want to leave it moored anywhere for more than a few hours. It might attract attention. So I rode the fifteen-minutes to Varenna and boarded the first *traghetto*, a ferry which linked the Lario side of Lake Como with Bellagio and also the Swiss town of Menaggio.

It was feasible that Peter, Paul or Martin had taken the ferry to Menaggio, but there was the possibility of a passport check and, unless he had the kind of resources I have, I doubted he would want to risk that yet.

'Stay calm, stay low,' Giacomo would say.

The short ferry crossing was uneventful. Cars and motor-bikes with number plates from all over Europe shared the deck. Predominately German, French and Italian there was a UK and Dutch plate and some from Poland, Rumania and Hungary.

I was at the front and the first to ride up the ramp. The ferry dock was right at the entrance of the town. I turned left and parked up in a row of other motorbikes, opposite a souvenir shop and next to the tables of a three-star restaurant, less than thirty metres from where I disembarked.

The hotel building was opposite, next to the shop. Tables with matching brown cloths and fabric chair covers on both sides of the road were a statement of ownership. It was busy even at this hour. Fortunately a table cleared on the roadside just as I removed my helmet, so I hastily sat down. Tables here were at a premium. I began to move the used cups, saucers and plates.

'I'll do that, sir,' a waiter said in perfect English. This was the default language of all the waiters in Bellagio. If the response came in Italian they would flip effortlessly into their own mother tongue. I did so now. Many spoke several languages and could easily help most customers with the five major languages of the European Union. Being a waiter was still a source of pride in Italy, unlike in many other countries.

I ordered a *cappuccio*, what the locals call the famous frothy milky coffee, along with my usual *brioche* and freshly squeezed grapefruit juice. I sat and waited. The waiter brought my order.

Typical in tourist regions he also brought the bill, which I paid in cash. I opened the small packet of sugar which had been placed on the saucer and poured the contents down the side of the cup. I don't know why I had developed this habit. Perhaps it was because, as a child, I didn't want to disturb the melting chocolate powder sprinkled across the top. I inserted the teaspoon also down the side and stirred underneath the foam.

The rituals completed, I took a drink. My first bite of the brioche was still being chewed when he appeared.

I couldn't believe my good fortune.

He walked straight out of the hotel door opposite and sat down at a table, he was clean-shaven and appeared not to have aged much from his Interpol photograph. I needed to get closer to him if I was to be sure he was the guy in the film. The marks I was looking for could not be seen from this distance.

The table next to him was vacant. I would need to move carefully and couldn't just pick up my breakfast and walk across. It was essential to bide my time and hope the table wouldn't be taken before I could get there.

I drank the last of the grapefruit juice and stood up. I was about to start and walk over to the souvenir shop before making my way to the target table, arriving from behind, when another man approached the Belgian.

This couldn't be true.

This was the third time I had seen this man. The first two times had been in London, now in Bellagio. He was one of the two guys outside the café the day I left. My mind went through a dozen possible scenarios. None of them good.

The man smiled as he approached the seated rapist. He raised his hands, palms upwards in front of his chest, then joined them together as if to pray. I had seen this gesture before.

'*Namaskār*,' he said. '*Tu kasā āhes?*'

I froze. This was the last thing I thought I'd hear. I left Mumbai a year ago, swearing never to return. Now, close to my home in Italy, I hear the familiar Marathi greeting by a man who seems to be tracking my every move. Worse than that, the Mumbaiker salutation was being made to my target. The repercussions of what was happening began to dawn on me. I needed time to think. The body of a young girl found virtually in sight of my home, the Interpol Notice, and now this.

I pulled on my helmet, went to my bike and powered up the engine. I drove once around the car park to check; the two men were sitting, talking amiably. I turned up the hill and around the one-way system for the five-minute ride. I knew where I had to go. I took the road towards Lecco and turned into the long private road that led back down to the lake and the house owned by Giacomo's family. His wife greeted me warmly.

'*Ciao, carissimo*,' she said. 'Do we need to talk?'

Chiara was formidable. One of the original Atenisti, she was the only person alive I could trust with this.

We talked.

CHAPTER 3

One year ago.
Lago di Como, Italy and Mumbai, India, day one:

The call from Giacomo came as I was relaxing on the terrace. 'I need your help,' he said. 'Can you come to Mumbai, or are you working anything at the moment?'

'No,' I replied, 'there's nothing which can't wait. What the hell are you doing in India?'

'I'll tell you when you get here. There's a flight booked for you under your BA Gold Card name and a hotel room is reserved in the name on the passport you can collect at the usual place in Malpensa. I'll come and meet you when you arrive.'

No names or specific details were ever given over the phone.

Giacomo must have known he might have needed my help. It was not a quick process to forge a passport, particularly one with a visa. Chiara had obviously been working overtime to sort that out.

'The usual place in Malpensa' was a restaurant car park about two kilometres from the airport. There, in a silver Mercedes, Chiara was waiting.

'Tell him to be careful,' she said. 'I don't have a good feeling.'

There were no direct flights from Milan to Mumbai, so I was booked on the overnight from Heathrow. I was pleased my business class ticket for the long-haul leg was upgraded to First and, after arriving in London, I enjoyed an extremely good steak and an excellent Bordeaux in the Concorde Room in Terminal Five before boarding Flight BA 199 five minutes before the gate closed.

The Cabin Crew director greeted me at the door with a smile. She looked at my boarding pass and showed me to seat 3A. Before I had a chance to sit down another member of the crew handed me pyjamas and slippers. I took these to the bathroom and changed, then hung up my jacket, shirt and jeans in the small wardrobe on the side of my seat. I intended to go to sleep as soon as the seatbelt signs were switched off and my bed could be made up.

The nine-and-a-half-hour flight turned into eleven hours, with delays taking off, due to congestion, and further hold ups on landing. Mumbai Airport authorities had decided to carry out repairs to the main runway and this had caused some flights to be cancelled and others, like mine to be delayed.

We touched down at the Chattrapathi Shivaji International Airport a little before one o'clock in the afternoon local time. The airport, named after the seventeenth century founder of the Maratha Empire in western India, was relatively new and only opened in 2014.

I walked towards passport control, which was so far away, after five minutes, I felt I should have taken one of the people buggies on offer at the end of the air bridge. However, the artwork and statues all along the walkway walls were worth the physical effort.

I had always imagined India to be a country of poverty. The magnificence of this airport belied that impression. Modern, yet traditional, this was a different world. Multi-limbed goddesses and elephant headed gods mixed with scenes of life in modern Mumbai and Bollywood films. Had I been so wrong about India?

Having expected crowds at passport control, I was pleasantly surprised. Despite the people buggies overtaking me at frequent intervals, there were only ten people in front of me in the queue reserved for First and Business Class customers.

There were no problems with my passport, visa or the arrival card I had been given on board to complete. I wasn't happy that my photograph was taken but there were some things beyond my control.

With no luggage to collect I headed for the exit. A long queue had formed.

What's this for? I asked myself.

It was another security control point for hand luggage. I was used to such checks leaving airports but never when arriving. I liked to get in and out as quickly as possible. There were always CCTV cameras and standing in queues gave people time to be spotted. It didn't matter I had never been to India before, was not on any wanted list nor under an international arrest warrant, at least in my present guise. Cameras make me nervous. I wanted to be out.

Once through, the arrivals hall was empty. Not the usual crowds of parents greeting children, men with flowers in their hands waiting for their girlfriends or *Welcome-home* banners. Through the glass wall I could see the reason for the emptiness. The crowds were outside. Security concerns, since the 2008 terrorist attacks, mean Mumbai doesn't allow non-passengers into the terminal.

The first thing that hit me as I walked outside was the heat and humidity. This was late May and the hottest, most sultry time of the year, just before the monsoon winds blow in the rains.

How was I going to find Giacomo in the horde of people which now filled my view? Hotel courtesy car drivers in their grey, black or brown suits, families straining their necks for a glimpse of their loved ones, a crowd of faces twenty or more deep all facing in my direction behind a steel barrier.

There were exits to join the throng both to the left and right. I looked but couldn't see any familiar face. Most exiting passengers seemed to move to the right, so I followed. It was the correct decision. As soon as I passed the barrier, I saw Giacomo standing next to a tea vendor. Beside him was a short man, in his thirties, wearing open toed sandals, jeans and a white shirt which was not tucked in.

Giacomo greeted me. The short man took my backpack and we followed him towards a car park. He stopped beside a small blue and white sedan with the words *Cool Cabs* written on the side. My luggage was placed in the boot and Giacomo and I sat together in the back. It took us over an hour to drive the sixteen kilometres to the Five Star Hotel in the *Ghandi Nagar* area of the city. Traffic was at a standstill

'Is the traffic always as bad as this?' I asked.

'No, sometimes it's worse,' replied Giacomo. 'It has, on occasion, taken me almost four hours to drive twenty kilometres particularly during monsoon.'

The rest of the journey was mostly in silence. The driver, whose name was Pathik, probably couldn't speak more than a few words of English, and he certainly couldn't speak Italian but we live in the age of smartphones where everyone has the ability to be a spy. Recording or filming can be done anywhere and at any time with translation coming later; better to leave conversation until we were alone.

The road was along the so-called Western Expressway. The name was at best ironic as I doubt we exceeded twenty kilometres an hour for any of our journey and most of the time we sat, bumper to bumper with yellow and black taxis, more blue and white cool cabs and private cars. This was worse than Brazil, and I didn't think anywhere could have been as bad as Saõ Paulo for traffic.

I picked up the *Hindustan* Daily newspaper which Giacomo had been reading; it was left folded at page 3. The headline read:

THREE-YEAR-OLD CHILD THROWN FROM MOVING CAR IN WHICH HIS MOTHER WAS RAPED BY TWO MEN, IS SHOWING GOOD SIGNS OF RECOVERY.

Muzaffarnagar, Uttar Pradesh: Another incident of gang rape sees 26-year-old mother raped by two men in a moving car. The woman's 3-year-old was getting in the way of the attackers so they threw the child from the moving car. The incident took place on Monday evening on Delhi-Dehradun national highway.

Local people discovered the injured child and rushed him to hospital. Doctors say the child is out of danger, now.

The young mother was later dropped from the car and reported the incident. The attackers were known to her and had enticed her into the car on the pretext of offering her some work.

I turned to Giacomo and pointed to the article. 'It seems like it happens every day here,' he said. Any person listening to a recording could think he was talking about the traffic. He held up five fingers. I turned to page five.

POLICE ARREST STEPMOTHER, THREE OTHERS FOR RAPE AND MURDER OF GIRL, 9.

I couldn't believe what I was reading. If the newspaper account was accurate, Indian police had arrested a woman and three boys or men after her nine-year-old stepdaughter's decomposed body was found, hidden behind bushes, about a kilometre from her home. The girl had been reported missing by her father ten days earlier.

Physical condition and preliminary forensic analysis of dead body indicate gang rape, murder and mutilation said a police statement issued on Tuesday.

A Police Inspector leading the investigation informed this reporter that the arrested woman, aged 34, was jealous of her stepdaughter, and on May 15 took the girl to a secluded wooded area. Signed confessions inform that she there directed her own 14-year-old son and his two teenage friends, aged 16 and 18, to take turns in raping the child.

The woman's son has admitted that under direction of his parent, he used a belt to strangle the girl while one of his friends hit the child on the head with an axe. Another friend went to his home and returned with car battery acid which the woman sprinkled on the body whilst one of them gouged out her eyes before dumping the corpse in the bushes.

I felt physically sick. I had heard some horrific stories in my life and learned of disgusting things being done to innocent children, but this far surpassed anything I had ever come across.

I looked at Giacomo, he shook his head. 'Later,' he whispered.

I finished reading the article.

'A local police Superintendent later confirmed to this newspaper that the teenage offenders confessed to the crime and their stories corroborated the evidence. They will be sent to a juvenile home and will be dealt with by the courts according to the juvenile law,' he said.

I dropped the paper on the floor and gazed out of the window.

An enormous bridge structure came into view. It looked as modern as the airport. Two giant wishbone shaped pylons tied down with rows of cables dominated the skyline.

As we approached I read the sign. Anything to try and avoid thinking about the newspaper articles.

'Rajiv Ghandi Sea Link. Toll Charges Car: Single Journey 60. Return Journey 90 Day Pass 150.'

Without stopping, Pathik handed a piece of paper to the toll booth operator. I assumed it was the return part of the ticket he had bought on the way to the airport.

We drove along the eight-lane bridge, four for each direction. Speed limit signs showed eighty kilometres per hour and there were frequent signs saying *No Stopping* and *No Photographs*.

'Five minutes, we arrive, sirs,' Pathik said, as our journey over the sea ended and we were back on dry land.

'Thank you Pathik,' Giacomo replied.

I remained in stunned silence. The slight diversion of reading signs and seeing a small ship half submerged less than fifty metres from the bridge could not remove the images in my head.

I hadn't even read beyond the first few paragraphs of the first article about the three-year-old thrown from a moving car. I couldn't believe how desperately depraved both of these stories were.

Arriving at the hotel, the car was halted inside the large metal gates. A security Guard signalled Pathik to switch off his engine and open the boot. He held a mirror under the bonnet whilst a second guard with an overweight and disinterested Labrador circled the car and opened the boot access.

It would have been relatively easy to place a bomb which that search wouldn't have found, however, I would never put an explosive device in a car in which I was being driven.

All safely checked, we drove around to the main door. The car doors were opened by red coated porters.

'Welcome to Mumbai, sir,' the one on my side said.

'Welcome back Mr. Fratelli,' I heard being directed to Giacomo. I realised I hadn't ascertained which name Giacomo was using. At least now I knew his surname.

We passed through a metal detector into reception. My backpack was taken off for x-ray checks.

The 2008 terrorist attacks on several five-star hotels and other targets in which 164 people died, was still fresh in the memory of Mumbaikers and extra security concerns were not restricted to airports. This particular hotel had escaped the atrocities being well away from the access point the terrorists had used, but like everywhere, security had been stepped up. From what I ascertained it was, however, half-hearted and more for show than being an effective deterrent.

I checked in, Giacomo said that everything was to be posted to his corporate account and I went up to my room accompanied by the receptionist and a porter carrying my backpack.

'I've arranged a room on the same floor as me, so we can

communicate more easily. You can only have access to your own floor in this hotel. It'll save having to meet in the lobby or at the rooftop bar which is open to all keys,' Giacomo said as we arrived on the thirtieth floor.

'Room 3028 for you, Mr. Johnson. This way to the right,' said the concierge, whose name badge told me was called Dakota. Real name or not I was unsure.

'As soon as you're settled come and see me in room 3001 in the opposite corridor. Are you hungry?' asked Giacomo.

'A bit,' I replied.

'I'll order room service, they do a great *rajma masala*.'

I entered my room. It was much bigger than most rooms I had ever stayed in. I removed my jacket and threw it down on the large, white linen covered King size. The porter came and placed my backpack on a long stool at the end of the bed. He looked as if he was waiting for a tip but I was totally bereft of Indian currency. I pulled a five euro note from my pocket.

'No that's OK, sir, it is not necessary to tip.'

His lips and eyes were telling two different stories.

I unpacked the backpack.

Trousers, jackets and shirts I placed in the walk-in wardrobe. Underwear and socks in a drawer in the mahogany chest underneath a fifty-inch TV screen. My computer, I placed on the glass covered writing desk, the wood matched the drawers where I had placed my underwear. I opened the sliding door to the bathroom and placed my soap bag on the shelf between the twin sinks. I pushed open a door in the bathroom to find the toilet. There was a shower and bathtub which was situated beside an uncovered window. Returning to the main room I was faced with a bowl of apples, pears, kiwi fruit and grapes

34

in the middle of a small glass table placed between two green armchairs. A postcard, which showed a man carrying a great number of small tins on a wooden board balanced on his head, was beside the fruit. I turned it over.

'Welcome to Mumbai, Mr. Johnsson,' it read in neat black ink, misspelling my false name. I hope you enjoy your stay. Best wishes A.P. Singh General Manager.'

I walked over to the built-in fridge, found it fully stocked with beers and spirits and chocolate. This was luxury.

At least I thought it was until I entered Giacomo's room, 3001. He opened the door, dressed casually now and the first thing I noticed was a dining table surrounded by six chairs. An L-shaped settee dominated one side of the room and behind that was a desk, twice the size of that in my room. Doors led off in all directions. One, I assumed, was a bedroom, another the wardrobe but there were still three or four doors leading to who knows where.

Giacomo saw the expression on my face. 'I got an upgrade,' he said and laughed.

We sat on the couch.

'Am I here because of the reports in that paper?' I asked.

'No,' said Giacomo. 'Those stories are more horrific than most, but that is the kind of thing you read here every day. Our job is to deal with one or more kidnappers and hopefully the safe return of the seventeen-year-old daughter of one of the richest men in Mumbai. I'll give you all the details.' A doorbell rang and Giacomo got up to answer it. A well-dressed young woman in a red coat came in with a wheeled table.

'Your food, Mr. Fratelli. Shall I serve?'

'Just leave everything there thank you,' replied Giacomo.

'We're not quite ready.'

'OK. Please call room service when you are finished and we'll clear everything away.'

She handed Giacomo a bill and pen, he signed, took a five-hundred-rupee note from his pocket and gave everything back to the girl.

'Thank you,' she said and walked out through the door, closing it quietly behind her.

We sat at the table and ate the Punjabi rice and bean dish, which I enjoyed as much as did Giacomo.

'The chef has given me his recipe. I'll make it for Chiara when we get home. The *rajma* are simply red kidney beans, soaked in tomatoes and onion and then cooked together with a wide range of spices; coriander, turmeric, Kashmiri red chilli, cumin, *amchoor*, *garam masala*, garlic, ginger and anything else you want to throw in.'

'That sounds like a complete spice shop on a single plate,' I said. 'But it is delicious.'

The meal was accompanied by a well-known Italian wine, which I usually bought in my local supermarket for fifteen euros.

'That's more than a hundred euros here,' Giacomo said.

'Then I think I'll drink beer from now on,' I said. 'That price is outrageous.'

'Tax,' said Giacomo. 'India is a country whose religion doesn't like alcohol, but which can't do without the revenue.'

We talked until the sky outside started to lighten and the soulful sound of a *muezzin* chanting out *Adhan* from a nearby mosque, filled the air.

CHAPTER 4

Present Day
Bellagio, Tuesday 4 p.m.

I descended the seventy-five steps to the lakeside terrace and waited for Chiara to return. She had driven into Bellagio. With a greater number of contacts she would be able to access hotel records better than anyone.

She returned with a photocopy of a passport.

'He's using the name Peter Martens. Room 236. He's booked in until the day after tomorrow,' she said. 'There's no other Belgian registered there. Of the Indian, there is no sign. I don't think he is staying in Bellagio.'

'He's probably renting a house next to mine across the lake,' I said, only half joking. There were too many elements of this crime which were pointing in my direction. Am I being set up? Or is there something else being planned for me?

'I have the access codes for the CCTV from the hotel where Martens is staying. Let's go take a look.'

I walked up the steps behind Chiara who, despite her seventy years, managed them effortlessly. We went across the gravel courtyard and passed the table, big enough to seat twenty, and entered the house. We sat in the office she had shared with Giacomo, with a view over the lake. Pictures of him and them together were on every spare piece of wall and free surface. I didn't see a single picture of their son, but then I didn't expect to. His protection was too important to them.

She sat down and logged on to her computer. A large TV screen was attached and it was on that we watched the morning meeting between my target and Shadow. It had lasted no more than ten minutes. The Indian shook hands, passed something over to the Belgian and left, heading towards the ferry terminal.

'Let's leave Martens for now,' Chiara said. 'Let's follow the Indian.'

She quickly pressed a few keys on her computer and another CCTV image appeared.

'This is from the ferry terminal.'

The Indian, now nicknamed *Shadow one*, walked straight in line with the camera as if he didn't know it was there or as if he wanted to have his image captured. My suspicion fell on the latter. He didn't go to the ferry. He entered a car which was in the line waiting to board the next boat. This car, driven by another person, pulled out of the line and drove off in the same direction I had taken when I left.

'They could be heading anywhere,' Chiara said. 'We have their registration, so I'll start investigating.'

'Thank you Chiara. I think I'll head back into town and see if I can make sure Martens is the person we're looking for.'

'Stay and have something to eat. Miguel has prepared ceviche.'

'When I've finished what I have to do, with pleasure. For now I don't want to delay. Thank you for everything,' I said.

'It was nothing, a piece of paper and some CCTV.'

'I don't mean today, Chiara. I mean for everything.'

She smiled, kissed me on both cheeks and walked with me to my waiting motorbike.

'Take care, *carissimo*, Giacomo and I are very fond of you. If I find anything I'll let you know.'

I parked in the same place I had this morning. I walked over to the hotel and asked for a room. They had one available. I took it, and paid cash for one night. The receptionist didn't ask me to sign any register, or for a copy of my ID, so I assumed he was going to pocket the cash for himself and pretend I didn't exist. That suited me. If Martens was only staying here two more nights, I would need to act quickly.'

There was no sign of him around the hotel, so I went out for a walk. With my leather biking jacket removed and tied around my waist, my mirrored sunglasses and white T-shirt, I looked like a hundred other bikers in Bellagio that day. Strolling through the town I kept to the low streets.

I wanted to walk to a restaurant at the very end of the peninsular, with its open views towards Switzerland. The food was good but at tourist prices. I wasn't heading there for the food, although I was hungry. Sooner or later everyone visiting Bellagio comes here. I hoped my early luck this morning would be continued. I tried to forget the Indian connection.

'Deal with one thing at a time, concentrate. Prioritise and concentrate.' Giacomo's instructions were clear.

Priority one: Always make sure of your own safety.

Priority two: Identify and eliminate the perpetrator.

Priority three: Identify and eliminate the patsy.

I agreed with everything he said. Today, though, I might move the priorities around a little. I owed it to Kiki to get her justice. I owed it to all the young children in India I wasn't able to help, and I owed it to Giacomo and Chiara. My debt to them I could never repay.

At this time, between the lunchtime rush and evening service, the restaurant was quiet.

Sitting down, I asked the waiter for a non-alcoholic *apperitivo*, which he promptly brought. The orange liquid served with ice and a slice of orange accompanied by potato crisps, peanuts and olives which added several euros to the price. Still, the foreign tourists enjoyed this and they paid the waiter's wages.

I preferred to take my *apperitivo* well away from tourist traps, in bars and restaurants filled with lively conversation. Men from the ages of sixteen to ninety sitting around arguing about football, politics or both, drinking prosecco and beer. Where the food, served with the drinks, consisted of small slices of pizza, squares of focaccia, bruschetta, frittata and dozens of other bite size delicacies. *Stuzzichini*, the Italians call them, from the verb *to tease*. The French do not have a monopoly on *amuse bouche*.

Today I contented myself with the olives and the days-old peanuts. I sat, drank, snacked and waited. After the second drink a man walked past and sat down at the table next to me.

I vaguely recognised his face, but couldn't place him. I hated when this happened. I generally only took note of faces if the person meant something in relation to my work. It could have been an old case. I tried to concentrate but nothing came to mind.

He placed a newspaper on the table, and ordered a beer. He spoke Italian but his accent was Germanic. The beer arrived with the trio of tourist tit-bits and he picked up the paper and began reading. It was the *Frankfurter Allgemeine Zeitung*. It must have been from yesterday or earlier. Foreign papers took a day or so to arrive in Bellagio. If it was from today, he must be a new arrival and have brought it with him. He appeared too comfortable to be a new arrival. He was reading the front page attentively. It was taking him a long time. An occasional half-smile altered the shape of his mouth.

Who is he?

Perhaps he was reading an article several times. He was half way through his beer when the person I was hoping to see walked up the steps to the restaurant terrace. The German obviously saw him, folded the paper in half and put it on the table in front of him. I saw Kiki's smiling face peering out of a photograph. Images from the film hit my consciousness. There were no smiles in those flashbacks. The German stood.

'Peter, *Wie geht's?*'

Using the informal verb showed they knew each other well. Many Germans even after knowing a person for years, still used the formal, *Wie geht es Ihnen,* when meeting. Knowledge of language was important in my work. The way a person spoke could tell you a lot about interpersonal dynamics or how a situation was likely to unfold.

'*Schlecht, danke,*' Peter replied.

Saying it was going badly meant all was not what he hoped. 'Our Indian friend told me the Italian is on to me. I'm leaving in the morning.'

They were standing right beside me as they shook hands. It gave me the opportunity I prayed for to check what I needed to see. On the Belgian's right hand, on the fleshy part between thumb and index finger was a small but clear tattoo. I hadn't been able to make it out properly from the slightly out of focus single frame it appeared on the screen but now I could see that it was a kind of monogram, combining the letters *J* and *K* in a

41

very floral style. Like the German, it seemed vaguely familiar, but I couldn't place it.

That wasn't the only thing I needed to see on his hand, the handshake also enabled me to see his thumb nail.

It was there!|

I've got you, you bastard, I thought. The only way you're leaving tomorrow is in a body bag.

The clinching mark for me was a subungual hematoma. These two marks together would be sufficient to convict him in a Court, but I couldn't wait that long for justice.

As their hands separated, I saw something else. Not on the Belgian, but on his German friend. He had exactly the same tattoo in the same place. His thumb was clear of any blood blisters so he was not the rapist but there was obviously a connection. I wished I could remember where I knew him from. It would come to me, if I concentrated I was sure of that. Was he the one behind the camera? I would deal with that next.

As the two men continued their conversation in German, I was only half listening. I had my target and I knew where he was staying, at least for tonight. The snippets of their conversation I did catch infuriated me and made the task I was to do even easier.

'*Ein anderes Mädchen kommt.*' Another girl is coming

'*Acht Jahre alt.*' Eight years old.

'*Aus Thailand.*' From Thailand.

The bastards were planning another, this time the girl was only eight years old. I hoped by killing these two she would be safe, but maybe all I would achieve is for her to be passed on to another in the gang. I had to get to the bottom of this.

I kept going back to the tattoo. J and K, I repeated over and over, as my silent thought processes moved through the gears. Or is it K and J? No, that would be too much of a coincidence, and such things don't exist. Kiki Jachenholz was the victim; they were her initials. Maybe some kind of trophy mark, like fighter pilots put on their jets?

I soon discounted that. It was already on his hand when he performed the disgusting rituals I was forced to watch last night.

The same tattoo on the German meant something else. Was it something sinister and more threatening?

Perhaps my belief in an organised group was not far away from reality after all. I needed to find out the meaning of the tattoo. Some form of sign for members of the group? A rank in an organisation? Or innocent friends who had tattoos done after a drunken night in Amsterdam or Hamburg? The possibilities were endless.

I needed to prepare. I called the waiter over and paid the bill. I spoke in the same Oxford English I had when I arrived, which drew no attention from the two men. There was more English and German spoken in this town than Italian in the tourist season.

The German's face was still bothering me as I reached the Hotel. In reception there were a number of foreign papers, the *Allgemeine* was one of them and the same edition as I had just seen at the restaurant. I took the paper folded it and went to my room. There were a number of things I needed to do. I called Chiara.

Information obtained, I changed clothes, packed my few things and went out to the bike, pushed my used clothes into one panier and from the other collected a bag Chiara had given me earlier. I returned to the hotel, entered the Belgian's room.

Having completed my preparations for what was to come I walked back downstairs. The receptionist nodded as I passed.

I took a seat on an outside table by the hotel entrance and ordered a glass of prosecco, it's what tourists do. I occupied my time people watching, and there was plentiful opportunity for that.

It was two hours before Peter Martens came walking down the street on his own. His gait was random. I hadn't stayed long enough at the restaurant to see what he had ordered to drink, but it was clear he hadn't stopped at one.

He leaned against a wall and leered at a couple walking in the opposite direction with two small children. The look on his face made me want to go over and slit his throat. I had seen what he was capable of and needed to make sure no other child was subjected to what I had seen him do last night; not by him; never again.

Chiara had been sitting on a table on the opposite side of the road. As I followed Martens into the hotel, she walked over and sat down in my place. The Belgian paid no attention to me following behind him up the stairs; he paid no attention as I matched his pace along the corridor to his room; he did, however, pay attention when, as he unlocked the door, I tapped him on the shoulder and broke his nose with the grip of the pistol I held in my gloved hand.

He continued to pay attention as I crammed a damp cloth into his mouth, the intricate chemistry of the liquid immediately calming him. The anaesthetic-imposed atrophy made him less attentive as I tied him, hands and ankles, to the bed, using the straps I applied earlier. Any muffled sound he made was inaudible outside of the room.

I touched my finger to my lips and picked up the knife I had left on the bedside table. It was big; it was sharp. I saw the fear as I held the blade fractionally above his left eye.

After the rape, that's where he had started with Kiki.

'You're going to die,' I said. 'That much you know already. The manner of death will depend on what you now say.'

He nodded. I removed the gag, its work was done.

I had a maximum of ten minutes, but he didn't know that.

'Who paid you?'

'I don't know his name.'

'That is not what I want to hear. After this, I will ask you questions only once and I want an immediate answer. Understand?'

He nodded. 'But I don't know their names. They send me instructions on a secret App and pay me straight into my bank account.'

'Where are they from?'

'All over.' I lowered the knife until it touched his now closed eyelid. 'Mostly Russians and Indians living in Dubai,' he added quickly.

India again.

'What does the tattoo mean?' He seemed surprised at the question.

'I waited one second, then two. I looked him in the eye so he knew my intention.'

'It's a sign so we can recognise each other if we meet,' he said.

'Who?'

'The group. The ones we share the videos with.'

'Who is the German you were with tonight?'

'Just another member of the group.'

'Where have I seen his face?'

'I don't know.'

His speech was beginning to become unclear. I didn't have as much time as I thought.

'What do the initials K and J mean?'

'Kinderjäger,' he said.

'Child hunter.' I was going to have to find that German.

I didn't want to ask, but the image would not go away. I needed to know.

'Why did you take her eyes?'

'They're for him. He collects them.'

'Who?'

His facial contours changed as if he was having a stroke. Cerebral dysfunction and heart failure was setting in. The final phase had begun.

'Indian,' he slurred, pronouncing the word as if he was in a black and white cowboy film talking about a Native American. 'Keeps them in a jar.'

There would be no more useful information from Mr. Martens. I waited until I was sure he was dead. I removed the straps checking they had left no marks or indents which might excite an over enthusiastic forensic scientist. Meticulously, I put everything belonging to me, back in the bag and left him there. If it wasn't for the broken nose he would have looked as if he had collapsed in a drunken stupor.

I straightened his nose and wiped away the blood, flushing the tissues down the toilet. A post mortem would show he died of heart failure. The poison, which also acted to help liberate any secrets he held, would dissipate within six hours.

The Russians were experts at such things.

His death had not been as uncomfortable as I would have wanted. His associate would not be so fortunate. However the circumstances were such that today had to be quick and quiet. I took the newspaper and threw it on the floor beside the body, perhaps the local police would make the connection with Kiki.

As it fell I saw the bottom half of the front page. Kiki's smiling face was still there. Underneath, was another photo, this time of the family. Kiki with her mother and father, in happier times. A normal family in a normal family pose. Except this was no normal family. The father in the picture was the German I saw meeting Martens only a few hours before.

Vomit rose in my throat. I forced it back and ran out of the room.

I had to appear calm but sweat poured out of every pore as I walked down the stairs. I saw concern in Chiara's eyes as I walked past. She nodded slightly and followed me. I went straight to my bike, she to her car.

At her house, I told her about the German. She confirmed she had taken the CCTV recordings from the hotel and planted the necessary virus in the computer system to ensure no visual trace of our being there would ever be found.

I had found my next target, but I would need to calm down before I approached that task. The way I felt now would not be conducive to a cool and calm execution.

I kissed Chiara as I left and went home. I needed to be more at ease and, for that, I needed to be alone. As I rode along the narrow lakeside *cul-de-sac* towards my house a car passed me going in the opposite direction. The registration was familiar, so were the occupants. It was Shadow One and, beside him, was the second guy from London. These had to be my new priority.

I parked my bike at the end of the road and logged into the house CCTV on my mobile phone. The images were clear. What had they left in the post box?

CHAPTER 5

One year ago
Mumbai, India; day 2; 6:30 a.m.

Giacomo recommended room service breakfast. I ordered a fresh fruit platter and orange juice to start. They didn't have grapefruit. To follow, poached eggs, bacon, beans, wheat toast and peanut butter. All washed down with a strong Assam tea.

I was ready to start the day, even though I only managed about three hours sleep. My mind was still reeling from the horrors of what I had read yesterday. This wasn't helped when I opened the newspaper delivered with my breakfast.

UTTAR PRADESH - 35-YEAR-OLD MOTHER OF TWO GANG RAPED BY FIVE, DRAGGED TO TEMPLE AND BURNT ALIVE ON YAGYA SHALA

Residents of Uttar Pradesh's Sambhai district have been left shell shocked by the news of the 35-year-old woman allegedly gang raped by five men and later burnt alive in the yagyashala of a temple in the close vicinity of her house. Police have taken evidence from the victim's husband and have issued an FIR against five named suspects. All efforts are being made to nab the perpetrators before they can leave the district.

Reports indicate that the victim had called up UP Police's Dial-100 emergency help line but that her call remained unanswered. Unable to call her husband or brother as their phones were not reachable, the victim called her cousin and was able to name her five attackers who unlawfully entered her home at around 2.30 a.m. on Saturday morning and took it in turns to rape her. She was able to relate the events prior to the accused coming back to her house before Police could be informed, dragging her to the temple and after dousing kerosene over her, set her on fire and ended her life.'

Uttar Pradesh, a state in the north east which borders the area of Delhi, seems to be at the centre of many sex related crimes. The depravity of burning her in a Temple on the *Yagya Shala*, the platform on which religious fire ceremonies are held, seems to plunge new depths.

Such actions cannot be possible in the twenty-first century. How can someone who professes to adhere to the teachings of a religious sect perform such vile perversions?

Only my first full day in India and already I was beginning to regret coming here. I tried to reason with myself. This cannot be possible. The country, ruled by Hindu values, of not harming others and the benefits of *karma* could never allow such things.

How wrong can a man be?

There were, of course, many articles bemoaning the number of rapes in India. Bollywood stars crying out for action; they were wasting their tears. The editorial stated that 106 rapes occurred in India last year. Not in the whole year, not every month, or even every week but 106 each and every day. What horrified me even more was that forty percent of these were attacks on minors. My head couldn't fully comprehend.

According to the paper, In any given period of twenty-four hours more than forty children are raped in this country. Five or six of those under the age of twelve.

Perhaps the stories I read yesterday were more horrific than most but it didn't deflect from the fact that this was a horror beyond imagination. It got even worse as I read on;

in almost 95 per cent of these crimes, the perpetrators are the victim's relatives including brothers, fathers, grandfathers, sons or connected with work or school.

What kind of morality can permit such things? What kind of religion could give succour to these degenerates?

I ripped the newspaper into as many small pieces as my temper dictated and threw it into the waste bin. I must find Giacomo, I want to get this job done, salve my conscience by dealing with a few of these animals and then get the hell out of the country.

The television was on without sound, a preview of a film to be shown this evening about English retirees coming to a non-existent hotel in India to live out the rest of their lives. I had seen the film and much of what I thought I knew about India was based on that idealistic blend of chaos and humour. An internationally renowned film industry, passion for cricket and exotic spices.

Everyone knows India or do they?

I called Giacomo's room and he told me he was ready to go whenever I was. I must have been knocking on his door before he put the receiver down.

'Where in the name of God have you brought me? Forty-two kids a day raped in this country, and that's only the reported cases'

'You need to stay calm,' he said. 'Yes, there are many problems with Indian society, particularly among the less educated, but you can't change the world.'

'I can change a few people's world,' I said. 'We have to start somewhere. Rome wasn't built in a day but it all started with a single brick,' I clichéd.

'Let's concentrate on what we are here to do,' Giacomo said. 'After that, you can return to doing what you want. I need your full concentration on this task.'

I nodded but my mind couldn't escape the horror that, while I had been eating breakfast, at least one child had been sexually violated.

'We are meeting the Indian private investigators who believe they know where the girl is being held,' Giacomo explained. 'Our job is to get her out and eliminate her kidnappers.'

'All in a day's work,' I said, knowing that Giacomo hated clichés.

We walked down the short driveway of the hotel and hailed a very small yellow and black cab.

'Where's your suitcase?' I asked Giacomo. 'Remember what you taught us. Always leave as if you will not return.'

'I'm sure I'll be OK in this hotel and on this occasion,' he said.

'Do as you say not do as you do?'

Giacomo smiled. 'That's three clichés. You're not going to get me riled, but please, enough already!'

He gave the driver the name of the hotel we needed to go to and we sat, cramped together, in the back. We crawled along for about ten minutes when the wishbone supports of the Sea link came into view. All along the sea wall multi coloured plastic elephants were having their photographs taken with lines of people.

Walking or jogging the length of the Seaface, as it was known to the locals, seemed to be the daily exercise for many in the area. We crossed the bridge and turned left soon afterwards. The signs told me we were heading for Bandra. Our destination was a hotel I had seen out of the taxi window twenty minutes earlier. Mumbai roads were certainly complicated.

Giacomo was greeted formally by a man wearing a suit. His hair, the colour of jet, was oiled to his head.

That has to be a wig, I thought, immediately nicknaming him, Slick.

After introductions we moved to a raised area and ordered the local *masala* tea. Spicy, sweet and milky it was another new experience for me. With Slick were two other men, neither of whom spoke during the entire meeting; Slick did enough of that for all three of them.

'Our observances have procured for us a very valuable information,' he said. 'The girl is in an apartment less than half a hundred yards from here.'

What's wrong with saying fifty? I thought, already disliking this man.

'Rohtakji instructs us to act immediately, without hesitation and rescue the girl today itself. She is in mortal danger and must be saved.'

Along with the other five women and children raped while we've been sitting here, I wanted to say; but resisted.

'Wait,' Giacomo said. 'We can't just go knocking on the door. We need to watch and wait. Assess the risks, act in the best way to ensure the safety of the girl.'

'We don't have time. Rohtakji is leaving for Dubai first thing tomorrow. This must be resolved by then. He has matters which need to be organised and he must know the girl is safe. Freedom must be secured by today only. He agreed for you to bring in help. He is paying very handsomely and he demands a return for his investment.'

'He is not paying enough for us to take a bullet by going into a situation without full reconnaissance. No money could buy that.'

'He is paying you enough that his instructions are to be obeyed without question.'

Giacomo and Slick exchanged glowering stares. It was Slick who broke the silence. I would have bet on it.

'Furthermore,' Slick continued, 'you are not to speak with the girl, or allow her to say anything. She must be passed over to us and then you must deal with the foul perpetrators. Rohtakji wants silent efficiency and no conversation.'

I knew how Giacomo's mind worked. We thought very much alike. There was something not right about this job. We both knew it. What is it that Rohtakji doesn't want us to know? We would find out, of that I was sure.

The kidnappers' hideout proved to be a large apartment on a very expensive road. There was a crowd of people outside of one house we passed.

'Famous Bollywood actor,' Giacomo answered my unasked question.

At the security gate three doors down, Slick talked with the guard. Several red-coloured notes changed hands and we were ushered through. Another security guard was standing on a tiled entranceway beside a lift. More cash, this time the notes were light-brown, passed from hand to hand and the guard accompanied the three of us to the lift. The silent assistants remained at the entrance.

On exiting the lift, Slick walked up to a door and pushed the bell on the side. A three-tone sound was announcing our arrival.

It was all too casual, too low key, what was going on?

My hand moved to the pistol Giacomo had given me this morning, tucked in my belt under my jacket.

The door was opened by a boy, late teens, bare feet, brown slacks and striped T shirt. He didn't look like a kidnapper to me.

Slick pushed him against the wall before he had a chance to speak.

'Take him out,' he said, far too easily and casually.

He's been watching too many bad TV shows, I thought.

Giacomo walked over to the boy curled up in a corner trying to push himself inside the plaster wall.

'Please don't, uncle. I haven't done anything.'

'Do as you're told. Kill him.'

Giacomo stayed silent. He always did when working.

'We are not murderers. He seems harmless to me,' I said.

Giacomo shook his head. This was one of those times when waiting and watching were needed, and preferably in silence.

Slick moved across the lounge area. As he approached a door, on the far side, a girl in jeans and a bright yellow shirt with a rabbit motif, walked out. She saw Slick and screamed.

Another boy came out from the same door followed by a second girl.

The girl in the yellow shirt turned and tried to push past them, but Slick grabbed hold of her long black hair and pulled her down on the ground. He knelt on her stomach.

'Get off me, you're hurting me,' she said. This was followed by a string of words in Hindi or Marathi. I had no idea what she was saying but it didn't sound pleasant.

Slick responded in kind, simultaneously taking a cloth from his pocket and stuffing it into her mouth.

'You be silent,' he said to the girl in English. 'It's time to come home.'

She shook her head vigorously.

'Ne, ne, ne,' was all she was able to say.

Slick pulled out a gun and pointed it at the young couple. He motioned them in the direction of Giacomo and me.

'Mr. Fratelli, your job is to dispose of those three kidnappers. I'll take the girl home.'

'Wait,' said Giacomo. 'This doesn't seem like a kidnapping to me.'

'She was removed from the care of her loving family, by these criminals. That is kidnapping.'

The girl's wide brown eyes seemed filled with fear and she shook her head furiously.

'She must be returned and they must never be allowed to speak about it,' Slick continued. 'Rohtakji was informed you would do that without question. He paid you and now you must do as he asks.'

'Please uncle, we haven't done anything. Priya is our friend. She asked for our help.'

'Shut his mouth or I will,' Slick said, standing up and pointing the gun at the cowering figure in the corner. Giacomo nodded, releasing me to spring at Slick and in one move disarm and floor him.

'We don't murder innocent people. Money is not our

motivation, it's justice. This isn't right,' I said, my face so close to Slick I could smell the minty odour of the sweets he sucked constantly.

'Priya, you're safe,' Giacomo said, 'and if your friends are telling the truth, no harm will come to them. I promise you. What is going on?'

She pulled the gag from her mouth. 'It's my father,'

'No,' shouted Slick. 'I told you, don't let her speak.'

Giacomo walked over.

'I don't take orders from you, Rohtak or anyone else. I also do not take money. Rohtak is paying me nothing. I was asked to come here by Diamond Insurance under the policy Rohtak has against family kidnapping. He pays them. I do my job which is limited to the needs of the insurance company, the safe return of the kidnapped person, nothing else,' he said.

It didn't go unnoticed that Giacomo dropped the respectful 'ji' suffix to Mr. Rohtak's name always used by Slick. 'Please, Miss Priyanka, talk to me.'

'My father is evil. He's forcing me to marry a business associate living in Dubai. I'm supposed to be there tomorrow for the *Sakhar Puda*,' she said. 'The engagement ceremony is scheduled and my father cannot lose face by not producing me. My friends have been trying to hide me so I can't go. The man is fifty years old and I've never met him. I am only seventeen I don't want to be married. My father is forcing me to marry him.'

Giacomo looked down at Slick.

'Ben, you stay here with Priya and her friends,' he said, using the name I had checked into the hotel with. 'Mr. Deepak Shitole and I will pay a visit to Mr. Rohtak. I need to make some things clear to him about who we are, what we do and where our obligations end.'

'OK,' I said, thinking that, to my European ears, Slick's real name was a better description of him than mine.

'Protocol three,' he said, as he walked out the door.

That was the last time I saw him.

CHAPTER 6

Present Day
My house Lago di Como. Wednesday 4 .a.m.

The instructions in the letter, left in my post box by the Shadows, were clear.

I was to be in Mumbai, at the same Hotel I had stayed when I last saw Giacomo, next Monday. I would be contacted there. To encourage me, there were a number of photographs. Two were of Giacomo. In one, he was gagged and tied in a chair. The other was similar to the photograph I had seen before. Giacomo with his face and throat savaged. This photograph had one major difference. The dogs were still attacking him.

The other photographs showed Priya's three friends. They were sitting together in a bar. I thought they were safely out of Mumbai. They certainly were when I left. Someone clearly knew their whereabouts. In the foreground of one of the photos was a newspaper, obviously held by a person next to the photographer, perhaps trying to disguise the picture being taken. It showed a date five days ago. Under the photograph was a caption in red ink.

The dogs are hungry.

It was a trap, of course it was. I had two choices. I could ignore it and let them do whatever they wished with the three young, innocent teenagers. Alternatively, I could accept their invitation and succumb to whatever game they wanted me to play. The first option was not a good idea. They clearly knew how to find me and if I didn't go it might be worse. The second option seemed to have no advantages over the first.

I always thought best in the early hours. Perhaps there was a third alternative, but even this was not one I liked very much. It would mean I'd need help. Not something I dealt well with.

Help meant reliance and trust in others.

There were only two people I could totally rely on in my professional life. One was dead, the smoking embers of the photographs of his corpse fluttered in the downdraft of the *caminetto* in the corner the room. The other was a seventy-year-old woman who was too precious for me to place in danger.

My bike pulled up outside of Chiara's gate. Removing my helmet I rang the video call system. It was 6 a.m. but she answered the call herself and when I drove down the drive to park outside the garage she was there to greet me.

'I've been expecting you,' she said. 'Don't look so surprised. I accessed your CCTV and saw your Indian friends posting an envelope.'

'Is there nothing secret from you?' I asked, trying to feign exasperation.

'Not much,' she replied. 'So what was it?'

I handed over the note and the photographs of the three teenagers.

'Is that it, or are you hiding something from me?'

'Not hiding, but I did burn the other photos. They were of Giacomo. I didn't want to look at them again and you certainly don't need to see them.'

'I saw the photographs from the Indian police. Were they

any worse than those?'

'No, in fact one of them appeared identical. It was the other that was a concern. The dogs were still attacking.'

'And?'

'And what?'

'What did the other photo tell you? What do the photos together tell you?'

'I'm not sure what you mean.'

'No,' she said. 'That's what worries me. You are becoming emotionally involved.'

'Of course I'm emotionally involved. It's Giacomo for God's sake.'

'And you're not helping him by failing to focus. Be careful, *caro*, you are risking your life as Giacomo risked his.'

A silence fell between us, giving me time to think. What was it about the photos?

I broke the silence, Giacomo would have bet on that.

'How could the photo have been identical?' I asked.

'That was my first question too,' she said.

'They came from the same source,' I said. 'But how?'

'There are several possibilities. The Police were implicit in the act. The photo you received yesterday was lifted from the police files. The similarity was pure coincidence and a photo taken from the same angle of the same scene. All of those are possible.'

'No,' I said. 'The photos were not similar, they appeared identical in every way.'

'What did the second photo tell you?'

'That Giacomo was already dead or so heavily drugged he couldn't react to the dogs.'

'Anything else?'

'That's it.'

'Are you sure? I wish you hadn't destroyed the photos. I would have appreciated seeing them for myself. I have some suspicions, but without the photographs to check them against, they remain only suspicions.'

'How can you even think about looking at the photos of Giacomo?'

'I have, in my life, seen many much worse. Other members of my family. I have to ignore who the person is and concentrate on the evidence.'

'Even when it's your own husband?'

The horror must have shown in my voice as she appeared hurt by what I'd said.

'Especially when it's my husband. Do you think this is the first time I've seen family snaps like this? My parents were killed by a car bomb. It exploded directly beside them. There were only pieces of them remaining. I had to bury those pieces. I had to study the photographs of the scene and look for the evidence. Find the truth, hidden behind the obvious. There is always a story to be told by photographs. I had to track down the bastards who had ordered the hit. I slit their throats and watched them die. One of them was living near Milan, with his wife and an Alsatian dog. Do you know what he named his dog?'

I remained silent.

'No? No? He called it "Bomber." 'The arrogance of the man.'

She pronounced the dog's name like most Italians, vocalising every letter; *Bom-bair;* but her meaning was clear.

'His wife was spared because she had walked out and left him the day before I arrived. The dog was not so lucky.'

'I'm sorry,' I said. 'I didn't know. You told me they died in a car accident.'

'Did I? Are you sure?'

Then I realised. In Italian the word for 'accident' and 'incident' are the same - *incidente*. She had told me they died in a car incident but let me believe it was an accident.

'You were in South Africa when they died, Russia when I buried the pieces of them that could be found, Germany when I killed the first murderer and Brazil for the second and his dog. You didn't need the extra pressure.'

'I'm sorry.' I repeated.

'I don't want *sorry* from you.' She paused. 'I want clarity. I want you to deal with this exactly as Giacomo and I taught you. I want you to be professional, but most of all, I want you to be safe. Please don't let me have to look at photos of you.'

'I'll try,' I replied weakly.

'What I don't understand, is why?' Chiara's eyes looked far into the distance.

'Why what?'

'Why they want you to go to Mumbai.'

'They want to kill me.'

'But why Mumbai? Why not just kill you here?'

'Maybe they don't like the odds here.' My attempt at humour fell on stony ground.

'Don't be facetious. There is something not right about this. If they just want you dead they don't need you in Mumbai.'

'Perhaps they want to make me the star of a snuff movie, like Kiki, and they need the comfort of somewhere under their control to do that.'

'Even if that was the case, that could be done here as well as anywhere. It doesn't make sense to me.'

'It didn't make sense last year when they got Giacomo and me to rescue Priya. Slick had a gun, he could have gone on there and done what he wanted. Why were we there?.

'They had the insurance policy so you didn't cost them anything extra – and if it went wrong it would be easy to blame the foreigners.'

'Maybe, but I'm not going to find the answer to those questions sitting here. I need to go.'

CHAPTER 7

One year ago
Mumbai, India Day 3: 3.30 p.m.

'Protocol three,' Giacomo had said.

The word *protocol* meant nothing; we didn't work with protocols. But the *three* meant simply: *If I'm not back within three hours, get out and deal with the situation you're in.*

I waited exactly three hours. With no sign of him I told the four youngsters to pack essential items only. I found a safe place to stash the gun. Airport security systems and personnel have a tendency to react badly to firearms. We went downstairs. There was no sign of Slick's friends. We couldn't go back to look for the taxi or my backpack. There was nothing in it of any importance, clothes are easily replaceable.

We hailed a cab. All four of them jumped into the back, I had the *luxury* of the front passenger seat all to myself.

'Airport,' I said.

'Which one?' asked the driver.

'Terminal 2.' It was Priya who spoke from the back seat.

'Terminal 2,' I repeated for no reason. 'Are you four OK in the back?'

'Sure,' came a reply from one of the boys. 'This is how we travel by taxi in Mumbai.' They all laughed.

We spilled out of the motor under the wide canopy. We

were stopped at the terminal entrance by a police officer. Only travelling passengers were allowed inside. Priya spoke to the officer who called over to a man in a blue shirt and matching name tag.

'Wait here,' Priya said. 'They will only let one of us in to buy the tickets. What's your name?'

'Benjamin Johnson.' I replied. 'No credit cards.'

Priya nodded and the rest of us moved to one side as rows of people with suitcases piled high on baggage trollies went in. All had to show tickets and passports as they did so. Priya returned after about half an hour.

'We have forty minutes to wait before our flight. Let's go.'

This time we were all allowed to enter. Priya and the others headed for security control.

'Wait,' I said.

They followed me to the first ticket office in Lane 3. I bought a business-class ticket for myself and economy tickets for them to Chennai. I deliberately paid with Ben Johnson's credit card. It was a tactic which might delay anyone checking our whereabouts.

'OK,' I said, 'Let's go to Delhi.'

I picked up a newspaper and soon wished I hadn't.

Not the headlines but at least this one made the front page.

RAPED 1-YEAR-OLD, FOUND WITH HEAD SMASHED IN. SUSPECT SEEN ON CCTV

I read on.

A one-year-old girl, asleep next to her parents on Mumbai street was allegedly picked up and taken to a nearby place by a man who then raped her and smashed her head to the ground, police said yesterday. The removal of the child from beside her sleeping family was captured on CCTV cameras in the area. Continued on page 7.

Priya, who was sitting beside me, noticed the article too.

'This is a sickness in my country,' she said.

'It's more than a sickness,' I replied. 'I can't believe how this can happen in the twenty-first century.' I was reluctant to discuss my opinions with a girl who was a child herself.

'It is because much of this country, particularly among the poor and uneducated, does not act as if they live in the twenty-first century. In parts of India, particularly in the north, it is not unknown for the *panchayat*, the local council, or its leader, to order rape as a punishment for a girl who they deem to have acted against the religion or tradition of the village.'

'Rape? As a punishment?'

'Yes,' she said. 'In one case a girl of twenty years only, was gang raped by all thirteen members of the tribal council. Her crime? She was having a relationship with a Muslim boy.'

I was dumbfounded. She continued.

'We, the young and educated people of India, are as sickened by this attitude towards women, as much as you are. But until the government decides education and moral guidance are more important than sending rockets to the moon, we can see no hope in things changing.'

One of the others joined in. It was Ganesh, the boy who had answered the door to the flat when Slick rang the bell.

'Even the educated are living in the past,' he said. 'This is a country where marital rape is not a crime, unless your wife happens to be under the age of fifteen that is.'

'Under fifteen? What age can people get married?' I asked.

'Legally, eighteen for girls and twenty-one for boys. That's what the law says, but it's widely flaunted. Even in my case, I am not eighteen for another six months but my father has arranged my marriage for two weeks' time only.' Priya said.

'But, you're almost eighteen. What about the children as young as seven or eight who are married in the villages? They never go to school and spend their lives in virtual slavery to their husband's family,' said Ganesh.

Our flight was called. We were all in boarding-group one so were amongst the first on board. I sat in the aisle seat next to Priya. A short round-faced man with a moustache sat by the window on the far side. Ganesh and the others were together in the row opposite.

'My father's a lawyer,' Ganesh continued the conversation interrupted by the boarding announcement. 'He was in the Supreme Court and heard a judge say that it was not possible to have a straitjacket formula for the marriageable age of girls to fit every case.'

'Indian society is full of complexities,' Priya said. 'Age-old beliefs, many condemning women and children to lives of drudgery, infest society. We suffer from cultural and social interdictions, outdated rites and customs. Ours is a country dominated by ignorance and poverty. Many in rural areas perceive marriage as the only option for girls even before they reach puberty. Early marriage can be a means of securing both the parent's and young daughter's future.'

I was admiring the knowledgeable and erudite way in which these two teenagers were talking when the moustache by the window started shouting at Priya.

He was speaking in either Hindi or Marathi. His spit was heading in my direction. Priya let him carry on. When he had finished she turned to me.

'This gentleman says that I should shut my mouth and not speak lies about my country to a white monkey. He says that girls with tongues like mine deserve anything that happens to us. We should be grateful for what God has given us and be silent.'

I guessed she had translated reasonably accurately as moustache decided the view from the window was fascinating.

'Excuse me Priya,' I said as I leaned across her. I grabbed the man above his knee with my large hands and squeezed my thumb and forefinger against the ligaments. This was painful, both to his leg and his pride.

'Don't rattle this white monkey's cage,' I said. 'He bites.'

I let go of his knee. The man said a few words.

'Does he understand?' I asked Priya.

'I think he does, finally,' she replied. 'That is, he understands to stay quiet. I doubt his attitude to women and children has moved out of the dark ages.'

We continued our conversation and I learned a lot on that two-hour flight. Particularly about these four teenagers, whose education had not been limited to the school classroom but augmented on the streets of Mumbai and Delhi. Helping in voluntary organisations trying to better the lives of desperate prostitutes and their fatherless children, they saw much of the underbelly of modern Indian society.

They spoke with a maturity and knowledge which belied their years. I had been condescending in my thoughts that they were children. These were young adults, and impressive ones at that.

I learned of the work being done in Kamathipura and

Garstin Bastion Road in Mumbai and Delhi by social workers and volunteers of all ages trying to bring safety and education to the workers in two of the biggest red-light districts in Asia. How young Nepalese and Bangladeshi girls are bought from their fathers in their home countries and brought here to make money for their owners. This is slavery in its most vile form, but it is up to NGOs to try and help the hundreds of thousands of young women and their children.

'HIV and AIDS have forced the Government to take some action, but this is pushing the trade further underground.' Priya said. 'It is not enough. We have all participated in the *Rakshin* Project workshops and our numbers are growing, but we are still just a small voice, we need to be able to roar.'

'Rakshin project?' I asked.

'Rakshin is a pan India youth led project aimed at stopping child sexual abuse. In a country of more than a billion people the four or five million involved in the project is still a fractional amount,' Ganesh said.

'Five million people is a significant and impressive number.' I responded.

'It needs to be fifty or a hundred million, then we might get near to addressing the issues in the country and fight the denial, stigma, shame and silence associated with this problem.'

'The *Rakshins* are a step towards a responsible India, but the journey ahead is long and arduous,' Priya added.

We arrived in Delhi. Ganesh's parents had sent their driver to collect us and we were all invited to stay at his house. It was more than a house. It was a mansion with some ten bedrooms. Ganesh had said his father was a lawyer. He had not said he was a Supreme Court judge and had once been advocate general for the State of Maharashtra.

The law obviously pays well in India, I thought.

I was shown to my room and invited to join the family for drinks and dinner in half an hour. By the time I got downstairs the four youngsters had obviously filled in Ganesh's father with what had happened.

'Ah, Mr. Johnson,' he said when he saw me. 'What can I offer you to drink?'

'Sweet *masala chai* will be fine,' I replied.

He nodded to the servant standing in the doorway who immediately went to fetch my tea.

'Mr. Johnson, I have to thank you for bringing my son and his friends safely to me. However, I am concerned why Priya's father would think you capable of killing a child. Should I be calling the police?'

'Sir,' I replied; 'I cannot speak for Priya's father, I have never met him. I came to India to help out a friend who had been asked to free his daughter from her supposedly dangerous kidnappers. My friend and I help out, from time to time, an insurance company which specialises in kidnapping cases. We were duped into believing she was in the hands of potentially murderous criminals. Neither I nor my friend are killers of innocent people. So he was much mistaken.'

'Call me Chirag,' he said. 'Are you a killer of non-innocent people?'

'That's a blunt question. I've been in the military and have killed,' I replied, not lying but hoping he wouldn't delve too deeply into whether the two statements were connected.

'So my family is safe whilst you are in my house?'

'I hope, Chirag, that they are safe whether I'm here or not.

71

I can assure you that I am not a threat to anyone here.'

'Good, now drink your tea.'

I sat down and the servant handed me the white china tea cup. My throat warmed as the Indian speciality tea I had tasted for the first time only this morning, flowed from the cup.

Was it only this morning? I thought.

This *chai* was even better than the one earlier. The smooth, yet piquant, milkyness of the drink and the mellowing warmth of blended black pepper, ginger, cardamom, cloves and nutmeg; I would need to learn how to make it.

'This is good,' I said.

'It's a recipe handed down from my wife's great-great grand-mother,' Chirag responded. My wife claims it's the best *chai* in the world.'

'I wouldn't argue with her on that,' I said

'Best not to argue with her on anything,' Chirag replied. 'I'm a Supreme Court Judge and I can't ever remember winning an argument in this house. Anyway, you'll meet her tomorrow. She's been visiting relatives in Hyderabad, India's City of Pearls. Are you hungry?'

'It's very late,' I said. I think I'll wait until the morning, if that's all right.'

'No problem. The children have sent out for a MacDonald's.'

'I'll definitely pass on that one,' I said.

I was awake before dawn. I checked my phone. No messages from Giacomo. Concern was growing. Chirag told me some worrying stories about Rohtak, and the people he was involved with

'Priya has convinced herself that her father is a part of the sex trafficking mafia which controls many of the prostitutes in

Mumbai, Delhi and Kolkata. There is no proof of that, but he has become a very unsavoury character, or perhaps he always was and he hid it well.'

I was perplexed. If these men were as bad as Chirag and Priya believed, why had they asked the Insurance Company to deal with the kidnap and kill Ganesh and the others? Slick carried a gun and gave me the impression he was not afraid to use it.

I sent a message to Chiara, but her response was not encouraging.

'Nothing since yesterday before you left the hotel.'

Her reply had been almost immediate. It was about 2 a.m. in Italy. The fact she was not sleeping told me she too was worried.

I walked downstairs and into the courtyard at the back of the house. The humidity was unbearable. Servants were already going about their chores. An armed security guard was standing by the gate.

To keep people out, or me in? I thought, but didn't care about the answer. If I wanted to leave then I would. One slightly overweight security guard armed or otherwise would not stop me.

'Please, sir, breakfast this way,' one of the servants said.

'OK thank you.'

'How would you like your egg preparation, sir?'

'My egg what?' I replied not having caught what she had said.

'How you like your eggs cooked? Boiled, fried, poached, scrambled, omelette?'

'Oh, I'm sorry. Yes of course. Fried, over medium on brown toast if that's possible.'

'On wheat toast? Yes no problem, sir. Tea, coffee?'

'Black coffee please.'

My seat at the breakfast table allowed for a panoramic view of the artwork which filled the walls of the well-lit room. The original, signed paintings all had an oriental flavour and feel to them. Deep red oils with diminutive white figures undertaking various tasks, all wearing the distinctive, white, upside down wok shaped hats. Each painting similar but subtly different. On one, the figures were ankle deep in water, sowing rice, in another they were walking through fields of tall vegetation, a third, riding bicycles along muddy tracks. These were unusual. I liked them.

Priya was the first to join me as I was finishing my second cup of coffee. She was wearing intricately designed pyjamas and looked very childlike. I couldn't believe her father was trying to marry her off.

'My dad is very angry,' she said as she sat down. 'In the end I had to put my phone on DND. This morning I have twenty-three missed calls either from him or Deepak. They are trying every few minutes.'

As if on cue, her phone rang again.

'It's not them, it's my mom. Hi mom, where are you?'

Silence whilst she listened.

'Already? That's fantastic. When do you arrive?'

More silence.

'Uncle Chirag will send the car. OK I'll see you then. Love you.'

Indian youngsters seemed to call all older people 'Uncle' or 'Auntie' whether they were related or not.

She put the phone down on the table.

'She's coming, arriving tomorrow morning. Thank god I

can go back with her.'

'Where does she live?'

'Toronto.'

'You'll be safe there, I suppose,' I said.

'I think so. Her husband is head of the vice squad. My dad wouldn't go anywhere near him.'

'Did she know about your dad's plans to marry you off?'

'She was the first to know, after me of course. It was only a few weeks ago that I was told. It was her idea for me to get away from him. I thought I would be safe at Ganesh's apartment until she came. My mom's been sorting out my visa. It came through only yesterday. It seems my dad was using some influence somewhere to block the process, but my step-dad got around that.'

Her phone rang again. I saw the name. I pushed Priya's hand away and answered.

'Mr. Deepak Shitole, good morning,' I said, emphasising and probably miss-pronouncing his surname. This didn't produce the response I had expected.

He laughed.

'You're next Johnson. Your friend Fratelli was only the appetizer. The hounds are still hungry. You wasted your money on those Chennai tickets. We know where you are. You can't hide there forever. I'll be waiting. Tell the little bitch she can't escape either.'

He hung up.

'What did he say?' Priya asked.

'A couple of things I've no clue what he was talking about. Then he says for you to have a safe journey and a good life.'

'You're lying. He wouldn't say that.'

'They weren't the words he used but, believe me, that was the meaning. I won't let anything happen to you between now and when you get on board your flight to Canada.'

Giacomo was only the appetizer? 'The hounds are still hungry? Various scenarios presented themselves. None of them pleasant, especially for Slick and Priya's father.

CHAPTER 8

Chiara and I watched the television news together in total silence. It was detailed. Kiki had died from strangulation but had a total of forty-two knife wounds on every part of her body. Traces of cocaine had been found on her skin, but not in her blood. This was no surprise. I had seen the movie and knew what had been done. They didn't mention the extent of the mutilation and for that I was grateful.

The female newscaster had tears in her eyes as she told how the body had now been released and Kiki's heartbroken parents were taking her home for burial. There were pictures of the child size coffin and the couple with jackets covering their heads to avoid the cameras.

'Too late,' I said, finally breaking the silence. 'I've got your name, I know your face and I'll find out where you live.'

The report continued. Kiki had been rescued by the couple from an orphanage in Cambodia three years before when she was only seven. They had hoped that they would have provided her with a safe future but all their dreams had been shattered.

'The lying bastards,' I said. 'I think they must both be in on this. That poor child has almost certainly been subjected to sexual abuse since she arrived in Germany. Marten's knife

77

made sure there would be no evidence of that to find.'

'I advise you to concentrate on what the *Shadows* have been doing and what they want of you in India. *Herr Rechtsanwalt* Jachenholz will still be around when you have sorted that out. What are you going to do?'

'I have no choice, I have to go. There are still a few scores to settle, I need to know who the eye collector is. I want to find Giacomo's body and bring him home.'

'I doubt there's a body to find. The police told you the body was 'lost' on the way to the morgue.'

'The police can't be trusted. They must have been bribed. A body doesn't go missing.'

'Anything can happen. Especially in India.'

'I've spoken to Chirag. He says Ganesh and the others are in Hyderabad. He's organised for them to fly back to Delhi. They'll be safe with him.'

'I doubt they were ever in danger. Whoever's looking for you want's you on his home ground. But I still can't think why.'

Breaking News flashed up on the screen. 'The body of a man has been found in a hotel in Bellagio,' the newscaster said. 'Initial reports say that he is a tourist who has been staying at the hotel for about a week. Police sources say there appear to be no suspicious circumstances but are to conduct a post mortem examination.'

'They won't find anything there.' I said.

'The nose might be problematic if they do a thorough examination,' said Chiara.

'They're not going to examine him that minutely. They'll find excessive alcohol in his blood and he'll have all the signs of dying of natural causes. Anyway, I fixed his nose.'

'It's the small details that can sometimes unravel us.' Chiara was always ultra-cautious. 'If you insist on going to Germany, when are you planning to go to India?'

'The instructions in the letter state I must meet them on Monday. I think I'll fly out from Frankfurt on Saturday.'

'You can't sort out Düsseldorf in two days. You're going to need time to plan and execute.'

'I want to find where Jachenholz lives. If the opportunity arises I'll take it. If not I'll sort it when I get back from India.'

'Let things settle. I'll search and see what I can find. Go home. Plan for India, you don't know what you're going to face.'

'Then how can I plan?'

'*Caro mio*,' she said.

I hated when she started a sentence with those words in the slow deliberate tone she now used. 'My dear one' meant she was going to give me a real bollocking. I wasn't wrong.

By the time she had finished I was like a schoolboy awaiting the cane outside the headmaster's office. I attended school in England when the wanton infliction of physical pain in a vain attempt to maintain discipline in schools was still permitted. I was no stranger to the rattan cane across the palms of my hand.

'From the palm to the palm,' our headmaster would say before starting the ritual punishment, finding the linguistic twinning of the wood and the hand sadistically amusing. Corporal punishment didn't do me any harm, but then it didn't do any good either. Its sole effect was to make me more careful when I broke the rules. Not because I was afraid of the physical pain, that was a passing irritation, I despised the time it took, to get dealt with. Time is precious. It is the only thing in this world that once it's gone can never be retrieved.

'Chiara,' I said finally. 'We both know that everything you have just said is true. We also both know that I'm going to leave here, go home, pack the things I need and take my bike for a ride to Düsseldorf. I'll be there by morning. On Saturday I'll ride to Frankfurt Airport and fly to Delhi. I will take a train to Mumbai. In the fifteen-hour journey I will think of what I'm going to do. That depends on them.'

'Why not fly to Mumbai from Delhi?'

'I might but they'll think I'm on a train. They're going to try and get me before I ever get to that hotel.'

'You can't know that,' she said.

'Exactly. But despite what you think, I always assess the endless possibilities and prepare for the worst of them. I will be unarmed until I can get to Mumbai. I need to avoid premature confrontation.'

'I'm afraid you are more like Giacomo than you realise. Don't make his mistakes. Don't end the way he did.'

With tears running down her cheek, she hugged and kissed me before I left.

I don't make mistakes, but I must have done. But I don't and I hadn't, I was sure of it, even if all the evidence against that profound belief was clear. The Shadows were one step behind me or more worryingly perhaps one step in front. There was something not right.

I went over everything in London again and again. There was no way they had followed me.

How did they know where I was? Not on one occasion but two.

How had they arrived in Bellagio, seemingly on the same day I did?

What was their connection with the paedophile ring?

How had they found my house?

Why do they want me in India?

Why can't they get me here, or at least try?

The more questions I asked the more concerned I became.

I needed to pack. I smiled as I pulled the motorbike friendly backpack and roll from the top of the wardrobe. As always, Giacomo's voice was there.

'Never carry a gun across borders,' he had taught me. Now, with around twenty-four countries all linked by politics and road, with no border checkpoints, at least in this part of the world, his words could be taken with a degree of flexibility.

I'd need to bring a pistol on this trip and leave it somewhere secure, before I took my flight in a few days. There would be no time to obtain one on this first leg and I hoped I'd have use of it.

Underwear and socks first. Never worn for more than a day, ten pairs of each should be enough. If I'm away longer I'll find laundry facilities, or a shop.

I took a Beretta M9 from the hidden gun safe and carried out the ritual checks. It went between several layers of folded pants. Three spare fifteen-round magazines inside socks, then a pair of rolled jeans.

My favoured travel suit hung by the door. Bought in Saville Row, Giacomo hated me rolling this up into a backpack.

'You should show more respect for such fine tailoring.'

'Thomas, taught me how to pack it properly, and he made it,' I would reply.

With the suit jacket face down on the bed, I held one shoulder and folded it back, turning the other shoulder inside out. A vertical fold followed by a horizontal one, I placed the prepared garment in a plastic dry-cleaning bag. Now for the trousers. Laid flat, jacket on top and both ends folded to the middle. Perfect size.

Equal care was taken in folding the five shirts I assessed as sufficient. As with the underwear there were ways of dealing with the situation if I needed more. I always prefer folding to a rolling technique for shirts. Giacomo and I debated for hours about the pros and cons of non-iron over wrinkle-free material, sharing several bottles of wine of course. I miss him. Those bastards will pay.

First, there was another job on my agenda.

An airline friendly plastic bag containing shaving gear and toiletries fitted neatly into a side pocket. A pair of shoes and a pair of trainers went into the detachable roll bag.

Strapped and clipped together it was small enough to be used as hand luggage for my forthcoming intercontinental flight and weight, minus the firearm and accessories, would be no problem. For now it would fit, neatly and securely, on the motorbike's luggage rack, which waited outside, fuelled and ready for the 900-kilometre trip.

I locked up, fired the engine and rode off. As always, I wondered if this would be the end.

I relished the wind in my face as I raced along the *superstrada* in Italy and the *autobahn* in Germany. Between those two stretches of road, I enjoyed the danger of the narrow mountain pass connecting Italy and Switzerland, with its winding road. I had decided against the more traditional, motorway route through Switzerland into Germany. Quieter and more exciting was to take the Splügen pass open again after winter snow.

I remembered the words of Mary Shelley who more than

a hundred and fifty years ago came in the opposite direction along this same road.

Look back and see the country you had left, through the narrow opening of the gigantic crags, set like a painting in this cloud-reaching frame, she wrote.

Except I didn't have to look back, those same crags were directly in front of me. The road twisted and turned exactly as she had described.

Whenever I travelled along this road I tried to imagine where Baron Adelburt Gruner had murdered his wife by throwing her off a precipice. Sherlock Holmes had never been able to prove it was murder but anyone who ever read that particular Conan Doyle short story was left in no doubt.

Thoughts of Kiki and the similar fate she had suffered came suddenly. Baroness Gruner was probably still alive when she was thrown over the cliff edge. Kiki most definitely couldn't have been.

I had witnessed her death with my own eyes, albeit through the lens of the camera, held by the man I was now going to find and kill. It may have been a technical legal issue and the suspicious death of a witness which saved Baron Gruner, but I didn't need any witness or legal consideration. I possessed Sherlock's certainty. Jachenholz was guilty; as guilty as Gruner.

I would make him pay in a way Dr. Watson would never approve of.

Despite taking the narrow pass with its hairpin bends and sheer drops, I arrived in Düsseldorf a little over ten hours after I left home. I parked outside the budget hotel next to the Hauptbahnhof. Minimal checking-in formalities, I paid by cash and went to get two hours sleep. That would be enough.

I bought a newspaper from reception and went to my room.

I didn't read the paper. I collapsed on the bed and went to sleep immediately. I woke up feeling as if I had overslept but a look at my watch showed I had only been lying down for half an hour.

All attempts to get back to sleep failed. I turned on the television News 24 channel. I saw many of the same pictures I had watched yesterday with Chiara. Here too, the main story was about Kiki and her adoptive parents, now returning to Germany. Nothing more useful than I had already learned in Italy.

I decided to make a start on locating him. My single trip use tablet connected quickly to the hotel Wi-Fi. I was only going to be looking at non-descript public sites so there was no need for complicated routing.

I was looking for an Italian speaking lawyer in Düsseldorf, so I typed, *Italienisch sprechende Anwälte in Düsseldorf.*

I was amazed at the number of answers that came up. According to the Search Engine I used it was 56.700 results in 0.45 seconds. Impressive.

I wanted to narrow the results down so, following my instinct as Giacomo taught me, I added *für kinderadoption* to the research. It reduced to 20,300 results. I thought I would try even further and added *Jachenholz* to the search.

This brought it down to 14,600 results. A quick browse did not show up the name I was looking for. There was nothing for it but to start an entry-by-entry search.

A couple of hours later I found a Jachenholz and it looked promising.

Schneider Jachenholz Anwaltskanzlei was the entry and

underneath was written amongst other things: *Fachanwalt für Kinderadoption* - Specialist lawyer for child adoption.

I went into the home page. From the drop-down menu I selected *Über uns*.

'That's interesting,' I said.

The law firm consisted of two partners. There was a picture of Herr Jachenholz and, making allowances for ten years, twenty kilos and stress, I was convinced this was the guy I saw with Martens in Bellagio.

Above this was another photograph of *Rechtsanwältin* Ulrike Schneider.

'Is this your wife?' I asked the ether.

The woman in the picture was young and fresh-faced. The woman in the televised press conference was an advertisement for why attractive woman should not have plastic surgery. Bee stung lips, an impossibly small nose and an ironed face incapable of showing any emotion or even motion other than the vaguest movement of her swollen mouth. She had dabbed her eyes with a paper handkerchief throughout the conference, but I didn't get the impression that the tissue was any wetter after the conference than it was before. I was always cynical.

Their office address showed they plied their trade on *Königsallee*. The *Kö*, as it was known locally, was regarded, at least by the people of Düsseldorf, as the equivalent of Fifth Avenue in New York, filled with high end brand shops and very expensive offices. I would need to go there; it was only a fifteen-minute walk along *Friedrich-Ebert Strasse* and *Steinstrasse*.

As a student I had walked those streets many times on my way to the Altstadt. Fondly known as the longest bar in the world, Düsseldorf's old town is a conglomeration of bars and restaurants and a focal point for the night life of the city. Filled with students, business people and tourists, it would always be a special place for me.

I needed to make one stop on the way. I entered the shop through its narrow blacked out door with the intricately designed Chinese-dragon motif.

Inside, the small shop was brightly lit. A woman with long blond flowing hair, in a short white dressing gown, was lying on a couch facing away from me. She was leaning on her elbow and seemed to be scanning through a magazine. Her right thigh was fully exposed.

Kneeling down beside her was the person I came to see. In her hand she held a thick, pen-like instrument. A small motor whirred as she applied the pen's ink-filled needle to the woman's skin. A snake with its head somewhere above the line of the dressing gown, twisted and curled down the firm flesh of her thigh to just above her knee. This was the part the tattoo artist was now working on.

'*Ein Moment bitte,*' she said as she heard me come in, never taking her eyes away from the work she was doing.

I said nothing as I sat down on one of the small chairs which were either side of the doorway and picked up a magazine which was filled with the latest must have tattoo designs. I flicked through it. I never had a tattoo, although I had thought about getting a snarling tiger on my shoulder once. Not a good idea though to have such a distinguishing mark, not in my job.

After about five minutes the tattooist stood. Momentarily eyeing her handiwork.

'*Fertig, Maria,*' she said, informing the woman it was

finished. The woman turned and admired the serpent which would now remain a constant companion for the rest of her life.

'*Fantastisch. Vielen Dank, Christiana. Du bist der Beste auf der Welt,*' she said.

I have no idea if Christiana is truly the best in the world as her client claimed, but she is certainly talented. For the first time Christiana turned towards me. Her eyes widened, her lips stretched into a broad grin, her perfect teeth gleamed.

'Ricci? *Häschen?* Is it really you?' she said as I stood. She launched herself at me. Arms tight around my neck, her legs wrapped around my waist. She kissed me on the cheek and then full on the lips. The woman with the snake leg smiled as she went towards the changing room in the corner, where she would have her new inking covered for protection.

By the time she came out, dressed in wide trousers and a very tight-fitting shirt, the top four or five buttons undone displaying ample, silicone-enhanced cleavage, Christiana had released me from her vice like grip.

'Maria, this is Ricci, my oldest and dearest friend. We were at University together.'

She then punched me hard on the arm.

'Why don't you keep in touch more, you bastard?'

'You know how things are in my life Christiana, I'm never in one place for more than a couple of days. I come and see you when I can. I did send you a message at Christmas!'

She punched me again.

Maria made her way to the door. As she walked past me, she touched my arm. '*Tschüss,* little rabbit,' she said, using the embarrassing nickname Christiana had called me, 'if Christiana gets fed up with you, you can always call me. She has my number.'

'Get out Maria,' Christiana said. 'He couldn't afford your tastes.'

'I'm sure we could come to some arrangement. You could play *find the snake's head* with me.'

'*Raus.* Out, out, out, Maria. Next time my hand might slip and the snake might bite.'

Maria laughed. She turned and gave an exaggerated wink in my direction.

Christiana picked up a magazine and threw it at her. '*Tschüss*, Maria. *Bis* nächsten Mal.'

Maria's laughter carried out onto the street.

'That's a dangerous woman,' I said.

'A very rich, dangerous woman. Her husband owns an Insurance company. She usually gets everything she wants – one way or another. Enough about her, what are you doing here.'

'I want a tattoo of course,' I replied. I showed her a photograph on my mobile phone. 'Exactly like that, but not permanent. I'll need to get rid of it tomorrow night.'

After university, Christiana had gone to study at a School of Visual Arts in America. She became a renowned traditional illustrator. A fellow student introduced her to body art and she became hooked. Now, much of her body, from her shoulders down, was covered in multi-coloured ink.

She was in demand in Hollywood and Milan. Like Maria, many film stars and models regarded her as the best. Christiana's tattoos, both temporary and permanent, adorned the bodies of some of the most beautiful and glamourous women in the world. Maria could be included in that group.

She looked at the photograph of a hand. She didn't need to

know it was a dead hand, so I didn't tell her.

'That's simple' she said, 'but it will cost you dinner tonight.'

'Tomorrow might be easier.'

'So, you are here two days at least? Then you've no excuse. Bring your things tonight. You're staying over. You owe me something else, after the last time you were here, and I have a new tattoo I want you to see. Don't expect to get much sleep.

CHAPTER 9

I sat with Chirag, in his study, awaiting the arrival of his wife. The car had been despatched to collect her. She would be here any moment.

I picked up the newspaper, the Times of India. In the entire paper, there was not a single mention of rape or murder. I felt I was growing obsessed with this topic.

'Why is rape so prevalent in India?' I asked.

'That's an impossible question to answer. Or, more correctly, it's impossible to give a definitive, short answer,' replied Chirag. 'India is very complex. Its caste system is impossible to understand unless you have been born and brought up with it.'

'What has caste got to do with rape?' I asked.

'Everything and nothing,' Chirag replied. 'It is all about position in society. No-one knows the precise origin of the caste system. Academics have been arguing about it for centuries. At its simplest, and probably the most accepted of theories, there are four main castes and by omission of certain people from those four there must be a fifth.'

'Only five? I thought many more.'

'Yes, correct. I told you it's complex. Are you sure you want me to explain? It can get very boring.'

'No, please explain. I'm genuinely interested.'

'I'll try and keep it as simple as possible. I won't go into every theory and stick to the most widely accepted. Firstly, the name *caste* is not of Indian origin, but Portuguese. Prior to the arrival of Vasco di Gama and his successors, the Hindu system had been established for millennia. According to some ancient Hindu texts the creator god, *Brahma*, created four *Varnas* from different parts of his body. The *Brahmins*, he created from his head; the *Kshatryas* from his hands; the *Vaishyas* from his thighs and the *Shudras* from his feet. The part of *Brahma's* body dictated the hierarchy.'

'So that is why the *Brahmins* are regarded as the leading caste?' I asked.

'Yes. Your *Varna* dictates many things about your life; your work, your diet, social interaction, marriage; the list is long. In the main, *Brahmins* were destined to become intellectuals, priests and teachers; *Kshatryas*, warriors and rulers; *Vaishyas*, farmers, traders and merchants and, at the foot, *Shudras* were to be the labouring class. Then the complications arose. Over hundreds and even thousands of years, each *Varna* became subdivided based upon the actual work done. This created about three thousand *sub-varnas* which themselves became sub-divided into perhaps twenty-five thousand.'

'So you're telling me that there are more than twenty-eight thousand different castes?'

'As a minimum,' he replied. 'It depends on how you count them. Following the 2011 census it was reported that there were around four-point-six-million different castes.'

'Four million, six hundred thousand?'

'Yes, but I think that's because we Indians have a great habit of spelling the same thing in many different ways so it's probable that in various areas people used an alternate spelling and it became a new caste. I think twenty-eight thousand is more accurate.'

'That's more than enough, but what is the link between that and rape?'

'It's impossible to say that there is a direct link. I'm trying to explain some of the background, which may explain some of the incidents we see, particularly in rural communities. I told you that there are four main *Varnas* or castes. Below that is another caste, which did not come from the body parts of a god and is therefore regarded as of having little or no merit. Ghandi referred to this group as *Harijan* meaning Children of God. He tried to incorporate them into society.'

'Are these the Untouchables I've heard about?'

'We don't like to use that term in modern India, but yes, these were the people who traditionally did the lowest of the jobs, rubbish collection, latrine cleaning and the fact that they came into contact with bodily fluids meant they were deemed polluted and by touching them their pollution would affect you.

Today this community prefers to be called *Dalit* meaning supressed or broken and, although the law does not allow discrimination in India today most intellectuals and high-ranking officials are *Brahmins* and most street cleaners are *Dalit*.'

'Is there no hope of changing this?' I asked.

'Things are changing but it will take generations and we need to have better education open to everyone in our country. A *Dalit* can, and has, become a President of our nation. Kocheril Raman Narayanan, was our tenth President. He was a *Paravan* from Kerala which is a *Dalit* caste. He made it to the top, and we have examples of actors and sportsmen from the *Dalit* classes, but this is a small minority. India can never be regarded as a true democracy until the caste system is dead and forgotten.'

'We still haven't explained what this has to do with the number of rapes in India.'

'Hopefully you realise the hierarchical system we live in. That has always been traditionally dominated by men...'

'Not in this house it hasn't,' a voice came from the doorway.

A tall woman with long, straight, coal-black hair, stood smiling, exuding elegance. She was wearing a yellow and red sari, her bare midriff showing toned muscles. I guessed her to be about forty years old, and no stranger to the gym and exercise.'

'Ben, please let me introduce you to my wife, Sushma.'

I was already on my feet, having jumped up as she entered the room. Chiara would never have forgiven me if I'd remained seated when a lady entered a room. I walked over to her and held out my hand. She took it in a strong, confident grip.

'Mr. Johnson, Ganesh tells me you saved his life. I am grateful to you for that.'

'I think Ganesh may be exaggerating slightly,' I replied.

'Whatever you did, my son is here, safe and well. Now what have you been discussing?'

'Ben was asking about our nation's rape crisis. I'm starting to try and explain our caste system to him.'

'It's not the caste system alone,' Sushma said. 'When a religion glorifies rape amongst the gods how are the uneducated masses able to differentiate? It's about control, about showing men's strength and as a punishment to women, for dressing provocatively, or being alone at night.'

'Sushma, you are being too generic.'

'I am not a Supreme Court Judge, like you Chirag. I see what I see, in the way that I see it. I don't want to analyse every angle before reaching a conclusion. I think my views reflect those of many educated Indian women, sooner or later we will be heard.'

'What do you mean, Hinduism glorifies rape?' I interrupted their discussion.

'There are stories in the ancient texts where the gods have raped a woman, pretending to be their husband. Vishnu raped Tulsi, the wife of his enemy, in the knowledge that Jalandhar could only be defeated if his wife's chastity had been taken. Brihaspati raped his own pregnant sister-in-law, Mamata, after telling her he didn't need a lecture from her on morals.'

'Hinduism is not alone in that kind of story. In Ancient Egypt, the god Amun appeared to Mutemwiya, the wife of Pharaoh disguised as her husband and she became pregnant with his child who too became Pharaoh.'

'That story is different, Ben,' Sushma said. 'It is said that Mutemwiya knew that it was the god and rejoiced in their lovemaking. That is not rape. When Tulsi discovered the real identity of Vishnu she was horrified and attacked him for outraging her modesty.'

'You know about Egyptian history?'

'Many of the Hindu texts were written around the time of Amenhotep, Akhenaten and King Tut. At University I studied the similarities of the *Vedas* with other contemporary religious cults.'

'The colleague I was with in Mumbai is an expert on Atenism and the religious revolution which occurred in that period. You should meet him.'

'I would love to,' she replied.

This morning's phone call from Slick came back to me. I doubted Giacomo would ever be able to meet Sushma.

'Women in Hindu society have always been regarded as secondary to their husbands. *Sati* was common practice for centuries.'

'Please excuse me but what is *Sati*?'

'It is the ritual self-sacrifice of a widow on the funeral pyre of her husband,' Chirag replied.

'Not always self-sacrifice,' Sushma said. 'The widow was often coerced into the act, sometimes simply so that her husband's family could claim her wealth. It was neatly justified by adjudging it to be an act of peerless piety, purging the widow of sin and ensuring salvation for her dead husband and the following seven generations.'

'Isn't suicide condemned by Hinduism?' I asked.

Sushma laughed. 'Here we have one of the many dichotomies of Hinduism, which denounces suicide, but at the same time can applaud it as an admirable act of self-sacrifice. The difference is in the motivation of the act. Suicide to relieve oneself from the burdens of life is selfish and therefore evil; suicide to assist your husband to achieve salvation and protect his family is a sacred, sanctifying sacrifice which is to be applauded.'

'Nobody believes in *Sati* anymore Sushma.'

'Are you sure Chirag? It was banned by the British colonialists in 1829, but we still needed to have an Act of Parliament in 1987. We still needed to prosecute the father-in-law and brother-in-law of Roop Kanwar for forcing her, aged only eighteen, to sit on her husband's pyre and be burned alive.'

'They were acquitted,' Chirag replied.

'That sums up Indian Justice, right there,' said Sushma. 'It took ten years for their trial to end. They were acquitted but Roop is still dead.'

'*Sati* is ended. There has been no reported case for ten years and in the years before that it was only a rare occurrence, perhaps linked with mental illness of the widow.'

'No, Chirag. Do not go there. There is absolutely no evidence of mental illness being involved. That is a biased excuse trying to divert blame away from the cultural norms to make it the fault of the poor women who died horrific deaths.'

'You can see Ben,' Chirag said, 'that this is a subject which animates our society.'

'Animates?' said Sushma. 'It animates us because the Government turns a blind eye. Modi will not even condemn acts of rape and violence if it affects only *Dalits* or Muslims.'

'That's not true, Sushma. You should not say such things.'

'I should not say such things? Newspapers report it all the time. Modi's BJP party and senior members are involved in some of the attacks. Modi has never once referred to the rape of girls and women. He talks platitudes, promising justice for our *daughters* but refuses to recognise the role his own party supporters play in perpetrating and celebrating the horrors we see every day.

'What about Sengar? He raped a sixteen-year-old girl when she came for a job interview. He had her father arrested on drummed up firearms charges. He tried to kill the girl and her two aunts on their way to court. One aunt died, the girl was lucky to escape with her life. Modi said nothing. Sengar was a senior member of Modi's party in Uttar Pradesh.'

'That is your view Sushma, but not everyone agrees.'

'Let us not argue this in front of our guest, Chirag. He is wanting to understand the reason India is becoming reviled by other nations because it cannot protect its young whilst sending satellites to the vacuum of space.'

I wanted to reduce the growing tension. 'India is not reviled Mrs Patel. It's simply not understood.'

'How diplomatic you are Mr. Johnson.'

'Please call me Ben.'

'And you must call me Sushma. You are a guest in my house. We should not be arguing in front of you.'

'I prefer to think you are debating, not arguing. Also you are enlightening me about Indian culture and society in a way I doubt tourists would ever be.'

'Tourists see nothing of India. They visit the Taj Mahal, they go to Jaipur and other places which are geared up to show them an idealistic view of our country. They go to the beaches of Goa and they think that is India. They never go to Haryana, or Uttar Pradesh, to the villages run by men living in the past. Where to raise a daughter is likened to watering a neighbour's garden. Where selective abortion, to ensure a male child, was so prevalent laws had to be passed making it illegal to reveal the sex of a baby before birth. Where council leaders can order rape as a punishment.'

'Selective abortion is blamed for India having a much higher ratio of men to women,' Chirag interrupted. 'Some also blame that for the high incidence of rape. Together with pornography which seems readily available on every computer and smart phone in India.'

'We've heard all the arguments, Chirag. Pornography, lack

of prostitution, no hope for young men without means to marry, having to satisfy their lust by rape. These are all excuses not reasons. Until our young men realise that rape is wrong and not acceptable under any circumstances things will never change. Until the Hindu religion accepts its liability in this issue we will have more cases like Asifa Bano, eight years old and Muslim, held in a Hindu temple for five days by an eight strong Hindu gang which included four serving police officers and a minor. Asifa was strangled and stoned in the head, not once but twice, to make sure she was dead. Before they killed her one of the policeman demanded to rape her one last time. This led to her being gang raped again by all of them. Can you imagine the horror and pain that little child went through?'

'I think I've heard enough for one day,' I said. 'This is horrific.' I wanted and needed to know more, but I felt this was not the right time. There is, clearly, a deep-rooted problem in India that has nothing to do with paedophiles or organised crime, or maybe it is, in part, a mask precisely for those.

'What makes it more horrific is that it is real and endemic,' Sushma said. 'Thank you for listening. It's something in our society which must be driven out, but nobody seems to know how. Perhaps I should check my cases have been correctly unpacked,' she said. 'I'll see you both at lunch.'

CHAPTER 10

Present day
Düsseldorf, Thursday afternoon 2 p.m.

After I left Christiana with the promise to see her later, I walked back to the hotel and collected my bike. It was pointless leaving it by the station if I was going to spend the night in her apartment.

I parked in a small side street off *Steinstrasse*. The hand-made Italian brand attracted some attention from other bikers. The limited-edition, high-priced bikes were not often seen in Germany being more popular in the lucrative American and Japanese markets.

I still felt self-conscious about the tattoo Christiana had so carefully applied earlier. Impossibly I could feel it; I wanted to scratch at it but knew I couldn't. Her skill had made it look permanent and old. I couldn't present my hand to the German with red scratches around it.

Königsallee was nearby, across a busy street. Cars were turning the corner oblivious to the growing number of people wanting to cross. The traffic lights had broken and this gave the drivers the excuse of keeping their eyes looking straight ahead, ignoring all things pedestrian.

It was the guy with the camera who changed that. He put his hand out, slammed the bonnet of the silver Mercedes, screamed and fell over. The car stopped immediately and the driver got out. As he did so the crowd divided. Some crossed the road through the gap that had now been created. Others went to see if the cameraman was OK. I leaned against a shop window watching the scene develop. The cameraman had hit the car, not the other way around. He had fallen and not been knocked over.

As the driver approached him, he stood.

'*Vielen Dank*' he said to the dazed driver, 'now we can cross the road.'

Laughter erupted. Red-faced, the driver turned to walk back to his car. All eyes were on him and not the cameraman. It could have been missed, it was so professional. The cameraman was quick. In his apparent rush to cross the road he bumped into a guy in a blue jacket. The merest movement of the jacket and a wallet was removed and passed behind him to a waiting accomplice, in a black hoody.

As the driver hurried back into his car the remainder of the crowd crossed the road. All except for the man in the hood; he came the other way crossing in front of me. I grabbed his arm and pulled him into the covered doorway as he did so. Fortunately, the shop was closed and I pinned him against the door.

'*Gib mir die Geldbörse*,' I said.

He looked at me with an expression that said 'Fuck off, I don't know what you're talking about,' but his mouth never moved. His hand started towards his belt and the knife he had tucked inside it. As his hand reached the handle I grabbed it and twisted. The knife blade was not covered and I could feel the resistance of his clothing and skin as it started to draw blood.

'Give me the wallet,' I repeated and you can walk away with no more harm. A slight scratch is all you've got at the moment, but if you would prefer, I can remove your appendix.'

He was still defiant so I plunged his hand down slightly more. He couldn't scream and draw attention to us so he bit hard on his lip.

'OK, enough,' he said. 'You can have the fucking wallet, take it.'

I watched his eyes. He was hoping I would release his knife hand so he could make himself feel better by causing me some damage. That wasn't going to happen.

'Release the knife,' I said. He resisted, so I started to force his hand further down. 'Release it; we are heading toward an artery.'

He loosened his grip. As he did so I grabbed the knife handle and pulled it out. Making sure it was hidden from view inside his open jacket.

'Pass me the wallet,' I said. He took the leather wallet from his pocket and held it out to me. I still had one hand on his arm and other on the knife. 'Drop it into my top breast pocket. Now, you can walk away, taking your knife with you. I am going to put it back inside your belt.'

I did this but pushed it further in so he would have difficulty taking it out without undoing his trousers. He wasn't going to do that on the street. I was certain that by now he would be feeling blood trickling down his leg. He would need to see how badly he was hurt. That would override his desire to hurt me. I let him go.

He ran off, but before he did he said, 'I'll get you for this. I know your face. This is a small town.'

'I look forward to our next meeting, then,' I replied.

I opened the wallet and looked at its contents. Credit cards and about 200 euro in mixed notes. I could see nothing which would be of use to me, so there was no reason to keep it. I headed for the *Kö*. I didn't wait for cars to stop but crossed between two holding out my right arm towards a driver as I did so, like a policeman, telling him to stop.

The blue jacket came hurrying in my direction. A worried expression across the man's face, verging on panic. 'Are you looking for this?' I asked, as I held out the wallet towards him.

'*Gott sei Dank!* Where did you find it?'

'I retrieved it from the guy who stole it. You should be more careful, pickpockets are everywhere. I happened to see him take it.'

'Thank you,' he said opening up the wallet. 'Please let me give you a reward.'

'No. There is no need. I'm happy you found me; it saved me having to go to the police. I hate paperwork.'

'I cannot thank you enough,' he said.

'*Kein Problem*,' I replied; 'but in future try to be more careful.'

He sped off, in a hurry to get somewhere. A couple of hundred euros and two credit cards mean so much to the lives of so many people.

An abundance of reporters and TV crews outside one building told me two things.

This was the building I wanted to find and the occupants were in.

Journalists were hoping for a glimpse, a word, a face shot anything that would make their editors happy. A happy editor and a Pulitzer Prize were the ambitions of most journalists I have met. Neither ambition easily achieved.

Like many shoppers trying to get to the Gucci or Armani outlets and other famous brands which lined the *Kö*, I pushed through the outer ring of gossip columnists and news anchors who were chatting and waiting for the next photo shot opportunity or newsfeed request. I noticed the brass plaque '*Schneider Jachenholz Anwaltskanzlei.*' I was definitely in the right place.

I turned quickly into the doorway. Showed my *Bundespolizei* ID card to the security guard. He didn't look beyond the obvious, they never did. Just as well as the photo and I bore little resemblance to each other. I had my story ready, in case. 'I know, I've shaved my beard and lost a few kilos, since then. Oh and now I use contact lenses,' but it wasn't needed.

I went to the lift and hit the button for the fifth floor. As I came out of the elevator I saw them standing in a doorway. I walked up to them.

'*Herr* Jachenholz, Gunter,' I said 'we need to talk.' I held my tattooed right hand out to shake his. He saw the tattoo and the initial shock that had crossed his face passed. He held out his hand, I pressed my thumb against his matching tattoo as I had seen Martens and he do at the restaurant in Bellagio. He reciprocated.

'Martens is dead,' I said to him. 'You might be next.'

'What do you mean?' it was Frau Schneider who spoke. 'Who is Martens? Why might Gunter be next? Do we know you?'

'Which question do you want me to answer?' I said, buying a little time. Is it possible she doesn't know about this? I pondered.

'All of them.' She turned to her husband, 'Gunter, who is this man?'

I could see Gunter struggling to reply. He didn't have a clue who I was, other than I had the tattoo and knew the handshake.

'Martens is Luc. Luc Peeters,' he said, avoiding the most difficult question. 'He sometimes uses the name Martens.'

'Luc?' she said. 'Dead? Luc dead? How?' her voice rising several octaves as she spoke.

'I don't know the details,' I replied, 'other than he was found in his hotel room in Italy. It doesn't seem as if they suspect foul play, but we believe otherwise.'

She reached into her Michael Kors handbag and pulled out a tissue. She dabbed at her eyes. It was there, on her right hand. The intertwined 'K' and 'J,' removing the momentary doubt I harboured about her involvement. This sick bitch would die too.

'What makes you think we… I mean Gunter is in danger? There is no connection between us and Luc, or Martens or whatever you want to call him.'

'There was no link between Martens and Kiki. Someone joined the wires.'

'It'll be that fucking Italian,' Gunter said.

'What Italian?' I asked, hiding my amusement.

'I don't know. Some Indian acquaintances of Luc's warned him that an Italian would be looking for him and that he was dangerous. The last time I saw Luc he was very nervous.'

'When did you see Luc?' his wife asked.

'I met him for a drink in Bellagio.'

'You idiot! Why in God's name did you meet him in Bellagio? Why didn't you tell me?'

'I didn't want you to worry,' he said. 'He sent me a message saying he needed to meet urgently. He wanted to warn me about the Italian.'

'What if you were seen together? What if the police connect Luc and Kiki? I can't believe how stupid this is.'

She walked into the office. Gunter took a deep breath and followed.

Once inside the office, she gave instructions to the receptionist sitting behind a counter.

'Greta, you and the others can go home. We are shutting for the rest of today and tomorrow. Tell the others we are grateful for their support and we'll see them on Monday.'

'Are you sure *Frau* Schneider? We are all more than happy to stay and help.'

'No. Thank you Greta, but no. *Herr* Jachenholz and I need to have some more time alone. This gentleman is here to help us try and get through this. Please, go. Find your daughter and hold her close. Do something nice with her this week-end.'

Tears ran down Greta's cheeks. Ulrike Schneider was a fine actress.

After Greta and her fellow workers left, Ulrike showed me into another office. Her name was written in gold letters on the opaque glass which filled the top panel of the door.

Inside was a small, round conference table. Four leather chairs surrounded it. Beyond the table was a large desk with a green leather centre panel. Bulging files of varying colours covered large parts of the desk and the floor surrounding it.

'Please sit,' she said, pointing to one of the conference chairs.

I did so, she and Gunter sat facing me.

'Now,' she said; 'who the fuck are you?'

'My name is Siegbert Schuster,' I replied.

'I'm not interested in your name, it's probably false anyway. I asked you a simple question. Who the fuck are you?'

'Who do you think I am?'

I regretted the reply as soon as I said it. They were getting to me more than I thought. I had left myself open to a trap. How I answered the next question would be vital.

'I think you are an arsehole who has been sent to get information from us. Perhaps you think to kill us if you feel we are a threat to the group.' Not the difficult question I had been expecting, perhaps I was giving her too much credit.

I laughed. 'Do I look like a killer?'

'Killers have no looks,' she said. 'That's why they're difficult to catch. I asked you a simple question and I am awaiting an answer.'

'I was sent to warn you both to be careful.'

'Who sent you?'

'Someone who cares what happens to you.'

'Who?'

'It doesn't matter.'

'It matters to me. Who sent you?'

'I've told you. Someone who cares what happens to you.'

'No-one gives a flying monkey's shit what happens to us. Who sent you?'

'There is absolutely no point in my giving you a name. It's probably false anyway,' I said repeating the line she had said about me. 'I don't know by what name he or she is known to you, so a name now is nothing more than a nonsensical noun.'

'*Herr* Schuster, or whatever your real name is, get out of my office. I don't know you. I don't believe Gunter knows you and I don't trust you. If KJ informs me who you are and tells me, in the standard communication format, to expect you on a certain day at a set time, I will talk to you again. Until then, I want you out of here and as far away from us as is possible. We have work to do. Gunter, see him out.'

'OK, I'm leaving but please take notice. Your lives are at risk. I could help with that. Here is my telephone number, it's a burner and will be destroyed tomorrow night. After that you'll be on your own. May I use your bathroom before I leave?'

'Show him the way Gunter, then get him out.'

I had learned a lot. Ulrike was in control, Gunter her lapdog. They had a busy legal practice. I needed to find out more. I went to the bathroom. Gunter did not come all the way. As we crossed an office he said, 'Out that door, then third on the left. Don't be long, I'll wait here.'

Third on the left, so I went into the first. An open-plan office like the one we had just passed through. Four desks. More files. I opened the first I came across. Adoption papers. I picked several files at random. All the same. Adoption of foreign kids into European families. Not only in Germany but also in Luxembourg and Holland. There must have been thirty files in Ulrike's office, at least the same again here. Sixty ongoing adoptions at least. How many of these kids would suffer the same fate as Kiki?

None, if I can help it, I thought and moved onto the second door.

A kitchen. Kettle, cups and herbal teas on the counter. More teas in the cupboard with instant coffee and hot chocolate. Nothing of interest, apart from the bunch of keys in a drawer. They moved from drawer to pocket and I walked out and quickly into the third door which was indeed a bathroom. I turned on the tap and pressed the soap dispenser, allowing the drops of soap to fall onto the sink. I wet my hands then dried them on a paper towel and walked out as Gunter entered the corridor.

'What have you been doing?' he asked.

'What do you think?' I replied. I don't like to lie unless it's unavoidable.

He escorted me to the lift and pressed the down call button. When the doors opened, I entered; he pushed his head in and pressed the button with the letter L. He pulled away as the doors started to close.

'*Auf Wiedersehen, Herr* Schuster,' he said. 'Best you don't come back. Ulrike doesn't like you.'

'I will do as I am ordered,' I risked saying, hoping Ulrike wasn't the one giving all the orders.

Once the door was closed I pressed the button for the third floor and exited. Finding the stairs I walked up to the fifth floor, found a place from where I could see the office door without being conspicuous, and waited. By the time I left the building and headed for Christiana's apartment, I had all the information I needed.

CHAPTER 11

One Year Ago
Delhi, India Day 4: 2:00 p.m.

'Lunch was wonderful Sushma, thank you,' I said.

'My pleasure, Ben. At least Chirag and I managed to get through it without having a, what did you call it earlier? Ah yes, a debate.'

Chirag smiled. 'Healthy debate is good for a relationship,' he said.

'Ben, have you seen today's newspaper?' Priya asked.

'No, not yet. Anything interesting?'

'Just more of the same that we were talking about yesterday,' she said. 'Two gang rapes in different hospitals in Uttar Pradesh. Both girls were patients in ICU. One, a student, aged seventeen, the other, recovering from a snake bite, was raped by five men, one of them a nurse. She's only four years old.'

'Oh God no,' said Sushma. 'When will this sickness end?'

'The cops have arrested the nurse but they are still looking for the other four. Here's the paper if you want it.'

The headline hit me as I took the paper and put it on the floor beside me. 'I'll read it later.'

HOSPITAL GANG RAPE CAUGHT ON CCTV: 4-YEAR-OLD RECOVERING FROM SNAKE BITE RAPED BY HOSPITAL WORKER AND FOUR OTHERS.

I couldn't say anything.

'That's the death penalty for him.' Chirag said. The debate free lunch ended abruptly as Sushma let Chirag know how she viewed the Indian Court System.

'What's the estimate? Three hundred and twenty years just to clear the backlog of cases?' she asked.

'Including civil cases, yes, something of that order' he replied.

Ganesh interjected. 'I read recently, Dad, that of the twenty odd million cases awaiting a judgment two-thirds are criminal and, of those, ten per cent have been waiting more than ten years to be decided on. By my calculations, that is nearly one point four million criminals who have not been sentenced ten years or more after the offence.'

'Or acquitted,' Chirag said.

'What? Oh yeah, right. That nurse will die of old age before he gets hanged.'

'Why am I always blamed for the vagaries of our court system?' Chirag asked.

'You're a Supreme Court Judge and in a position to try and do something about it,' Sushma replied.

'Let's not argue… I mean debate that now,' he nodded towards me. 'We simply do not have enough Judges at the courts of first instance and they are under extreme pressure. Some have on average less than three minutes to hear each case.'

'That's impossible,' I said. 'Three minutes to hear arguments and decide?'

'It's an average. Some might have longer, maybe as long as fifteen minutes, but the average throughout the country is less than five minutes.'

'Three-minute decisions cannot bring Justice,' Sushma said.

'Something has to be done. Also the environment in Court with lawyers shouting, talking over each other, verbally abusing each other and witnesses, cannot be conducive to a judge even being able to hear cogent argument, let alone reach a fair decision.'

'Everyone agrees, Sushma, but nobody can find a solution. You tell me how it can be done and I will petition the Chief Justice, Ministers, Prime Minister, even the President. One billion people know the system is broken, but not one single person knows how to mend it.'

'Where did you say these rapes happened?' I asked.

'The four-year-old was in Hapur, the student in Bareilly.'

'How far away are these places?'

'Why Ben? Are you thinking of going there?'

'I don't know Chirag. I feel the need to do something.'

'Forgive me, Ben, but what could you do? You don't speak Hindi or Urdu. You have no contacts in Hapur or Bareilly. Nobody will trust you. You're a foreigner. You won't get help, you'll be looked on as a white, would be, saviour who thinks he knows better.'

'A white monkey you mean. I know I've been called that already.'

'That's a very derogatory term Ben and no right-thinking Indian would ever use it.'

'Many will think it though,' Sushma added. 'You are white, that cannot be denied. India is not free of racism and here you can be regarded as an ethnic minority. If you really want to learn more, let me introduce you to some of my friends who have contact with the Rose Alliance, a group of mostly women in Uttar Pradesh who are fighting back against these disgusting crimes.'

'Sushma, I've warned you about those people. It's a copy of the *Gulabi* Gang in *Bundelkhand*. They're no better than vigilantes; they'll get into serious trouble one day so will anyone connected with them.'

'Chirag, The *Gulabi* Gang is estimated to be ten thousand strong. They are being derided when Politicians and journalists refer to them as a *Gang*. They are more akin to an army, the start of a movement which will one day be victorious. The Rose Alliance doesn't use *lathis* and is more politically motivated, seeking to change things from the top. It has already published lists of Members of the Indian Parliament who are awaiting trial for offences of rape and murder. This rottenness goes to the core of our Government and our society. Boys as young as eleven or twelve are getting involved in rapes. How can this be tolerated?'

'The bigger they are the quicker they get bail.' Ganesh interrupted. His attempt at humour not working to ease the atmosphere.

'Sushma, we are running around in circles. It's time we changed the subject. We know that many in our country are still corrupt. Modi is doing his best to eradicate it.'

'Sometimes best just isn't good enough. His own party members join marches in support of releasing rapists and he says nothing. He doesn't condemn rape as a crime. The *Gulabis* with their bamboo *lathis* beating abusive husbands and criminals, have done more to stop domestic violence and crimes against women, in their region, than the courts have done in decades.'

'Please, Sushma. Enough. Let's all go and watch the cricket.'

'Let's not,' replied Sushma as she walked out the door.

'I'm sorry Ben,' Chirag said. 'Sushma is very passionate about this cause.'

'We all are,' Priya joined in. 'If the government doesn't do something soon we'll become a pariah state.'

'I think I might like to meet this Rose Alliance,' I said.

'I'll go and tell *mammii*,' Ganesh said.

'Ben, you shouldn't get a completely wrong idea about our justice system. It isn't as bad as it sounds. The three-minute thing isn't accurate. It's arrived at by dividing the number of cases on a daily list by an estimated number of minutes a judge sits in court.'

'Is it true it can take more than ten years to get a judgment in a criminal case?'

'Depending on the parties, yes often much longer. The case of Sumedh Singh Saini, a senior police officer in Lhudiana, arrested on murder charges in 1994 has still not been finalised.'

'But that's more than twenty-five years. How can that be possible?'

'It might be an exceptional case as the body of the victim was never found. He was last seen being driven off by the police officer. In India the trial can get bogged down in spurious applications, which can themselves take years to resolve and the trial is halted in the meantime.'

'That cannot be justice. Whether the man is innocent or guilty he surely must have the right to a timely trial.'

'The majority of the applications in this case have been instigated by the accused. In many cases particularly where a prominent police officer or politician is involved, especially when they are guilty, they play the system. Put on an application to be excused from a court appearance, that can delay things for months.

'Then appeal any decision made; that can be a further six months to a year, or longer if it goes to the Supreme Court. In the Saini case, the mother of Ashish Kumar, the victim, was in ill health, she was seventy-two years old when her son died. She was eighty-six when she was called to give evidence and appeared on a stretcher.'

'Fourteen years?'

'Yes. She petitioned the court on numerous occasions to be able to give her evidence, she worried she would die before doing so. When she finally got her chance, the judge decided part way through her evidence to break for lunch and told her to come back in a month to continue.'

'That was a long lunch.'

'It's the way the system works. He would have assigned other cases to his afternoon list.'

'It seems to me to be open to corruption.'

'The whole of Indian society is open to corruption,' he said, 'but we hope and pray that our judges are above that.'

'I've only been in India three days and I fear that it's a vain hope and your prayers are not being answered.'

'Maybe it's the prayers of the corrupt which are being answered. "Please God, don't let me get caught today" is a common request.'

CHAPTER 12

Present Day
Düsseldorf, Thursday, 5.30 p.m.

I should have anticipated the situation.

Perhaps it was the internal planning I was going through. How I would use the information just obtained, how and when the two lawyers would die, or maybe, it was the thought of meeting Christiana later that made me too relaxed.

Whatever the reason, I didn't see him until the last moment and significantly I didn't see him before he saw me. The guy with the knife, from earlier, was standing on the corner of *Steinstrasse*, waiting and grinning.

He seemed too relaxed, too happy to be alone. I needed to know what I was dealing with. I changed direction and crossed over *Königsallee* and continued along the *Stadtgarben*. As I passed his position he nodded at unseen person or persons and crossed the street towards me. About five metres behind was another man, dressed similarly.

That's two, I thought.

I kept walking under the shade of the trees which lined the street. I walk fast naturally so didn't increase my pace. I would choose when to start running. This would be done on my terms not theirs. It was just a glimpse, in my peripheral vision, but number three was matching my pace on the far side of the road. I didn't want to risk looking around and revealing I had seen him.

I approached *Heinrich-Heine-Allee*. Using the excuse of checking for traffic to look over at number three. He seemed on his own so I was satisfied there were no others, unless they were directly behind me with knifeman. Three made sense. Most thugs believe in their own legends. Attacking me in greater numbers would deflate their egos. They would be thinking two were enough and the third was a guarantee.

I felt safe whilst he was on the other side of the road. The others were unlikely to attack me from behind without him. They would need to act quickly. Stabbing me around my kidneys would be the most likely using the second and third man to hide the act as much as possible. They were thirty paces behind when they crossed the road, they would have to run to catch me and there was no sign of that.

As I reached the end of *Königsallee*, they would be feeling confident. They knew, as I did, I was heading towards a much quieter area, fewer witnesses. Now was the time to test their athletic prowess. As I passed the *Galleria Kaufhof* I started to run. Ignoring the red pedestrian light at the end of the road, I ran between the traffic. A police car was passing, a horn sounded.

'Come on then,' I said, 'arrest me for jaywalking. It'll save me a lot of bother.' But they drove on.

As I entered the *Hofgarten*, I took the path to the right, away from the *Deutsche Opera am Rheine*. Like all opera houses this is much more beautiful on the inside than on the outside, and is a theatre where Christiana and I have spent many entertaining evenings. I wondered if there were any tickets available for tomorrow night. Stravinsky's 'Petruska' was on, Christiana would enjoy that.

My intention was to go to the area by the *Märchenbrunnen* but decided to take the long way around. The further they had to run before they caught me the better.

The twenty-seven-hectare park, known as '*Die grüne Lunge*,' green lung of Düsseldorf was busy. Had I been running in a tracksuit I would have drawn absolutely no attention, however dressed in black leather and biking boots I drew glances. What people must have thought when they saw three guys chasing me I could only imagine. 'Maybe they're undercover cops, we should have tried to stop him,' or similar.

The chasers needed to think I was worried, so I kept glancing behind. The distance between us was increasing. That was good and bad. Good, as it showed me they were unfit; bad as I could simply keep running and get away from them. That couldn't happen. I needed to move freely in this town for the next thirty-six hours without wondering if I would come across them.

'Get it done when the opportunity is right,' Giacomo would have said. Now was right. I stopped for a couple of seconds bending over feigning tiredness. This allowed them to gain a few paces then I set off again slightly slower than before.

The knifeman from this morning was getting ahead of the others, I hoped that would continue. I ran towards *Maximilian-Weyhe-Allee*, named after the guy who, in 1804, extended Nicolas de Pigage's 1769 original work. Giacomo would have been proud of the historical knowledge I retained.

As I reached the road I quickly turned off the path and cut along the tree line. This would give me a better chance of dodging the traffic which was busy at this hour. I assessed the traffic and jumped the low fence, sprinting across the road, jumping the matching fence on the other side and feigned hiding behind a tree to watch my followers.

They arrived at the end of the path at the pedestrian crossing, the lights were red. The knifeman looked around as the others caught up with him. They obviously hadn't seen me. '*Arschlöcher*,' I swore, as I moved from one tree to another. A shout from across the street indicated the arseholes had finally seen me so I set off running again. I couldn't believe they waited for the lights to change to green before they crossed.

I hadn't been in the park since the glass vivarium built by an American artist for a 2002 exhibition had been destroyed by a falling beech tree during Storm Ela in 2014. It was now completely gone. I came out onto the pathway still about thirty paces ahead of the trio following me.

Time to stretch them out. I varied my pace, ten steps sprint, ten steps jog. Once again knifeman was ahead of the others, but no closer to me. After about 200 meters, following the path parallel to *Kaiserstrasse*, I turned left, past the children's play area, and carried on to the small hill named after Napoleon Bonaparte. The two following knifemen were flagging. I needed a change of strategy. Too much further and they would give up this chase.

I dropped the idea of heading to the statue of the children and frogs and cut back to the old vivarium site. There was good tree cover there and fewer people, and most helpfully for the chasers it was closer.

I changed direction again and headed back towards *Max-Weyhe-Allee*. As I reached the open ground with the trees beyond I stopped and faced the oncoming knifeman.

He slowed his pace and pushed his hand inside his jacket. He pulled out a knife. It wasn't the small stiletto type I had seen this morning. This was bigger. A hunting knife with a fixed blade, I estimated four inches. He intended to do me real harm. I presumed that the others would be similarly armed. I saw one of his companions still running up. Number three was missing.

Has he given up already? I asked myself.

I let knifeman take the first lunge towards me, I stepped slightly to the side and grabbed his wrist, behind the knife. I twisted and pulled, unbalancing him, he fell to his knees. I kept hold of his wrist and held his arm rigidly behind his back. He knew I could easily break both his wrist and arm and as I bent his wrist harder and harder he loosened the grip of the knife and let it fall. His friend arrived; he too was wielding a similar knife.

'An internet job lot?' I asked.

The first knifeman was immobile; I kicked the incoming assailant in the knee and then as he fell forwards kicked him again in the face. I completed breaking the arm of the first and walked over to the second grabbed his head and twisted, not enough to break his neck but sufficient to knock him unconscious.

It had all taken a matter of seconds, fifteen or so I guessed though I hadn't set my watch as I sometimes did.

There was still no sign of number three. I bent down to talk to the guy I had seen this morning. He was curled up in a ball, holding his arm.

I heard the footsteps before catching sight of the blade on the periphery of my vision. I instinctively ducked to the side. The blade caught my right cheek. His forward movement had taken the attacker past me. He turned; I slammed my left fist into his nose, shattering it. I grabbed his knife hand, kicked him firmly in the groin and used all my strength to displace as many of the eight carpal bones as I could. He had cut me, he needed to regret that.

Trapezium, Trapezoid, Scaphoid, Lunate, Triquetrum, Pisiform, Hamate and Capitate. I had learned the names of the bones which linked the arm to the fingers. I wanted to make sure that as many as possible on this man's hand would be repositioned. He would need surgery to repair the damage I was now doing, even with that he would have to learn to do things with his left hand.

Another twenty seconds had passed. I bent over the first guy and whispered in his ear. I wanted to make sure he understood that he was dealing with a professional, who today had decided to let him live. That concession would not be granted if I ever saw him in my vicinity again.

As I stood and walked away I felt the flow of blood from my cheek. I had a silk scarf in my pocket which I wore around my neck under my crash helmet. I held this to the wound, trying to look as inconspicuous as possible as I headed for my bike. The opera house tickets would have to wait.

With my crash helmet on, no-one could see the blood. I fired up the engine and headed towards Christiana's apartment near the University. Her reaction when she saw me was typical of her.

'Need patching up again, *Häschen*? Why is it I always get you when you're injured?'

She was matter of fact. If curiosity was burning inside I couldn't tell. She never asked questions like, What happened?

or What were you doing? It was as if she understood I wouldn't like her asking and maybe it was better she didn't know. Her total lack of judgmentalism was one of the reasons I loved her.

The wound was only superficial, I'd been lucky. No stitches required, antiseptic cream and a large plaster. It wasn't going to stop either of us enjoying the evening and night.

CHAPTER 13

I sat in the car with Sushma, Priya and the driver. We arrived at a five-star hotel near the airport and were shown to a private dining area where Sushma had organised a dinner with some of her friends in the Rose Alliance.

The heavy red alder round table could easily seat twenty. The raised centre portion, created a giant version of a 'Lazy Susan' on which the many dishes which form part of formal Indian meals could be shared and passed from one diner to another. A carousel of convenience which avoided the need for waiters to stand around listening to conversations which they should not be party to.

To the side there was a seating area with a self-service, non-alcoholic bar. I took a cola after Sushma and Priya helped themselves to Mango juice.

'We'll have wine and whisky with the meal,' Sushma said.

'Whisky? With a meal?'

'Certainly. You are in India now. Men in particular, but now also many women, drink whisky with food in much the same way as the French drink wine.'

'Almost half of the world's whisky is drunk in India alone,' Priya joined in.

'Amongst wealthy professional groups, whisky pairing dinners are very common,' said Sushma. 'Chirag knows more than me, but I understand *palak patta chaat* goes very well with rum-seasoned-casked whiskies, peaty Islay and Skye whiskies are great for Tandoori chicken.'

'It's a whole new level of education for me,' I said. 'However, I think I'll stick with a glass or two of wine or beer for the moment. I'm not big on highly alcoholic drinks.'

'If Manisha is here tonight, I'm sure she'll try and educate your taste buds. Her husband runs a big drinks importation company, in fact he supplies most of the wines and whiskies to this hotel.'

The other guests arrived in ones and twos and it was almost two hours before Sushma said, 'Let's go and sit.'

I quickly learned that, in India, a dinner invitation for seven-thirty meant if you arrived at any time before nine you were still regarded as on time. Having endured Mumbai and Delhi traffic I could easily understand this concept.

Manisha arrived, one of the last. As we went to sit I positioned myself strategically between Sushma and Priya, I'm not a heavy drinker and, if I do occasionally like a single malt, it should be with chocolate, not *chaat*. I didn't want to start tomorrow with a hangover. Eighteen of us were sitting around the table. I was the only man. Manisha was not afraid to shout across the table to me.

'Sushma tells me you are not a drinker of whisky with food; we'll have to change that.'

'Maybe on another evening. Tonight I want a clear head.'

'He feels threatened by so many women surrounding him,' another said, which led to loud laughter at my expense. I felt myself reddening, wondering if this had been a good idea.

Food arrived; dish after dish was placed on the central carousel. Manisha ordered wine and whisky from her *special reserve*, which I assumed meant a stock which her husband supplied and kept here so he didn't have to pay the exorbitant cost on the menu.

'*Ayurvedic* tradition dictates that all of the six flavours of food should be present in our meal,' she said. 'Sweet, sour, salty, bitter, pungent and astringent each have a place and order on the table. You don't need a diet plan if you listen to your taste buds and take each flavour in the quantities your body tells you. Now, please, enjoy.'

I resisted all alcohol, for which Manisha feigned insult. This was India and although Hinduism did not ban alcohol, many Hindus do remain teetotal and, at the table, I wasn't the only one abstaining tonight.

'A strict *Brahmin* diet forbids alcohol and eating of meat, although not everyone adheres to that,' said Sushma.

'This is India. Nothing is forbidden, Sushma. Hinduism allows for anything and everything. It is not a faith-based religion, but spiritual.' Manisha was in her element.

'Ben, we Hindus must understand *dharma*, the natural laws controlling us and the universe around us. If we want to do something we only have to think about how our *karma* will be affected. The basic tenet is "if I drink alcohol, or eat meat, will this cause harm to my spirit or that of another person?" If we are happy that it will not, then our religion allows us to consume whatever we wish. The so-called *Brahmin diet*, where meat, eggs, all animal products, mushrooms and alcohol are regarded as *Tamasic* or *Rajasic* and must be avoided leaving only the *Sattvic* foods to be enjoyed, is followed by very few Hindus in reality.'

I had studied Yoga so the concept of the three *gunas*, *Tamas, Rajas* and *Sattvas* were well known to me. Our being and behaviour, even the food we eat, are dictated by the varying combinations of these, philosophically complex concepts. My own self-analysis indicated to me I was almost entirely *Tamasic* – beyond hope.

At the table there was no lack of conversation. I was able to enjoy the food and not feel pressurised into thinking of topics to discuss. These were a strong, capable group and by the end of the meal I believed that if anyone could change the damaging parts of Indian culture, these were the ones to take the first step.

The distasteful topic we had all come to discuss was left until the food had finished. It was Manisha who seemed to be the unofficial leader of the group.

'So, Ben,' she said. 'You want to know about the rape culture in India and what can be done to stop it.'

'Along those lines,' I replied.

'The first thing is get people with political clout to take it seriously, and try and put pressure on our government, instead of cow-towing to a Prime Minister who doesn't care. He just wants foreign money and investment and foreign governments faun over him because he is the leader of a billion people.'

'I'm not sure I have those sort of connections.'

'Well, make them.'

'I'm not sure that is helpful, Manisha,' Sushma interrupted. 'Ben is here to try and understand. He rescued Priya from her father's clutches. He was trying to marry her off to some dubious associate, three times her age, in Dubai against her will.'

'Rohtak is the essence of evil,' replied Manisha. 'I can't understand how, or why, your sister married him. I only met him a couple of times, but each time he left me feeling unclean.'

'She was barely older than a child, when she met him.'

'That would figure,' Sushma replied. 'He seems to have a penchant, even now, for young girls.'

'Can we change the subject away from that monster? Please?' It was Priya who spoke.

CHAPTER 14

Present Day
Düsseldorf, Friday morning, 7 a.m.

Christiana brought me coffee in bed. We sat and talked about times gone by. Carefree times when two kids loved spending hours and days together walking or taking a boat on the river.

If I could ever marry, it would be Christiana I would ask, and I hoped she would say yes. I couldn't do that to her. My way of life was not conducive to a happy marriage, or indeed any marriage. It had worked for Giacomo and Chiara because they shared the passion and the work. I believed Christiana could never accept what I did.

'Why don't you come to see me more often *Häschen*?' she asked.

'You saw how I was when I came in last night. I never stay in one place for more than maybe a week. Sometimes, the job I do is dangerous. That cut yesterday, could have been more serious. I couldn't have you worrying all the time.'

'I worry about you anyway,' she said. 'Each time we're together like this, I search your body for new scars.'

'So that's what you were doing.'

We both laughed.

I broke the subsequent silence.

'You never ask what I do.'

'No,' she replied. 'I figure when, or if, you want me to know, you'll tell me.'

'Shall we go to the Opera tonight if I can get some tickets? There are usually some returns.'

'We'll need three. Freddy is flying in from Edinburgh this afternoon. Johann said he'd meet us later at *Zum Uerige*. He's at a conference in Frankfurt and will drive back when it's finished. The Opera will be over by the time he gets here – so yes, try and get tickets.'

'What are you saying? I have to fly to India tomorrow. I'll need a clear head not an *alt bier* and *schnapps* hangover.'

'Don't worry. Your Frankfurt flight isn't until late tomorrow night, you could fly down instead of taking your bike. Then I would know you'd come back. Anyway would it be such a bad thing if you postponed this Indian trip for a few days?'

'It would be a very good thing to postpone this India trip forever. But, it is also an impossible thing. I must go and it has to be now. Once this trip is done, let's all get together again and really make a holiday of it. The three musketeers and Christiana D'Artagnan wreaking havoc in the *Altstadt*!'

'Who knows what might happen after this trip. That will depend on any new scars you bring back with you.'

I didn't reply. She'd hit a nerve. The two most important people in my world were both telling me not to go.

Their instincts, one with full knowledge of what I would face and one completely in the dark, were identical.

Mine were not so different, but were tinged with, you have to, this is for Giacomo, and who knows who else? Maybe it could be for Kiki too and the sixty or more other kids whose files I saw in the lawyers' offices yesterday. Whatever the motivation, I knew I had to be on that plane tomorrow and in Mumbai on Monday morning.

I showered, shaved and dressed. Christiana made a fresh jug of coffee and we sat in the kitchen looking out across the street, to the apartments opposite.

'Does Brigitta still live over there?' I asked.

'She does and seems to move in a different girlfriend every month,' replied Christiana. 'I'm not going to tell her you're here or she'll come running and neither of us will get out for hours.'

'I'm one thing, but if she knows Freddy's coming, we'll never get them away from each other.'

'I'm sure she does know he's coming. He probably told her before me. He'll sleep over there tomorrow night, I can guarantee it'

'More likely, drink and talk all night. I doubt he'll get much sleep. Better to say he'll stay over there.'

In the days before LGBTQ openness, Freddy and Brigitta had found a unifying spirit. They formed the first Gay and Lesbian Society in Düsseldorf and were its first joint Presidents.

Brigitta, catwalk model, tall, blonde and sophisticated turned into a giggling mess whenever she and Freddy got together over cocktails, or wine or beer or vodka. Grape or grain, her propensity for alcohol was phenomenal. Freddy not so much, however they never entered into drinking competitions, more likely who could tell the funniest joke, or the most stupid, the crudest, or the most nonsensical depending on the stage of the evening and alcohol consumption. Going out for a drink with those two was like going to a comedy club, great fun but not something to do every day.

When Freddy was with our small group of four, he tended to be more serious. Brigitta was his steam release valve. He was an IT specialist for a UK governmental department affiliated to GCHQ but based in Edinburgh. He worked constantly and intensely. So much so that he had never been able to form any long-term relationship.

The men in his life had come and gone, mainly, he said, because he spent his life on his computer and most of the time didn't know they were there. He needed Brigitta and he needed the one holiday a year they spent together. A week in May at the Eurovision Song Contest in whichever country it was being held in. Christiana and I joined them one year and enjoyed the seven days and nights of partying as much as Freddy and Brigitta. We swore we'd go back, and meant it.

We never did.

I logged on to the *Opernhaus* web shop site and managed to book three tickets near the back of the first tier. Not the best seats but not the worst either. They weren't all together; Freddy would have to sit directly in front of us. He wouldn't mind. He watched ballet the way he worked on his computer, oblivious to everything around him.

Promising Christiana I'd be back in plenty of time, I set off to the small town about fifty kilometres away along the crowded A46. I would hate to commute this road in a car but my Italian two wheeled powerhouse weaved through the traffic without problems.

The house I was looking for was outside of the town, but nostalgia got the better of me and I went directly to the centre. In our final student year, Christiana and I had rented an apartment in this quiet municipality, half an hour by train from

Düsseldorf. I rode past the bright yellow four storey building on the narrow street which was our home together. I headed into the town a five-minute walk away, one on my bike. I passed the red-tiled houses with grey walls and small, square white-painted first-floor windows. This could only be Germany. I parked beside the twin towered church and walked the short distance to the *Altmarkt*.

In the old market square, I bought a *bratwurst*, served in a small, crispy bread roll, the sausage being twice the length of the bun. I did some window shopping as I ate. The expensive china and porcelain store was still there, dinner services and accessories dominating its displays. Waves, squares and wavy squares seem to be the modern trend. All white Villeroy and Bosch juxtaposed with patterned Meissen, antique and modern figurines displayed ostentatiously on shelves covered in white silk.

Next door a bric-a-brac store filled with cheap ornaments, candles and drinking games. A jewellers, clothes store and ice-cream parlour were all busy. I was chewing the last bite when I arrived at the café where Christiana and I had spent our Saturday afternoons drinking white wine and talking about everything and nothing. I stopped, ordered a coffee and wallowed in happy memories before turning to the reason I was here.

This was a strange case.

I felt the various strands of my life were becoming entangled. So much of the case revolved around me. My home in Italy, the lawyers, not just in Düsseldorf where Christiana lives, but here, in this small town where we lived together.

Have I always been wrong about coincidence?

Does it exist?

I was beginning to hope so, the alternatives worried me.

Two lawyers had to die. I hoped it would be today, I don't like to leave things undone. With a smile on my face, remembering the happy times here, I picked up my helmet from the back of the bike and headed up the steep hill for the short trip to the lawyers' house.

There were no TV or Press anywhere. The house was not visible from the road. Completely surrounded by dense trees, it would be easy to imagine there was no house there at all. Instantly-available satellite pictures told a different story. Strange how people believed that such tightly packed trees gave them more security. They tend to forget it also stops burglars from being seen from neighbouring properties.

As I parked my motorbike some distance away, I called Chiara.

'Everything is done,' she said. 'They seem lazy about their technology. Perhaps they believe the quiet position of the house is protection enough. I've managed to hack into the security systems and have control of the cameras and alarms. They have internal as well as external cameras so I can tell you there is no-one at home.'

'That's a pity,' I replied. 'I wanted to get things done quickly; I'm going to the ballet tonight with Christiana and Freddy.'

'Then leave everything. I told you before, these people can wait.'

'As I'm here, I may as well check things out. Give me five minutes and switch everything off.'

'OK, but don't be more than ten minutes inside.'

The problem with smart home technology is that there is

always someone smarter around.

Precisely five minutes after I finished speaking to Chiara the Jachenholz family home had a power cut. Forty-three seconds later I was standing in the hallway of this attractive white house with its red tiled roof. Internally the decoration was plain, minimalist and white.

White walls, white ceilings and white doors. The only contrast was given by the predominantly black wood furniture and door handles. In the hallway on top of a black table was a white ornament showing a man and woman in a tender embrace.

The black and white theme was repeated throughout the whole house. Black leather furniture in the lounge. Black chairs and a smoked glass table in the dining area. The large kitchen was white with granite works tops.

Everywhere was clean, too clean.

The faint smell of bleach lingered in my nostrils. Someone had gone to a lot of trouble cleaning this house. Perhaps in the knowledge that, after Kiki's death, there would be a visit from the police, they had cleaned it before she died. The stairs creaked as I walked to the first storey. Angled ceilings meant much of the time I had to bend as I paced from room to room. Nothing was out of place anywhere.

There was something not right, but I couldn't assimilate what it was. In the main bedroom the bed and linen looked brand new as if it had never been slept in. The second bedroom was obviously Kiki's. That too had a new bed and linen on which sat a single cuddly toy; a panda.

What else? I thought. There'll be no DNA found in here.

A book lay on the cabinet beside the bed. Like millions of

others, in different languages, I had read this book in childhood, *Das Wunder von Narnia*, only I had known it under its English title. I picked it up and flicked through a few pages. I still remembered the story and the snippets I read brought back the whole adventure. The change in language didn't diminish the enjoyment.

I thought of Kiki lying here and reading this tale of Susan, Edmund and Lucy facing perils and battles and ultimate triumph, losing herself, as I had, in its wonderful escapism. I placed the book back where I found it.

I wasn't going to learn anything from here so I turned to retrace my steps down the stairs. I hadn't gone far when it dawned on me. The house upstairs was smaller than down, yet on the outside the building was even all the way around.

There had to be another room. But where?

I imagined the space downstairs. The main bedroom with its en-suite shower room was above the lounge and dining area and the sizes matched. Kiki's room at the back was above the kitchen but was much smaller than the kitchen and laundry area downstairs. The bathroom on this floor didn't make up the difference.

Bounding back up. I searched, looking for a hidden doorway. There was nothing visible. Turning to face the bed the black-eyed panda stared at me. My eyes moved to the book. Its original name came into mind.

The Lion, the Witch and the Wardrobe.

Of course, the wardrobe. I flung open the door and pushed the pitiful clothes of a dead ten-year-old girl to one side. All looked normal. The back of the wardrobe was black the same colour as the outside. I ran my hand around its edges and found a small hole about the diameter of a man's thumb. Placing my index finger into the orifice, I felt a metal spring. I pushed down and a door swung open.

I moved inside. I scrambled for a light switch and found one. I forgot for a moment that Chiara had cut the power and my attempts to turn on the light failed. Taking a torch from my pocket I scanned the room. In the middle was a stone-coloured table, lying across it was the skin of a lion. A mannequin stood beside the table dressed in a witch's garb. Around the walls of the windowless room were pictures, tens of them, maybe hundreds.

These images could never now be unseen. I couldn't find Kiki's face, I was sure she must be there but she was lost amongst the dozens of other photos of children.

Maimed, molested minors, some with their eyes missing, others bound with plastic ties.

Frau Jachenholz was there, dressed as the witch, performing unspeakable sex acts on small boys. Her husband, the lion skin over his shoulders, doing the same to young girls.

I fumbled for my phone. I needed to record all of this. I had to show Chiara who we were dealing with. As I turned, I knocked over a white inverted umbrella shaped object. It was a translucent lighting unit; a sophisticated video camera was on a pedestal beside it. I was in a film studio. But this wasn't a make-believe place where actors learned their lines and, replete with costumes, performed their art under the eye of a director and producer for the enjoyment of the television or cinema audiences; where, between shots, coffee was served and cigarettes were smoked.

This was a place of visceral fear and unmitigated horror. A

sound proof box where children's screams would be unheard except for those watching the live screening across the internet, or later on a DVD or other device. Paying large sums of money to see the pain of innocents and satisfy their perverted sexual needs.

Horrified but determined, I left that place of terror-filled savagery. The Jachenholz evil would be eliminated. Unfortunately it wouldn't be today. They seemingly had no intention of coming back here and I had no quick way of finding them. My phone, set on silent, vibrated as I closed the front door. Chiara. I answered it as I made my way to the wooded garden at the back to go to my bike.

'Where are all the bodies?' she asked.

I realized I must have pressed 'send' on the video as I tripped over the light stand.

'Don't know, I'll ask when I see *Herr* Jachenholz.'

'Were all filmed in that room?'

'Looked like it, most of the time the kids were lying on Aslan's table.'

'I'll try and enhance your video. Videos taken by torchlight are never the best. And your hand was shaking.'

'Like their necks will be when I catch up with them.'

The profligate perversion I had just witnessed was made worse, in my eyes, by the fact they had taken a work of outstanding children's literature and twisted it.

The book beside Kiki's bed was not there for her to enjoy the adventures of children around her own age, but was to instil fear. To make her think of the wardrobe. Perhaps she had seen young boys and girls murdered in there. The book a reminder of what could happen to her.

The corruption of their souls was complete. They had destroyed Kiki mentally and physically. I would ensure they too would understand suffering before they died.

CHAPTER 15

One Year Ago
Delhi, India Day 5 05:00 a.m.

The house was awake early. The flight from Toronto, via Vancouver, was due to land at 05:40. Priya asked me to accompany her and Sushma. She didn't say why.

Once at the airport, Sushma approached the armed soldiers at the entry. She handed them a letter. They examined it. She beckoned us over and after a check of ID documents one of the guards accompanied us through the doors, and onwards through to immigration.

'It pays to have a husband sitting as a Supreme Court Judge,' Sushma said.

'India is a country of influential people and influence,' added Priya.

'I realised that by the end of dinner last night,' I said.

We saw the electric buggy arrive and a woman, instantly recognisable as Sushma's sister, stepped down. She could not have been dressed more differently from her sibling. Sports shoes, tight jeans and a figure-hugging hockey jersey. The royal blue shirt had a white band around her hips and two parallel stripes around her arms. The white shoelace ties at the neck looked more for fashion than use. The front was emblazoned with an enormous white maple design and 'Toronto Maple

Leafs' making it perfectly clear where she was from and who she supported.

There was no queue at Passport control at which she arrived beaming a perfect, veneered smile, waving excitedly at my two companions. After her passport was stamped she ran through and picked Priya up in a hug and twirled her around.

'Mom, I'm not six anymore.' Priya laughed. 'Love you,' she said.

She then kissed Sushma, who turned towards me.

'This is Ben,' she said. 'Ben this is my sister Jamini.'

'Call me Jamie,' her sister said, holding her hand out for me to shake. 'All my friends do.'

'Your Canadian and American friends anyway,' Sushma said.

I hadn't realised until then just how high some people can raise their eyebrows. Sushma's seemed to disappear into her hairline.

'Better than the *Mini* you used to call me.' She pronounced the name *Meeny*. 'Over there they wouldn't pronounce it the same way and I'd have the name of a cartoon mouse. Thank you for saving Priya.'

'It was nothing,' I said.

'What are you saying? Are you crazy? This little girl is the most important thing in my life. How can you say it's nothing?'

'Mom, stop being so argumentative all the time. Just smile and agree once in a while. Let's go, the car's waiting.' She grabbed her mother's hand and linked her other hand in my arm. We walked out smiling.

We must have both seen him at the same time. Priya squeezed me just above the elbow. To her credit she made no other sign of recognition. Standing by the internationally famous coffee shop outlet, in a grey suit, white shirt and no tie, was one Slick's sidekicks. He watched us as we passed. We walked to where the white Mercedes and the driver were waiting, and got in. I sat in the front, the women behind. As we drove off I couldn't see him at the coffee stand.

'Let's get back to the house as quickly as possible,' I told the driver as we got in.

We drove out of the airport and along leafy suburbs. I looked in the wing mirror to check for any trailing vehicle, but there was nothing obvious.

We passed lavishly ornate Temples and Bank HQs, Embassies and Official Residences. At this early hour there was little traffic on the road, making it easy to spot a tail. The sisters were chatting animatedly in the back. They had slipped into their native tongue. Priya had earphones in and I could hear the rhythmic, muffled, metallic sound damaging her tympanic membrane with every beat.

Still no sign of anything behind, we were getting nearer the house, I started to relax.

First there was the noise of crushing metal and plastic. Our car started to spin. Screams from the rear seat and me shouting.

'Shit, where the hell did that come from?'

Neither I, nor the driver had seen the black Range Rover, coming at speed from the side road, hitting the Mercedes firmly behind the rear wheel.

Physics, and Newton's First Law of motion, took over. We would have persisted in our state of uniform motion, in a straight line, had the Range Rover not impressed its force upon us to change that state. The driver was trying to control the spin; he was competent and winning the struggle.

'Glove compartment,' he said.

I pulled down the flap and saw the gun inside.

'I'm Supreme Court Judge Police protection,' he said, the obvious question not needing to be asked.

I pulled out the firearm.

'Browning?' I asked.

'Indian. Made under licence. Ready, catch on.' He was trying to speak and control the car.

This world standard-defining, self-loading, semi-automatic pistol, sat easily in my hand. His few words told me that its magazine, of thirteen 9×19mm Parabellum bullets, was in place and all I needed to do was flick the safety lever on the side and start pulling the trigger. There was no sign of a spare magazine so thirteen had to be enough. They would be.

This pistol had served armies and police forces throughout the world for eighty-three years before production ceased in 2018. It was a shame to think the life of this great hand gun, the last of John Moses Browning's designs to remain in production was now limited. Perhaps this impressive Indian copy would continue in production; a question for later.

'Stay in the car,' I shouted as we came to a stop, rolling out the door, crouching facing the Range Rover.

Bullet one hit the front offside tyre, bullet two its nearside partner. Number three smashed through the middle of the windscreen, I didn't want to kill anyone… yet. They obviously hadn't expected us to be armed and tried to reverse away. They couldn't get far as traffic had built up behind. People who thought this was a normal traffic accident stopped, when they heard the gunshots they ran, abandoning their cars, blocking the road. Two small motorcycles came from the side road and pulled up beside the now, motionless 4 x 4.

Slick got out of the rear door. 'Mr. Johnson, how are you?' he said. 'Just give me the girl, and we can all move on with our day.'

'That's not going to happen, Shitole,' I replied. 'How are you going to explain this to the police when they arrive?'

'Don't be concerned about that. The cops won't be here until we're well gone. It's Sunday, it's early, they won't have time to come to a minor traffic accident. There are hundreds every day in Delhi.' He started to move forward. Bullet four struck the road a few inches in front of him; he instinctively jumped as road fragments caught him on the leg. Irritation not pain.

He motioned to one of the motorcycles, which revved up and came straight towards me.

Was he testing to see if I would shoot or jump?

Was this a game of clichéd poultry?

He didn't know me or anything about me, or he wouldn't have gambled.

Bullet six broke the rider's clavicle. He received worse injuries as his bike slewed out of control and hit the kerb.

'Enough, Johnson. Give me the girl and you might see your friend again.'

'You told me he was dead.'

'Did I? Or did you just assume that I did? Do you really want to take that risk?'

'Can't do it Shitole. Leave now, before anyone else gets hurt. Get your lackey an ambulance.'

'Girl, ambulance, you gone. That's the order of things.'

'You're very arrogant seeing that I have a gun pointed at you.'

'You've just shown that you are not going to kill anyone on

an open road in Delhi.'

'Won't I? Or are you just assuming I won't?' I said, 'Do you really want to take that risk?'

'I've tried to be nice, Mr. Johnson. It seems you won't listen to reason.'

He jumped in the car as the second motorcyclist pulled out a pistol and aimed.

Bullet seven hit him mid chest. Bullet eight went through his visor. Shitole had assumed wrongly.

'Always keep a running total of the numbers of bullets used,' Giacomo's voice was clear; 'it will dictate your next moves and may save your life.'

I ran towards the car.

'You need to take the safety catch off,' I said to the driver who was pointing a pistol at me. I couldn't risk he would do as I said. Bullet nine went in the middle of his forehead.

A bullet ricocheted off the road. Instinct told me to roll away from the car. Bullets ten and eleven were discharged in the guessed direction, of the incoming shot. Slick was on the phone, I aimed my gun. Another shot missed me by fractions. I caught a glimpse of the grey suit behind the tree. Bullet twelve strewed splinters of bark in the area of his face.

The next shot had to count.

It didn't.

I thought there was enough of him available to hit, but he moved just as I was pulling the trigger and my shot went wide.

The laugh was manic. He came out from behind the tree. His pistol held professionally, two handed, blood trickled from a small splinter wound under his left eye.

'You wasted that last one and you have no fresh magazine.

Too bad. Now you will die. We will get the girl and you will never know if your friend is alive or dead. You will leave this earth with only questions and no answers.'

Bullet fourteen shocked him.

His eyes widened, his mouth fell open.

Bullet fifteen killed him. A perfect head shot. I turned around and saw Chirag's driver.

'Perhaps I should have given you this Glock instead,' he said, 'more rounds. Now get in the car, it's still driveable, and give me the gun.' An advancing siren warned of approaching Police. 'If anyone asks you, I did all the shooting. Understand?'

I nodded, and moved towards the driver's door. As I opened it I could hear the murmurings of tearful prayers from the back seat.

'Are you all OK?' I asked leaning into the car.

Jamie nodded. She was holding Priya tightly; Sushma was curled into a ball, hands clasped.

The white, Maruti Gypsy small jeep came from the same side road that the Range Rover had attacked us from. I stood and looked over the top of the car. 'Delhi Police' was written in red on the doors and below the windscreen, the flashing blue light above.

It pulled up beside the, now open, rear door of Slick's car. Our driver started to walk towards it. The lone policeman on board got out and pointed his pistol. He was young, thin and visibly shaking. 'S-stay back,' he said, 'and d-drop the gun.'

'I'm IPS,' came the reply.

'Who? I d-don't care. D-D-Drop it, or I'll sh-shoot.'

A man with a gun is threatening. A nervous youth, with a loaded pistol, is unpredictable and dangerous.

The driver hesitated. He must have sensed it too. There was something awry. The policeman was youthful, maybe this was his first confrontation with an armed man; bodies lying in the road could also be traumatic. Is that all it is? No. It feels wrong. His uniform's too big for him: His frame diminutive, Indian Police uniforms perhaps standard size? Even the pistol looked large in his undersized, quivering hands.

'The gun,' I rasped, hoping the driver would hear but the policeman not. Realisation hitting me hard.

'Yeah, I see it too,' he whispered back. 'Get in the car, driver's side. If anything happens drive away. Don't stop for anything.'

'Is everything OK?' Priya asked.

'Don't worry Priya, you're all safe now,' I said, hoping I sounded convincing,

I wished I could believe what I was saying. The gun in the shaking hand of the juvenile, faux policeman, and pointed in our direction, was not a standard police firearm.

It was too big.

Its barrel an inch or so longer than the regulated issue. That was no 9mm. It was a Desert Eagle .44 Magnum. I had fired these guns on a range, smashing concrete to demonstrate their force. My one hope, the kid's small hands would struggle with the extra wide grip on the gun. Being longer than 9mm, .44 rounds require a wider magazine; consequently the girth of the Magnum's handle is notably bigger so as to accommodate the extra size.

More sirens sounded in the distance.

Slick walked calmly to the opposite side of the jeep. '*Challo*, let's go,' he said, as he opened the door and slid onto the seat. 'Quickly, boy.'

The young 'officer' lowered his gun as he got in. He started the engine and siren and set off hastily, driving around our car and away.

Slick moved his hand through his oiled hair, and waved as he passed. His mouth set in a grimace. Our driver jumped in the passenger seat. 'Go,' he said. 'I'll make a call, but you mustn't be found here.'

He pulled out his phone.

'Personal Protection R2097,' he said. 'Shooting incident off Amar Shaheed Marg. I'm taking my party away from scene to safety. Inform Officers I will return to event parameter soonest.' He turned to the passengers in the back. 'All's fine now. No worries. But please, Mr. Johnson was not here if you are asked any questions.'

'Thank you,' I said.

'No problem Mr. Johnson.'

'Call me Ben.'

'And you can call me Arjun.'

'Thanks again, Arjun. I hadn't seen him hiding behind that tree.'

'I had a different angle so spotted him straight away. I didn't want him to know I was also armed, at least until he felt safe.'

'You were certainly calm. You've used a hand gun before.'

'A few times. I'm ex-MARCOS.'

'Impressive,' I said. '*The Few, The Fearless*. I did some training with the Marine Commandos some years ago.'

'I know. I remember you… Ben.' His emphasis on my name indicated had known me by a different one. I'd talk with him later.

CHAPTER 16

Present Day
Düsseldorf, Friday, 9:30 p.m.

Freddy chatted incessantly about the Ballet as we walked from the opera house into the *Altstadt*. It had been a wonderful performance and Freddy liked to relive it, in great detail. We approached the brewery-cum bar which was central to the old town and one of its best-known landmarks.

The night was warm, the tables, outside on the pavements, crowded. Johann was there already. Even in the throng of hundreds of people, he was easy to spot.

Firstly he's black and over two metres tall. Secondly he was, as always, impeccably dressed, in a blue Italian designer suit, white shirt and, I had no doubt, a tie bought in Naples from E & G Cappelli. Johann made a trip once a year, sometimes more, to his favourite tie manufacturer. He had Patrizio's number in his contact list, and his fiery assistant, Maria, on speed dial.

He smiled, as we approached. I hated that smile at university. We would walk into a room, he'd look around smiling, and what seemed like every girl in the room would rush up to be near him. I always had to fight my way through them to get the drinks from the bar.

I hated that smile, but loved the man who owned it.

We became family. Freddy and Johann, the brothers I never

had. We were inseparable. The three musketeers, we said, no doubt like hundreds of other students throughout the world, over many decades. For us it was important, if not original. Here we are, twenty or so years later, standing together, like brothers-in-arms. When Christiana entered my life she was accepted.

'The ideal D'Artagnan,' Freddy said. 'Headstrong, confident, with a touch of Don Quixote about her.'

I noticed that Johann's beer mat had three pen marks on it.

'On your third already?' I said.

'You told me you'd be late,' said Christiana.

'My new car needed a try out. It didn't take as long as I thought it might.'

'Johann's got a new toy, Ricci,' Freddy said. 'He obviously can't get the girls through the force of his personality so he's bought himself a Mercedes AMG GT'

Everyone laughed at the thought that Johann was ever short of a love interest. He was one person who did not need to flash cash, or drive a fast car to attract anyone. Brigitta and Christiana had lists of famous models and actresses who constantly asked them if Johann was free and eligible.

'Join the queue,' was the stock answer.

'It's a thing of irresistible splendour,' Johann said. 'Top speed around three-hundred and forty kilometres per hour, but I only took her up to two eighty-five on the autobahn today. Next week I'm taking her to Hochenheim, then I'll really let her horses loose.'

He hailed a passing waiter, his stainless-steel rimmed tray covered in glasses of the brown *altbier*, brewed in the top-fermented micro-brewery, inside the building beside us, and for which this bar is, justifiably, famous. The waiter unloaded four glasses, pulled a pen from behind his ear and added the number, with individual strokes on the cardboard mat. Every fourth stroke had a diagonal line through it to signify five. It made it easier to count the number at the end of the night.

'It's like Dantès, marking out the days in his cell in the Chataeu D'If,' Freddy once remarked making reference to one of his favourite nineteenth century novels.

We raised our glasses.

'*Alle für Einen und Einer für Alle,*' we said, quoting Dumas as if we were all nineteen again without the concerns and stress that passing years and work brings.

'*Prost.*'

'*Zum Wohl.*'

'Cheers.'

'Good health.'

The well-established, teenage pre-drink rites concluded, we started to imbibe. It tasted even better than the last time.

'I was talking to a literary agent friend of mine,' Freddy said. Johann groaned. Freddy slapped his hand

He was starting one of his stories. How I missed the company of these guys. I had to keep secrets from them, and I knew they too had to keep their own secrets from me. It didn't matter. With these three I was always the closest to being myself. Two, were the brothers I never had, and Christiana the only woman I could ever love.

'Anyway,' Freddy continued, 'he says that if Daddy Dumas tried to get *The Three Musketeers* published today, agents and the mainstream publishers would set a new record for the fifteen hundred metres. I mean, let's face it, four very heterosexual, white males, cavorting around France and London, drinking and carousing, saving damsels in distress, is so not PC.'

Johann chuckled. He loved Freddy and his stories as much as the rest of us.

'We, my agent friend and I, are thinking of doing a re-write, what you think?'

He didn't wait for an answer. 'And, we four would be the models for the new breed of swashbuckling ne'er do wells, determined to rescue the lady from the clutches of the evil Cardinal. Can you imagine?' Again he didn't pause for breath or wait for one of us to respond. 'A gay, and I must say, very handsome, Aramis, a tall, black, charismatic Porthos and then I suppose, Ricci as Athos.'

It was my turn to slap his hand, but he didn't stop.

'And of course a beautiful tattooed lady with a brave heart and a Sir Quixote of La Mancha zest for life, as the dashing D'Artagnan, who risks all for the Lady de Winter, based on Brigitta of course, to return her to her lover, the Duke of Buckingham's wife.'

'You have it all planned out,' said Christiana.

'Also,' continued Freddy, as it will be written by two members of the LGBTQ+ movement, one of whom, not me, has a shady past, including spending time in prison in some -istan country for campaigning for Gay Rights, we will be snapped up and lauded by the media.'

'All sounds great, Freddy,' I said, 'but I see one problem.'

'Don't spoil it for me, Ricci, please. What is it?'

'Plagiarism.'

'That's a mere technicality. Who's going to sue? Daddy Dumas died on the Fifth of December 1870, Nipper Dumas in November 1895.'

Freddy always gave nicknames to authors to distinguish them from each other. 'Pere' and 'fils' were never sufficient for him. His names for the Brontë sisters were extremely unkind.

'I look forward to seeing it in print,' I said; 'and you in court.'

'It's in the Public Domain – no copyright issues,' Johann interjected.

'Thank you,' said Freddy

'Spoilsport,' said I.

More beer, more strokes of the pen. By the time we called a halt, we were onto a second beer mat.

'Christiana tells me you're flying to India tomorrow. Are you sure it's a good idea?' Johann sounded concerned.

He couldn't know all the details, but he knew how close Giacomo and I were and that he had died, mysteriously in India. We were walking down by the river, a short distance from the bar, heading, very indirectly, to the Taxi rank. We made the normal three-minute walk to Burgplatz last more than twenty. None of us wanted these evenings to end. I, in particular, was not looking forward to tomorrow

'It most definitely is not a good idea, but I don't have a choice. It's something I must deal with.'

'I know how much Giacomo means to you. We all do. We all have happy memories of our holidays with you in Bellagio. Giacomo and Chiara have had influence on all our lives, mine in particular. We've never really talked about it but it's true.'

'Why do you say, you in particular?'

'It was Giacomo and Chiara who paid for my education. Initially in South Africa and then here. I didn't find out until afterwards. My mother told me just before she died. She had survived the Soweto Massacre, her two brothers didn't. Giacomo and Chiara were there at that time and helped many black families in the aftermath.'

'I never knew. So many secrets.'

'They asked my mother to keep it completely confidential, and she did.'

'Typical of those two. They never told me either. They must have done so much good with the money and business empire they inherited. Everything I am is due to Giacomo and Chiara; personally and professionally. I've let them down. They trusted me to work with them and Giacomo died on my watch. I was there; I should have been able to help him.'

'I'm sure you did everything you could, but why go back?'

'Gut instinct tells me I must.'

'Never mind your gut, what does your head say?'

'That there is something very wrong and I need to try and sort it.'

CHAPTER 17

One year ago
Delhi, India Day 5 12:30 p.m.

'Ben, Arjun has told me all I need to know. The women are safe. That's all I care about. Priya and Jamini will leave on the first available plane tomorrow. They will have heavily armed protection directly to the plane, bypassing the terminal. Arjun and I are calling in a few favours.'

'Chirag, these men need to be stopped,' I said.

'And just how is that going to happen? Priya's father will no doubt be out of the country, so he can't be associated with this morning's events and Shitole will no doubt have a hundred witnesses who swear he was in Mumbai praying at his Temple.'

'But we know he wasn't.'

'What does that mean? We cannot do anything; we can't take the law into our own hands.'

Before I could reply, Priya, and her mother, walked in. Jamie gave me a huge hug repeating 'Thank you,' over and over again.

'Please, Jamie, I didn't do anything, I wasn't there remember.'

'We know the truth Ben, and that is we owe you. We owe you big time.'

'Big time?' Priya said. 'Just how Americanised have you become?'

Jamie ignored her. 'Ben, you must come to Canada and meet

my husband. You'd get along so well.'

'Maybe one day I'll get the chance,' I said, as diplomatically as I could. I spent my life trying to avoid meeting with Police. As much as I enjoyed their company, any further involvement with Priya's extended family would be too dangerous for me. Especially as Jamie's husband is a cop. No, it was time to leave and try and find Giacomo.

'What are your plans, Ben?' Chirag asked. 'You're welcome to stay here as long as you like.'

'Thank you, Chirag, but I must return to Mumbai and see if I can find my friend.'

'Speak with Arjun before you leave. He may have some contacts you can use.'

Having left the family alone to discuss personal matters, I sat in the expansive marble entrance hall on a red couch and picked up the paper. I was becoming almost numbed to stories of child molestation, but my anger was raised by two stories in this newspaper.

The first article was headed:

SUPREME COURT TO INITIATE SUO MOTU ACTION TO CURB SPIRALLING CHILD RAPE.

The Court noted that:

From January 1st to May 31st this year, as many as 20,176 First Information Reports were registered by police across India on incidents of child rape.

I needed the calculator on my mobile phone to check. This number seemed very high. The official figures I had read in the newspapers a few days ago had told me it was, disgustingly, forty per day, now the Supreme Court is saying that the true number is more than three times that. One hundred and thirty-three cases of reported child rape each and every single day of the year. How many more were there that went unreported?

'What the hell is wrong with this country?' I said out loud, raising curious looks from the maid walking past.

The bad news wasn't finished. On page three there was the headline:

MUM REJECTS ADVANCES: MAN RAPES DAUGHTER AGED 4 IN REVENGE THEN BEHEADS HER AND PEELS OFF THE SKIN OF HER FACE TO PREVENT IDENTIFICATION.

The suspect is reported to have taken the girl from her home without the knowledge of her hearing-impaired mother. He sexually assaulted, then severed her head with a kitchen knife and dumped her torso 300m behind his house, where he attempted to set it on fire.

The man removed all skin from her tiny face so the police could not identify her.

A blood-covered knife and bloodstained clothing found in the man's home led to him admitting all details of the crime to investigating police officers.

Since the world was shocked by the Delhi bus rape in 2012, the government has passed new legislation increasing punishment for the rape of an adult to 20 years in prison. Despite this, it's rare for more than some days to pass without another brutal sexual assault being reported.

In order to try and alleviate world criticism following international reporting and outrage over the number of rapes and killings of young girls and other attacks on children, India has recently approved death penalty for people convicted of raping children under age 12.

In other news, primary school teacher Mahendra Singh Gond received the death penalty earlier this month after he raped a four-year-old girl so badly she needed an operation on her intestines. More details and comment Page 12'

I couldn't turn to page twelve. What would be the point? The headline and first paragraphs gave me more than enough information. I was powerless and frustrated to do anything. At least he had been given the death penalty, but from what Chirag had told me about the Indian Penal Justice system, I had no real hope that it would be carried out. I had to find Giacomo and get out of here before my anger consumed me. If that happened, I might make a mistake which was something I couldn't afford.

'Arjun arrived as I was heading upstairs to pack. 'Namaste, Ben, have you got five minutes?' he asked.

'Sure.'

'Let's go to the garage. It's more private.'

I followed him out the front door and across the courtyard and into his domain. The *garage* was on two floors. The ground floor for the cars and upstairs was a large apartment where Arjun lived. Come into my office he said. We entered a spacious room, and as in the main house there was a lot of marble on the floors and walls.

'Is marble cheap in India?' I asked.

'Depends. I'm no expert but I assume there is generally a vast difference in price between Indian quarried marble and that imported from Italy. The marble in this house is an exception. It's white Makrana marble, the same as was used in the Taj Mahal. It comes from Rajastan and is probably as expensive, if not more so than the best imported Carrara marble from Italy.

Whoever built this house originally, certainly didn't have to worry about the cost. But we're not here to talk about marble; we need to speak of other things.'

'About this morning?'

'No, something very different. I'll come straight to the point. I am in the Indian Police service, and my duty is to protect this family. I must be sure that you pose no threat. The last time I met you, your name was *Tenente* Luigi Pastorelli of the Italian Special Forces.'

'Not strictly true,' I responded; 'I was in the Fourth Alpine Parachute Regiment which was a unit used for special operations. It didn't become designated as part of the Italian Special Forces until 2017. I wasn't there then.'

'Now you're just being pedantic.'

'I like to keep the facts straight.'

He laughed.

'You want to keep the facts straight? How come you're going around claiming to be an Englishman by the name of Ben Johnson?'

'Perhaps that's who I really am.'

'Ben, or Luigi, whatever your name is, I want to help you, but don't mess me around. Please.'

'Arjun, my name or nationality is not relevant. You saved my life today and I'm grateful. My work means that I sometimes have to travel under different identities depending on the circumstances.'

'OK. I'll work under the assumption that you're working for the Italian or other Government.'

Work on any premise you like, I thought. They'll all be wrong.

If he was expecting any acknowledgment from me, he didn't get it. He continued.

'I've been in touch with some people I know in Mumbai. I have bad news. They have found a body. It has been very badly mutilated but documents found nearby suggest it is your friend Mr. Fratelli.'

I rubbed my eyes and looked out of the window. So many thoughts rushed through my head. Giacomo and Chiara, in a boat on the lake, in their garden, sitting in a restaurant; love and laughter palpable and ever present. It had always been the two of them for as long as I could remember. What would Chiara do now? She was strong, but she said she got most of her strength from him. Giacomo said the same about her. My heart was breaking for her loss. I concentrated on that.

Think of Chiara and don't think about yourself and how much you'll miss him.

'What did they find?' I finally managed to ask.

'Italian ID Card and hotel bills.'

'No passport?'

'No, but that's not unusual. Passports are a saleable commodity. They're going to send me some crime scene photos, but they've warned me, it's a gut-churning sight. The murder weapon, or perhaps I should say, weapons were, what can I say, unusual to say the least.'

'Animals, presumably dogs,' I said, remembering the conversation I'd had with Slick.

God, was that only yesterday?

'So, when I talked to Deepak Shitole yesterday, he knew that Fratelli was dead?'

Arjun must have thought it strange that I referred to *my*

friend by his surname. This was me covering my tracks for a potentially serious mistake I'd made. I never asked Giacomo what his full cover name was. I'd picked up on his surname at the hotel, but never discovered his first name.

Idiot!

I thought of the quote from the book by Maurice Switzer, wrongly attributed at times to Abraham Lincoln, or Mark Twain. *It is better to remain silent at the risk of being thought a fool, than to talk and remove all doubt of it.* Better for Arjun to think it strange, than for me to put my foot in it by giving him the wrong name.

'The Maharashtrian Authorities thought it was an animal of some description, but were not sure. Why dogs?'

'It's what Shitole said yesterday, threatening me on the phone. "The hounds are still hungry," were the words he used.'

'I don't know about hungry; he was badly savaged but not eaten. It was more a frenzied attack than a feeding frenzy. Anyway, if you feel able, as the only person known to have been acquainted with Mr. Fratelli, the cops there would like you to try and identify the remains. It might not be an easy task, whatever it was that attacked him, bit off most of his face and mangled his hands so fingerprints are not an option.'

As we spoke his computer pinged. I turned at the sound and saw in the bottom corner the message: New mail – open Mail Folder. Arjun swivelled in his chair and slapped his finger on Enter. His emails opened and there was one highlighted as unread. I couldn't see who it was from.

'This will be the photos,' he said, as he opened the email and then the attachments. 'My God, they were not joking about the horror.'

I leaned back in my chair, closed my eyes and breathed deeply to steel myself. I opened them and moved closer to the computer.

I gagged.

He was wearing the clothes I had last seen him in. The grey trousers now drenched in his own blood. The shirt, patches of white visible, amongst the sanguineous staining. His, normally impeccably polished, black leather shoes scuffed and hanging on his toes, the heels seemingly dislodged as he was dragged across the floor. His head leaning back at an awkward angle, a mass of blood and gore, his throat gone.

His face bore injuries like I had only ever seen from close-range shotgun blasts, his hands as if he had opened a letter bomb. These were injuries I was used to seeing in photographs or in morgues, but not of someone I loved.

I couldn't take more and stood up and walked to the window. A gardener was tending brightly coloured plants in huge pots, a maid was crossing the courtyard with vegetables freshly bought in the market. Life carried on as normal, despite the carnage in the photographs behind me and the rapes, molestation and murders of children which were going on all around me every ten minutes.

My thoughts were of the past. On leave from training in the Alps. Sitting at the large table in Bellagio having eaten a splendid *Fiorentina* steak accompanied by a wonderful bottle of Brunello. Giacomo and Chiara explaining *The Atenisti* and where they would like me to fit into the organisation. For years they had kept these details from me. There was never any doubt, in their minds or mine, that I wouldn't accept the role they wanted for me. They didn't go into the details of the

160

reasons they had founded such a secretive organisation, not then. However, I knew it must have been the result of something traumatic.

'Why *Atenisti*? I know your passion for Egypt why choose a name of an ancient deity?'

They both laughed.

'It's because Giacomo thinks he's related to Nefertiti – or maybe he just wishes he was alive then and he married her rather than me.'

'Ha, ha, ha.' Giacomo feigned a laugh. 'That's just not true. I don't wish I lived in any time other than now, with you.'

'Mmm,' Chiara pronounced, with the knowing look she had mastered over many years and which Giacomo and I both recognised, bringing a smile to our lips.

'Then what is the reason?' I asked.

'You know my father worked at the Italian Embassy in Cairo when I was young?' Giacomo continued.

'Yes, of course.'

'And you remember my mother's name?'

'Yes. Kartika Armana. What's that got to do with anything?'

'Two things. Firstly the surname Amarna. The modern name for Akhetaten, the city founded by Akhenaten is el-amarna. My love of Ancient Egypt stemmed from many visits to the museum in Cairo, my passion for Akhenaten and everything about him and his reign, came from the similarities in my mother's name to his City of the Sun. As soon as she realised my interest she would tell me her family originated there.'

'But wasn't she was born in Indonesia?'

'It was a joke, Ricci, but, whatever it was, I spent many hours and days rummaging around, in what I called *her city*. Our driver would take me there from Cairo, nearly 600 kilometres round trip. He must have hated me. In the early days there had not been much excavation on the site. I later joined Barry Kemp's annual expeditions and worked with him and his team.'

'OK, that explains the place, but why the name.'

'That's a little more complex. The name, Atenisti, I made up. As you know, because I have taught this to you, the reign of Akhenaten only lasted a relatively short time. After he died the religion was crushed and its followers forced into hiding.

'Some say, and I am inclined to agree, that the followers of Akhenaten were the persecuted people, taken out of Egypt by Moses, or I like to think, the Crown Prince Thutmose, Akhenaten's brother. But that's another story. My mother's first name, Kartika, means *shining star*. So we have *Shining Star from Amarna*. That star has to be the sun and represented throughout Egypt as a golden disk with hands emanating from its rays. Ergo a secret group of followers of the shining Armanan star – Atenisti.'

'All very complicated,' I said.

'Complex to explain, but a very logical and simple conclusion.'

'For you maybe. I think I need another drink.'

'Where was he found?' I asked Arjun eventually.

'An abandoned hut near Mahabaleshwar hill station.'

'Where's that?'

'A hundred or so kilometres from Pune. Famous for its Strawberries. It's where the Beatles got their inspiration for their song.'

I didn't have the mental energy to argue. If he wanted to believe that John Lennon was thinking about a place, which as far as I am aware, was miles away from anywhere he had ever visited in India, rather than his clandestine visits to play with the children of a local children's home in his youth, then so be it. It isn't a hanging offence. I smiled, thinking about the reference to capital punishment in the words of the song.

Giacomo and Chiara loved the music of the Beatles and I was the proud owner of a full set of their vinyl records and CDs. I knew most of the words by heart and could play most from memory on the guitar. It was fortunate that the cottage in Northumberland had no neighbours close enough to hear the caterwauling renditions of such classical music.

'Any chance they'll find evidence incriminating Shitole, or Priya's father?'

'I doubt it,' came the honest reply.

CHAPTER 18

Present Day
Düsseldorf Saturday Morning 7:30 a.m.

The coffee was lukewarm. Sitting alone in the business class lounge, my thoughts wandered to the eleventh of April 1996, my first year at University. Returning after the Easter break, my flight was diverted at the last moment away from here to Cologne/Bonn. As the plane banked sharply, smoke billowed from the terminal building.

As I became mesmerised by the shapes being formed in the smoke by the winds, I didn't realise people were dying below me, people who I knew. Mortality hit me as news filtered through about the events of that day.

Gunther and Erik, two of my classmates, spent a lot of their spare time at the airport. Erik loved aeroplanes and the roof of the parking garage was the ideal viewpoint with a clear view of the runways. Where Erik went, Gunther would follow. We jokingly called him '*Der Schatten*,' like a shadow, they were inseparable.

It is only speculation, but they must have seen the smoke rising from the terminal building and decided to get away. Why didn't they use the stairs? Had they never been told, or read, the warning: IN CASE OF FIRE DO NOT USE THE ELEVATORS?

They were not alone. In total seven people jumped into two different lifts with the same destination – ground. The doors opened into the smoke and toxic gases of the arrivals hall. They had no chance.

Eight others died in a business lounge, very like the one I now sat in. There was no escape for them either. It had taken five years for the airport to become fully operational again; it would take forever for Erik and his shadow Gunther to be forgotten. The thought of them gasping for air, their throats burning as carbon monoxide induced anoxaemia, altering their haemoglobin, fatally took hold, came back to me whenever I flew into or from *Flughafen* DUS. A spark from a welding torch enough to devastate the lives of so many families. Perhaps my detestation for meaningless death began at that point.

I fought against my dislike of this airport, and took Christiana's advice. I left my bike with her and decided to fly to Frankfurt. It was a short uneventful flight and I arrived at the gate for the onward connection to Delhi in plenty of time.

My thoughts were filled with the joy I'd experienced spending a couple of days with Christiana. I wished I could spend more time with her, and tell her about my work. That would be selfish of me and so unfair on her. I tried to tell her some, but she always shut me down. It was as if she knew she wouldn't want to hear what I would say. Freddy and Johann, too, seemed to avoid any conversation about my life and work. Perhaps it was for the best.

I slept most of the journey. I disembarked and made my way through Passport and Immigration control to baggage reclaim. Arjun was standing there, my small suitcase at his side.

'What are you doing here?' I asked, not entirely displeased to see him.

'We worry about you. We can't be sure who may be watching European arrivals. Come with me.'

There could be no argument, as he wheeled away through a door marked *Staff only* I found myself in the luggage loading bay. Hundreds of suitcases in containers or on trolleys manhandled onto the conveyor belts to the waiting passengers arriving from Bengaluru, Amsterdam, Hyderabad, Tehran, Goa, Zurich, Doha and Dubai. This was a busy arrival time at Delhi and baggage handlers bore the brunt of the work at this hour.

A black sedan pulled up and Arjun ushered me into the back. He sat in the front next to the driver.

'Where are we going?'

'You need to get to Bombay. We're just providing the transport. Wait and see.'

I trusted Arjun, otherwise I would be planning how to get out of this situation. As it was, I closed my eyes and relaxed. Arjun was beginning to prove himself invaluable. An honest, intelligent policeman not afraid of taking decisive and rapidly thought-out action. I liked him.

It didn't take long for me to have to open my eyes as the car came to a smooth halt. We parked up beside a small aircraft, even in the dim light, in this part of the airport, I could see it was a Learjet 45. I liked this plane, even if I had only rarely flown in one.

The Bombadier Aerospace top seller, with a cruising speed of 465 mph and a range of 1,800 nautical miles was more than capable of flying me to Mumbai in a little over two hours. This would need a change of plan. I had anticipated a sixteen-hour train journey to arrive in Mumbai on Sunday evening, now I would be there around dawn. How would I fill the time? My appointment was on Monday morning at the hotel Giacomo and I had shared last year. I didn't want to stay there overnight.

'There will be a car to meet you at Juhu airport, when you arrive. It will take you to Ganesh's apartment where you can stay for as long as you need. Here are the keys – and something else you might need.'

He handed me a small bag. As soon as I took it I felt the familiar shape of a handgun. Perhaps it was the Glock Arjun had used to save my life all those months ago, whatever it was, it was a welcome gift.

'That's not all,' he said as he handed me a telephone. 'It's untraceable. I've written down some telephone numbers you might need. Memorise them and don't store them on the phone. Delete call history after any call you make. You're going into dangerous territory against unpredictable and vicious people, who only want one thing. You, dead. Are you sure you don't want to get the first plane back to Europe?'

'Not an option,' I said. 'Anyway, they want more than me dead. They want to make me suffer, that opens all sorts of possibilities that a bullet in the head down some dark alley, wouldn't.'

'But why go towards the danger and possible death?'

'Several reasons,' I replied. 'For his wife's sake, I need to find out what really happened to Fratelli, bring his body home if I can. Also if I don't go, Ganesh and the other youngsters will be in danger; it's me they want but they would make others pay if I don't turn up.'

'Won't that be the same if you go and they don't kill you?'

'If they don't kill me, there won't be enough of them left to organise a hit on anyone else.'

'You haven't mentioned revenge.'

'That's a bad motive, Arjun. It's emotional, and emotion can lead to mistakes. Revenge is a good result of a calmly executed plan, not as a reason to execute a plan.'

'Take care,' he said as he shook my hand, or perhaps he had said, *theek hai*, meaning *OK* in Hindi, which sounded the same to my untrained ear. 'If you need anything, then please call me. Chirag wants you kept safe, just as you have protected his family, he wants me to do all I can to protect you.

I boarded the jet. I was the only passenger so I had the choice of leather seats to choose from. A hostess smiled as I took the first seat on the right, fastened the seat belt and closed my eyes. She walked past me and closed the door. The pilot came over the tannoy making the usual, legally required announcements, even for private jets. The engines started and we set off. I drank tea and chatted to the hostess about nothing for two hours, when the pilot advised us to make sure our seatbelts were fastened and we landed without incident.

As promised, a car was waiting as I walked down the steps. I said my goodbyes to the hostess and pilot, put my bags on the back seat and jumped into the front. My driver was wearing all white and had a white chauffeur's cap which looked strangely odd.

Arriving at Ganesh's Bandra apartment, my first priority was to check the handgun Arjun had given me. I was right; it was the Glock, or at least one identical to it. I had my own handgun I'd left it hidden in a wardrobe here last year so was comfortably armed.

I took out my laptop and called Chiara. I had promised to keep in touch. Despite the time difference she answered quickly. Having satisfied her that I was well and safe, she said she could sleep. I doubted she was telling me the truth.

CHAPTER 19

One year ago
Delhi, India Day 6 10:00 a.m.

I said my goodbyes, to Chirag, Sushma and Ganesh, making half promises, I doubted would ever be kept, to meet them all again. Arjun took me to the airport, and I took an uneventful flight to Mumbai.

I was getting used to half of the Indians I met still referring to the Maharashtrian Capital by its old colonial name of Bombay.

'It's a cultural thing, Arjun had explained. 'Mumbai is the *Marathi* name and the change from Bombay was not universally welcomed when the leading political party in *Maharashtra, Shev Shena*, did so in 1995. Even now, a quarter of a century later, many *Mumbaikers* still interchange the names out of habit. There remains the Bombay High Court and the Bombay Electrical Company.

'What's in a name?' I asked.

'Plenty, when it carries political significance. Even the reasoning behind the name change is not accepted by everyone. A book written about Gujarat in 1507 referred to the City as *Manbai* but the Portuguese later renamed it *Bom Bahia* meaning *Good Bay* this became anglicised by the English, when they took over the city in the seventeenth century, to *Bombay* and that name became known internationally. *Shev Shena* said it was renaming the city after the Hindu goddess *Mumbadevi*, but not everyone agrees.'

I found everything in this sub-continent was over complicated. Irrespective of the name, I landed and took the pre-booked taxi for the ten-minute drive to the hotel. As I arrived and saw how close it actually was to the airport I believed I could have walked it quicker, but that would not have been a good idea.

Check-in at the hotel was chaotic, due to the arrival of the aircrew, from a British Airways Boeing 777 minutes before me. I eventually got to my room. I was awaiting a call from a very high-ranking police officer, a contact through Arjun's connections who was going to send two of his more junior colleagues to show me the evidence they had found about Giacomo. Arjun was clearly persuasive, he had bought the story of my working for an insurance company and that we were looking at the disappearance of Giacomo as a part of the same investigation that had brought us here to Mumbai in the first place.

The phone rang at 15:32. It was a receptionist who informed me that there were two police officers in reception who wanted to see me.

'That's great,' I said. 'Tell them I'm on my way.'

She seemed taken aback by my enthusiasm. 'Er, no, sorry, sir. You can meet them… er, in the… er, private meeting room beside the business lounge on the eleventh floor. It'll be more… er…private. I'll send them there if you wish.'

Any objection would be useless; she had already decided that is where we should meet. Whether she didn't want to see the arrest she was imagining carried out in the main reception of this well-known five-star hotel or was really respecting my privacy, I didn't know. Whatever the reason within ten minutes I was grateful to her for that privacy.

As I arrived in the meeting room, the two officers were in the process of ordering coffees for themselves.

'Ah, Mr. Johnson, would you like a coffee too?' the taller of the two said.

'No thanks,' I replied. 'A *masala chai* for me, please.'

'Can I have your room number please, sir?'

'1620,' I replied, realising that these refreshments would undoubtedly end up on my bill.

Both men were dressed in the ubiquitous Khaki uniform of the Indian Police Service. The taller had a swagger stick tucked into his left armpit as he held out his right hand for me to shake. I was used to strong firm hand shakes, but he held his hand limply, it felt almost wet. I applied moderate pressure with my own hand but quickly pulled away.

'I am Superintendent of Police Bhatt,' he said. 'This is Inspector Chandra.' I looked at the second officer; he didn't offer me his hand to shake but instead placed his hands together. 'Namaste,' he said slightly bowing his head.

'Namaste,' I replied.

'Please let's sit,' Superintendent Bhatt said, assuming he was taking control of the meeting.

We sat around a large square coffee table which had ornately carved legs of an eight-armed Hindu goddess. The armchairs needed two hands and a fair amount of force to be able to move. The waitress arrived with the pots of coffee and my tea along with a bill for me to sign. I glanced at it as I signed. Fifteen hundred rupees, almost twenty euros for a local tea and two small pots of coffee. The tea had better be good for that kind of price, I thought.

'Please, Mr. Johnson, drink your *masala* tea,' Superintendent Bhatt said with a magnanimity that belied the fact I had paid for it.

I sipped the spicy brew, it wasn't as good as the ones I drank in Delhi, but it was passable.

'You have some information for me I believe,' I said as the two men were bringing the cups to their lips.

'Yes,' Inspector Chandra said, putting the cup down, before tasting any of the dark liquid. Bhatt's eyes widened and his eyebrows flicked upwards. My attempts to take control of the meeting hadn't gone unnoticed. He sipped his coffee.

'It is not very pleasant,' Chandra said.

'Drink your coffee first,' his superior interjected. 'We have time.'

Control going back the other way.

'Time is precious,' I said. 'My employers do not want me to waste any of this irreplaceable commodity.'

'Mr. Fratelli is in no need of speed. You cannot help him. It's too late.' Bhatt was insistent. 'Take your time, drink your tea and then we will discuss the issue in hand.'

There was no point in arguing. I sat in silence watching them down their coffees then drain the pots, a thick brown sediment forming on the sides.

'Did you enjoy Delhi, Mr. Johnson?' Bhatt asked.

'I didn't get to see much of it.' I didn't want to enter into pointless conversation.

'I could never work in Delhi,' he continued. 'The smog levels are far too high. It's not safe to walk the streets without a proper face mask. You got out in time Mr. Johnson. According to reports, the Central Pollution Control Bureau, air quality index in *Indraprashta Marg*, where our Police Headquarters sit, will reach over five hundred by today evening itself and five hundred in Noida. This is rising every day. If that isn't bad enough, the levels of the miniscule particles of less than two point five microns in diameter, that can enter deep into the lungs and even the bloodstream, shot up to three hundred and seventy-seven micrograms per cubic metre. This breaches the emergency threshold of three hundred. It's not a safe place to live or work at the moment.'

'I noticed the haze as I left, but there was a haze over Mumbai as we landed.'

Bhatt laughed. It was not a pleasant sound, more akin to a Halloween witch's cackle. A hubbling, bubbling cauldron and Shakespeare came to mind.

'The levels here are not half of those in Delhi. Here, the air is unhealthy; there, it is dangerous.'

'Irrespective of the air quality, I need to know what information you have, that is why we're here isn't it?'

'Correct. Inspector, please show Mr. Johnson the file.'

As Chandra handed me the file, Bhatt's penetrative stare filled my peripheral vision. He was gauging my reaction. Trying to take my measure. I opened the file. A full colour photograph of a man lying in a semi prone position, his neck and head against a wall with his face missing was the first page.

I looked closely. recognising the shoes, hanging loosely from his toes The trousers and shirt were those he had been wearing when I last saw him.

I had seen cleaner deaths and I had seen worse.

I imagined the four-year-old girl whose rapist had peeled

the skin off her face. She would have been as unrecognisable as Giacomo was from this photograph. Without turning the page, I returned Bhatt's glare.

'I'll need to see the body,' I said. 'Identification from these photos is not possible.'

'Why do you want to see the body? You can see it was in a very bad state when he was found. He was your friend and colleague. Why put yourself through this?'

'There are some identifying marks which would help me.'

'What kind of marks?'

'Just marks, which I have been informed about.'

'What marks?' he repeated. His voice was clipped, his mouth barely moving. I was getting to him.

'Superintendent, I want to see the body. I need to report to my employers, that I have personally identified Mr. Fratelli. There will be a large payment to be made to his family as a result of his dying during employment and they like to be thorough in their information gathering, before making any payment.'

'But if you tell me what the marks are that you seek, I can make enquiries as to their presence or otherwise.'

I flicked through the pages of the report there were not many and much was written in the *nāgarī* script of Hindi or Marathi, characterized by its long, horizontal strokes at the tops of the letters, joined to form a continuous horizontal line. It was meaningless to me.

'Where is the body? Is it with the Coroner's Office?'

Bhatt cackled again. 'How little you know about our legal system. We don't have coroners. We are guided by our Criminal Procedure Code, the police or a magistrate investigate. There is no separate judicial examination.'

'But how is that right? What happens if a man dies in police custody, for example, do the Police investigate that?'

'Depends on the circumstances. Usually yes. The idea of coroners' inquests was tried in Mumbai, or Bombay as it was then, and Calcutta during British rule, but once your people departed, the idea left too. Inspector Chandra, explain section one-seven-four of the CPC to our inquisitive guest.'

His temper was getting shorter; there was something he was not telling me.

'The procedure is quite simple and effective,' Chandra started. When the police receive information that a person has committed suicide, or has been killed by another or by an animal or by machinery or by an accident, or has died under circumstances raising a reasonable suspicion that some other person has committed an offence, the officer in charge must immediately inform the nearest executive magistrate empowered to hold inquests. The senior police officer should then proceed to the place where the body is, and there, in the presence of two or more respectable inhabitants of the neighbourhood, make an investigation, and draw up a report of the apparent cause of death. He must describe such wounds, fractures, bruises, and other marks of injury as may be found on the body, and stating in what manner, or by what weapon or instrument (if any) such marks appear to have been inflicted. That's the officer's report under the photograph in front of you. You'll see that the report has been signed and has been sent to the District Magistrate. As in this case, there is some doubt as to the cause of death, the police officer, as is his duty, considered it was expedient to forward the body to the nearest civil surgeon.'

'So are you telling me that Mr. Fratelli's body is with a surgeon undergoing examination?'

'Not exactly, Mr. Johnson. I am saying that the police officer considered it expedient to send the corpse to a civilian surgeon.'

'What Inspector Chandra is trying to say, is that the body never arrived at the surgeon's hospital.'

'So where the fuck is he?'

'Please refrain from using expletives, Mr. Johnson.'

I struggled to quell a desire to throw one or both of them over the open balcony beside me. Two floors below, the fake palm trees and marble floors of the hotel's twenty-four hour, open-plan, buffet restaurant waited to receive their plummeting uniformed bodies. 'It's not the fall that will kill you,' Giacomo's words came back to me; 'it's the sudden stop at the bottom that causes the damage.' Perhaps they were only saved by the fact that we were too open. No deniability was available to me.

'I'm sorry,' I said. 'Where and when can I see the body?'

'That's exactly what we are trying to tell you. You can't.'

Chandra looked down at the floor as his boss gave me this information. He was trying to avoid eye contact, but Bhatt wasn't. Defiance and arrogance flowed from him in ever increasing volume. He was challenging me. Now was neither the time nor the place, but I'm a patient man, I could wait.

Several deep inhalations through my nose and exhalations from my mouth before I spoke.

'I'm sorry I don't understand, what do you mean?'

'What I mean, Mr. Johnson, is that we cannot facilitate your request at this time, as we are uncertain as to the whereabouts of the said item. It seems to have disappeared.'

'Can you at least refer to him as *he* and not it, he deserves some respect.'

'These are just words, Mr Johnson. We should not get upset by words. Your friend is gone.'

'How can a body disappear, particularly one which is the subject of a police investigation and should have been in the safekeeping of the police at all times?'

'Sir, things work a little differently here. When the officer in charge made the, very correct and honourable, decision under Section 174 that the circumstances of the death merited sending the cadaver to the nearest civil surgeon he did so through a local, private ambulance company.'

'What do they say about it? They must know.'

'They have no record of one of their ambulances being used for the transportation.'

'Then how…?'

He held is hand up to stop me.

'Please let me finish. I am a very busy man, Mr. Johnson. I am trying my best to help you but constant questioning and interruption is delaying me.'

My indifference to this man was turning to extreme dislike and distrust. There was something about him, the way he raised his eyebrows when he thought I might take control of this conversation. Glints of anger in his eyes when he thought I was questioning the honesty of what he was telling me. He was hiding something; I determined to find out what.

'It is the duty of the police officer in charge, having determined that referral to a surgeon is expedient, to ensure that the state of the weather and the distance needed to travel, admit of its being so forwarded without risk of such putrefaction on the road as would render such examination useless. From *Mahabaleshwar* Hill Station to the nearest available surgeon on that day, which was in Pune, is approximately four hours travelling. As you know, the weather here has been extremely hot. Our ambulances are not equipped with air conditioning. It was decided that speed was very much in the essence. The OIC did not want to wait and, as the gods' good fortune would very happily have it, an ambulance was passing the scene, he commandeered the very same to take the decomposing cadaver to the hospital.'

'Oh, I see, so it was the OIC,' I said, trying not too hard to hide the sarcasm of my linguistic play.

He ignored me.

'So you see, we did everything possible. We will continue to do our utmost to locate the body, but in this weather, even if we locate it, I doubt that it will be of much use to us, or to you.'

The thought of seeing Giacomo's remains had been bad enough, but the thought of not being able to bring him back to Chiara, for a civilised burial in the family plot, created a tightness in my stomach, like a hangman's noose around the neck of a swinging prisoner beneath a freshly opened gallows trapdoor.

'Now, Mr. Johnson, if you will excuse me, as I said, I am extremely busy. I will leave you, in the capable hands of Inspector Chandra. He will arrange for you to see the scene of the crime.'

'Just one question. Who is the OIC in this case?'

'Everything you need is in the copy report in front of you. Now I really must go. Good day.'

He held out his hand to shake, I stood with reluctance and

stretched out my hand. As he held out his hand I noticed a faint tattoo on the flesh between his thumb and first finger. I assumed it had some religious significance.

He used his swagger stick to strike himself on his leg as he left. Removing a phone from his pocket, he made a call. He started to speak quickly into it as he left the room.

I flicked through the report in front of me. I couldn't understand the *nagri* script, but I could understand the typed name of the Officer In Charge – Superintendent Pawan Bhatt.

CHAPTER 20

Present Day
Bandra, Mumbai Monday Morning 5:30 a.m.

After a comfortable sleep in Ganesh's apartment, I was woken by the melodious and loud *Adhan*, from the local mosque. The *muezzin's* voice was vibrant and clear.

The *Takbīr*, repeated four times followed by the *Shahada*, *"ašhadu 'an lā 'ilāha 'illā –llāh'* there is no god but Allah, chanted twice. I always enjoyed the dawn Adhan and listened carefully. *'aṣ-ṣalātu khayrun mina n-nawm'* – prayer is better than sleep - my favourite line, only chanted in the early morning Sunni version, Shias preferring to hasten towards the best thing. My time in Saudi, training the royal bodyguards, had taught me a deep and lasting respect for Muslims and their faith.

The religion, grown out of the same historical roots as Christianity and Judaism with only one God, 'the Father of Abram.' Abraham's first born, Ishmael, whose mother was Hagar, became the leader of his nation and his descendants settled in the Arabian Peninsula; the Prophet Mohammed being in direct line from him. His second son, Isaac, born of Sarah was a direct ancestor of Jesus.

'All true faith, leads us to Ibrahim,' an Imam had once told me, 'and from Ibrahim to Allah, there is no deity but he.'

I couldn't argue with that. But now I had to prepare for

what would be facing me today. The instructions, left by the Shadows, hadn't given a time so I thought to arrive at the designated hotel around eleven o'clock and sit in the café drinking coffee and reading the Times of India as instructed. I wondered why they hadn't asked me to wear a red rose in my lapel or some other clichéd sign of recognition.

I dressed thoughtfully. I decided against taking the Glock which Arjun had given me, preferring my own smaller pistol which was still taped to the bottom of the wardrobe shelf, exactly where I had left it a year ago. I could slide this into my sock, hidden by the boots I decided to wear, and it would be less conspicuous than the larger Glock tucked into a belt. I was sure they would make at least a cursory search.

I wondered what they had planned. They were certainly angry with me after the events of last year. Priya escaping their grasp and the death of Superintendent Pawar Bhatt, which presumably they didn't believe was suicide, were both motives for revenge against me.

I couldn't understand how they had tracked me down. I hadn't kept up to date with the rape and murder investigation in Italy over the past few days, Chiara would be doing that. Although sure that nothing could connect me in any way to Kiki's death, their ability to find me might also indicate an ability to plant evidence leading to me. Silence from Chiara in relation to that was comforting.

I would just have to see how things transpired. I didn't feel that today was the day my life would end, but in my line of work that is something that has no relevance. Of course, no disease would kill me today, but the suddenness of a bullet or a knife could not be predicted. Many people, throughout the world start their days unaware that it is going to be their last. Martens and Bhatt were but two examples.

A year ago, Bhatt had started his last day, with a shower and coffee. I know because I watched him.

He was in, what is known in India as, his bungalow. The meaning is different to the English version of this kind of home. It was not far from the popular *Mumbaiker* hill fort escape of Lonavla. Near to, and in sight of the promontory affectionately named, Duke's nose, as it reminded someone of Wellington's proboscis. I am not sure the Iron Duke would be impressed.

I couldn't believe that a policeman's salary, even a superintendent's, would stretch to affording a villa like this. Chiara had managed to get me his address, I didn't know how.

'Just leave it with me, I need to make a phone call or two,' she'd said.

Three hours later, she called me back.

Four hours after that I was outside.

The garden area must have been more than half an acre, with thick bushes and a few banana trees, ideal for hiding behind and snacking at the same time. Here in the hills it was cooler than it had been when I left Mumbai.

The Uber driver was happy that he was getting a ride all the way out here. I gave him the address of a small privately owned hotel I found on the internet about a quarter of a mile from where I needed to be. I didn't want to have to walk too far. I checked in, a different name and passport, thankfully the receptionist hadn't asked to check my entry Visa, he was happy I paid the ten thousand rupees in cash. The internet site told me the price would be around six thousand and perhaps it would have been had I paid by credit card, when a record would have to be made. Cash payments were not treated the same. Being a foreigner made the price different for me. The receptionist had probably just taken a month's salary. I wasn't going to quibble, good luck to him.

It was around midday when I arrived at Bhatt's country retreat. The house was impressive and empty. There were no visible signs of security and I managed to prise open one of the many windows, this one it turned out was a downstairs bathroom.

I had learned a lot about marble when I stayed at Chirag's house in Delhi. This was high quality. I guessed Italian. The bathroom fittings were all Villeroy and Bosch.

Leaving the bathroom I passed through a walk-in wardrobe, a ground floor bedroom. No clothes were hanging only a variety of wooden and plastic hangers. Not the master suite, I thought. The bed was unmade.

The bedroom opened out, across a corridor leading to the main door, to an open-plan living space. Three, deep cushioned, contemporary style beige sofas were positioned in a U-shape around a large white coffee table, with a glass top.

Under the glass were several miniature models of various Hindu deities. I recognised the elephantine *Ganesha*, the solver of problems, and *Maa Durga Devi*, the eight-armed goddess of war. Others I didn't recognise.

In the corner were four models of what looked like baby Buddhist monks in the classic pose of *see no evil, hear no evil, speak no evil, do no evil.* Multi coloured scatter cushions were lain neatly on the sofas. I assumed that Bhatt had a housekeeper as he didn't strike me as someone who would clean up after himself.

The room was dominated by a huge television screen it must have been at least seventy-five inches, possibly bigger. A small white box sat underneath with a green flashing light. The TV must have been connected directly to the internet.

I began to think of what would be shown on that screen when Bhatt and his friends sat around the sofas.

Beyond the seating area was a glass dining table surrounded by eight chairs whose fabric matched the sofas. This part of the room was ceilingless with a glass balustrade surrounding the opening above.

Beyond that was a small kitchen with L-shaped units. A five-burner Bosch gas hob, with the same brand of built-in oven. They looked unused. I assumed he did all his own cooking in the built-in convection microwave and got someone in to cook if he was having guests. On the worktop was a filter-coffee machine.

A further bedroom was beyond the kitchen. Given the size, I assumed that this room was intended for a live-in housekeeper. Fortunately for me there was none. The presence of a third party might be awkward for a man with Bhatt's extra-curriculum activities.

A simple u-shaped staircase led off the dining area. Two parallel flights of straight stairs joined by a landing creating a 180-degree turn. A large painting hung on the wall at the top of the first flight. A multi coloured fish with a bright-orange face. Blue, red, orange and brown stripes were separated by black squiggles and swirls. The sea, what little there was visible, was represented by black, wavy lines. Its basic style was unappealing to me, but art is subjective. I'm sure it was expensive.

Upstairs there were two further bedrooms, exact copies of

the one I entered through on the ground floor. Each bedroom had a private terrace, with large sliding glass UPVC doors.

Looking down from one of these terraces, the private infinity pool set into the outdoor decking was impressive. So too was the view. Wellington's Nose and the lush, green valley below dominated. It was easy to understand why these Hill Stations were so popular. This countryside is not as beautiful as the Italian, English or Irish lake districts or the rolling Cheviot Hills, but everything is relative. This is a vast improvement on the smoggy, gridlocked, concrete labyrinth that is Mumbai and is the best available.

Going back inside, only one of the rooms showed signs of occupation. In the walk-in wardrobe, there was a spare Khaki uniform. Twenty or so shirts were hanging on an upper rail, each had the same handmade tailor's label. A matching number of trousers lined the bottom rail. I assumed they too would have the same label. Getting clothes made to order is commonplace for the wealthy in India. The hotel offered to arrange some shirts for me with a twenty-four-hour turnaround. 'Maybe next time,' I said.

Underwear and socks were neatly folded in drawers. His housekeeper was efficient. I wasn't interested in such things. What I was looking for wouldn't be easy for a cleaner to find by accident.

I tapped the wooden panels; they all appeared solid. I went into the other bedroom, the wardrobe was empty. Something was different though in this one. I couldn't work out what at first. The rails were the same, the same number of glass fronted drawers on each side. Then I realised. In Bhatt's bedroom there was a large, open, empty shelf. Here there was none. A matching wooden panel blocked it off. I tapped and the sound came back hollow. I felt around the edges, it seemed solid. No access this way.

Some people have no imagination. I walked out of the bedroom and down one flight of stairs to the fish. Sure enough, it swung on hinges and revealed a safe about half way up the wall and obviously sitting on the covered shelf inside the wardrobe. The most obvious of hiding places, it should have been the first place I looked.

The safe was a cheap one similar to those found in hotels all over the world. However I would need to get something to stand on to reach it. I remembered the chequered, red blue and white long stools, at the foot of each bed. They made me think of tartan. The stool was heavy and, due to its length, awkward to manoeuvre. But it was the right height. I stood on it, bringing the safe to eye level. It was a standard, now outdated, brand.

Perhaps Bhatt had been gifted this safe when a hotel was being refurbished. Digital with twelve buttons in four rows of three. Numbers one to nine and zero in the regular telephone layout. Beside the zero on the right side was a button with a C and to the left, an R. The word, safe, was inaccurate for this particular brand. Maybe, safer, would be more appropriate. Certainly safer than leaving valuables in a drawer, probably safe from room service personnel and an opportunist thief, but not from a professional.

Why hadn't he bought a new safe? I was pleased he hadn't. No electronic gadget and probe necessary to open this one. It came with a standard access code, known only to the manufacturer and the installation teams to open, in the event that a guest forgot their self set password. This means hundreds of people, in cities everywhere. Nothing known by that many can ever be kept secret. This particular safe should be opened by pressing C-C-R-C-1-4-1-4-1-4-C-R-C-C; it did.

Wads of cash, new five-hundred and two-thousand-rupee notes. When Modi had announced the immediate withdrawal of the old five hundred and one thousand rupee notes it had caused panic and shortages of cash. Queues formed outside banks with people desperate to change the old money. India is not a country suitable for queuing and people died of heat exhaustion waiting in line. But people like Bhatt would not have been affected.

As a senior police officer, he would have received prior warning about potential civil unrest. He could easily have changed his cash into smaller denominations before the announcement, then converted to the new notes later. I couldn't estimate the amount inside. I wasn't familiar enough with the currency, but I guessed many tens of thousands of euro value, maybe a hundred thousand euros or double that, or half that. I took the cash and placed it in my back pack. I could count it later.

Also in the safe were two manila envelopes. I opened the first. It was a list of names. No indication of what the list was connected to, just names. Were they members of a group, or names of people who paid him bribes? I didn't know, but took the list anyway.

The second envelope was thicker. Inside was, what I had thought I'd find, a stash of pornographic pictures of children. Some dead. Three photos were stapled together. The first was a tiny headless corpse, underneath was a picture of a child's head sitting on a table. The small girl's face had a look of horror, mouth gaping as if in a scream, eyes closed. The third picture was of the same head still on the table, but this time the skin had been peeled away and her head scalped. It was the most horrific thing I had ever seen. It was the judicial sentence of death I needed, to have no regrets about what I was about to do.

The only other thing in the safe was a set of keys. They looked like house keys. I took those to try in the locks. Being able to return without having to climb in through a window would be useful.

Having emptied the safe, I closed it by following the faded printed instructions on the front. Press C, insert a six-digit code then hold the door closed until the light goes off. I pressed six numbers at random. Bhatt wouldn't be able to open the safe, but he would think it was a fault and call an engineer, if he knew one. Maybe he hadn't thought that far ahead when he acquired it.

I replaced the picture and the stool. Tried a key in the front door, a perfect fit. I left, removed my gloves and made the relatively short walk back to the hotel. Another tourist returning after viewing the beauty of Khandala Lake and the valley.

The following morning I left before dawn. I needed to be in position before he got up. The house was almost all glass at the front and I could easily be seen if he happened to be awake as I crossed his manicured lawn.

Safely hidden by the long, broad foliage of the banana tree I sat and waited. Like many people who live in houses which are not overlooked, Bhatt had not closed any of the blinds in his home so, as daylight came, the sun shone directly into the house. I had a good view. Last night's crockery was still on the table, he wasn't a man capable of lifting a plate from the table to the sink or, heaven forbid, a dishwasher. He paid people to do that sort of thing. The picture on the landing was open on its hinges. A small white step ladder on the landing beneath it.

He had obviously tried the safe, for cash or sexual gratification I couldn't know. But, whatever it was, he had been unsuccessful. His last morning in this life began at around six thirty. He got out of bed and walked to the bathroom. He was completely naked. He came out about fifteen minutes later with a towel wrapped around his waist.

Bhatt walked downstairs. He stopped at the safe, obviously tried his trusted passcode which didn't work. His temper showed as he punched the safe. Judging by the way he shook his hand, it must have hurt. Slamming the picture against the wall, it bounced back, so he hit it again. Finally giving up, he continued down the stairs and set the coffee machine in motion.

Retracing his steps to his bedroom and into the wardrobe he returned fully dressed in a finely pressed khaki uniform. The epaulets I remembered from our first meeting.

The National Emblem of India, sitting atop two stars and the letters *I.P.S.* The emblem, an adaptation of The Lion Capital of the *Ashoka Pillar* in Sarnath, shows three of the four lions standing above the twenty-four spoked wheel of the *Ashoka Chakra*.

The four lions represent power, courage, confidence and pride. I wondered which attributes the three lions visible on the police uniform represent. Bhatt certainly had confidence and pride, he exerted power, the next couple of hours would determine if he also had courage.

He walked back downstairs looking hard at the safe, shook

his head and went to the coffee machine. Now was the time to make my move as his back was towards me. I ran around the house to the front door, inserted the key and walked in. He obviously heard me coming in and shouted out something in Marathi. When he didn't receive an answer, he repeated whatever he had said as he walked to the corridor leading to the front door.

I was waiting.

Before he realised what was happening, the muzzle of my semi-automatic pistol pressed hard against his forehead.

'Yes, thank you, Superintendent, I would love a cup of coffee.' I grabbed his arm and turned him around. I saw enough in his eyes to know courage was not one of his attributes. With the grey metal of the firearm now pushed against the base of his skull, we walked back to the kitchen. His movements were slow and shaky. He managed to pour two cups and carry them to the table. I made him sit against the wall and pushed the table tight against him. With his hands in full view all the time his ability to grab a hidden weapon, unseen under the table, was prevented.

'What do you want, Johnson?' he asked.

I said nothing. I let the silence hang. He broke it, I knew he would.

'What is it you want? Money? I have money.'

'Do you?' I glanced towards the open picture above his head.

His eyes narrowed, he was beginning to see.

'Yes,' slightly more hesitantly, 'I have money.'

'I am not motivated by money,' I said.

'Then what?'

'*Satyameva Jayate*,' I said, quoting the National Motto of

India, Truth Alone Triumphs. I had spent time over the previous two weeks learning a little Hindi. It was very little and it hadn't helped a great deal when confronted by Marathi. I was able to understand some basic words and salutations also in that tongue of the Maharashtrians, one of the more than twenty languages spoken in the sub-continent, but not enough. There are supposedly only two official languages in India, Hindi and English, but try telling that to the man on the street in Mumbai, or the residents of *Tamil Nadu*.

'I don't understand,' he said.

'Is my accent that bad?'

'No, I understand what you are saying; I don't understand what you mean.'

'But the motto is clear isn't it? It's something you live your life by every day. Don't you? You wear the symbol of *Ashoka Chakra* on your shoulder. Is the greatest treasure not attained by truth? Does not truth widen the pathway of the gods?'

'I don't need teaching of the scriptures by a *firangi*.' Some spirit was coming out.

'But perhaps you do, superintendent. The English also have an expression, *Truth will out*, so the cultures have a similar philosophy. The truth about you is discovered and truth will triumph by your death. Your deeds will see you suffer in your next incarnation. For do you not believe that you will have nothing to bring with you into *Devachan*, you will be nothing but a disembodied entity, a soulless being, where you will very soon be reincarnated, and *Karma* will ensure you will experience all the pain and suffering that others have had, at your hands or at your bidding, in this life.

I pulled out the envelope from the rucksack which was now

by my side and threw it at him. 'This is what *Karma* dictates you will suffer in your next life. I only wish I could be there to witness it.'

He didn't open the envelope, he didn't need to. The realisation that his safe was not malfunctioning must have hit him, because he started to shake.

'It's not what it looks like. These are evidence photographs of cases I am working.'

'Then why are they not contained in police files like the one you gave me in the hotel two weeks ago? Why are they before, after, and sometimes during, the rape, mutilation and murder of these children, and not always in that order? There are maybe one hundred photographs in there of twenty or thirty children – how many cases are you working on without files?'

'You looked at them then? Did you enjoy them?'

I slammed the table hard into his paunched stomach. His instincts took over and he tried to push back. I leaned over and struck him on the temple with the barrel of the gun.

'Enough,' I said; 'this ends now.'

I left him, lying on his bed, a single, close range shot from his own revolver, to the same place I had pistol whipped him. I scattered the disgusting photographs around him and stuffed a wedge of five-hundred-rupee notes into his mouth. I didn't want to waste the larger denomination. I would ensure that money would be used to protect children in this country, I wasn't sure how yet but I would find a way.

I walked out the door, feeling sorry for the housekeeper who found him, but sure that she would take the money from his mouth, in lieu of notice, before calling the police. If she didn't, the first police on the scene would. I assumed they would treat the death as a suicide, even though the scene would make that impossible to uphold, but it would probably be more expedient and less embarrassing than having to explain the photographs.

Back in the present, I called the Uber taxi to pick me up and take me to my meeting.

CHAPTER 21

I arrived at the hotel.

The taxi door was opened by a smartly dressed bellboy wearing pressed black trousers teamed with a gold-braided burgundy jacket and a matching small, round, brimless cap.

As a child my parents had encouraged my learning of French by allowing me to read a series of cartoon stories called *Spirou et Fantasio*. My father had a set of the Belgian comics from his own childhood. I remembered Spirou, with his spiky red hair and bright, crimson bellhop uniform. I had an ambition to be Spirou and have his adventures and perhaps, in some ways, I had become like him. I doubt even André Fanquin's imagination could have developed storylines which matched my adventures. They would not have made good children's reading anyway. I couldn't see the classic uniform without thinking of my childhood hero.

'Welcome, sir. Are you staying at the hotel?'

'No, just meeting someone, thank you,' I replied.

'You are most welcome, sir. May I please have your bag for scanning?'

I handed over my backpack and walked through the revolving door, placed my phone in a tray beside the metal scanner and waited to be called through the scanner. It buzzed and the sumo-wrestler-sized security guard asked me to stand, arms outstretched whilst he gave a cursory check with his hand-held metal detector. It pinged at my watch and belt and again when at my shin. He looked at me and I lifted my trouser leg to show the metal buckle on my boots. I deliberately showed him my right boot as the gun was in the left.

'That's fine, sir. Thank you.'

My phone was handed to me by a woman dressed in the same uniform as the bellboy outside, but without the cap. I collected my bag from the scanner and strolled past the first reception-type desk. Behind it, stood two black-uniformed, young men. A crossed keys symbol on their lapels. The international symbol for *concierge*; a word I had first learned from Spirou.

I walked on, passing through a huddle of aircrew from an Asian airline and a myriad of persons who had all decided to check out at the same time. Six receptionists were kept busy with discussions and disagreements about items on their bills and unaccepted credit card payments.

As I moved on, burgundy uniforms were replaced by black and now I was greeted by a young woman dressed all in white. She stood behind a wooden lectern at the entrance to the lobby bar and restaurant. I remembered her from my last visit, but she didn't know me. Easy for me as she was one of the few I had met when I was last here. I was just one of hundreds of different businessmen she met every day and it had been more than a year since I was here and met her only once and fleetingly. I could recognise her as she was in place and dressed the same. She had probably met fifty thousand others like me in the time between our meetings so there was only a miniscule chance that she would recognise me, or even think my features were familiar.

'Breakfast is about to finish, sir, a table for one is it?'

'No, I'm here to meet someone. I'll take the table over there in the corner.'

I sat down, my back to the wall, with a view through the glass to all the cars entering and leaving and straight ahead with a clear view of the entrance, concierge and reception desks.

I ordered coffee from the black-coated waiter and the cafeterie arrived along with a cup, sugar bowl and a small plate of biscuits in various shades of beige. I was beginning to wish I had ordered *marsala* tea. I pressed the plunger half way down, allowing the grounds to continue flavouring the bottom half of the pot. I might be in need of a stronger second cup.

I didn't want to appear anxious or nervous so avoided looking at my watch. There were ten tables in this part of the hotel bar/coffee shop. Most were empty. I wondered how many would come. They wouldn't know if I was going to resist them, so I anticipated quite a few. They would not want any commotion which would draw attention to either them or me. A few quiet words, a demonstration of force and an inconspicuous exit.

The black Range Rover halted at the security check. It was exactly the same model as had side swiped us leaving the airport a year ago. As it drove towards the car park I tried to see the occupants but the blackened windows prevented any view inside. This vehicle was followed by its twin, then it turned into quadruplets. Each stopping briefly at the automatic rising bollard traffic barrier. A cursory check of under the bonnet and in the boot, the bollards lowered and they drove in.

If it wasn't sufficient that the cars were identical, I noticed that each had the exact same registration number plate. This should be picked up by the security cameras, but I suspected someone was turning a remunerated blind eye. Four cars, this could be sixteen people inside, or maybe fifteen if they wanted to keep a seat free for me.

The first four came in, avoided the metal detector, shaking hands with the sumo wrestler and sat on the table nearest to me. Each was dressed in a dark suit, suitably different to not appear like a uniform but sufficiently identical for me to know it was. No obvious glances my way, but the way one of them was looking at his smart phone I assumed I was being filmed.

'Is he alone?' was the unasked question I guessed they were seeking the answer to. The other tables were similarly filmed.

'Does he have accomplices?' the second unasked question.

Four more came in, similarly greeting the security guard, and took up a position nearest the entrance to the restaurant. The only potential escape route, other than the front door. My guess at fifteen was proved correct when Slick walked in. He was jacketless, his dyed and oiled hair even longer than it had been when I last saw him. He was flanked by two black suited bodyguards. Bypassing the metal detector he received a deferential greeting from the man charged with keeping residents safe. He walked confidently and directly towards me, passing reception and ignoring the girl by the pedestal. Eleven of them were now inside leaving the four vehicles and their drivers outside.

A sickening smile, showing unnaturally white teeth, crossed Slick's face as he approached. He stretched out his hand towards me but quickly withdrew it as I greeted him in a whispered tone.

'Fuck off, shit-hole,' I said, deliberately mispronouncing his surname.

'Now, now, Mr. Johnson, what way is that to greet a friend?' They did not sit down, there wasn't going to be any small talk.

'No, but I don't see any friends, just ten, half witted, would be gangsters and a walking dead man.'

'Mmm. Not sure you understand the situation here Mr. Johnson. Now, pay for your coffee and walk out quietly beside me. Don't make this more difficult, or public than it needs to be.'

He motioned to the waiter. 'The gentleman's bill please,' he said.

I placed a five-hundred-rupee note into the wallet, closed it and left it on the table.

We walked out, like a wedding or funeral procession, into the steamy heat. The first car pulled up. Slick grabbed my arm indicating this one wasn't for us. Three of his team got in and the car moved slightly forward. The second car came and Slick motioned for me to sit in the front.

Could this be his first mistake?

Our car pulled across the driveway and waited for the last two cars to pick up their occupants.

'Fasten your seat belt Mr. Johnson,' Slick instructed. It wasn't a normal car seatbelt but more akin to a harness, seen in a racing car, or the safety belts aircrew use on an aeroplane. I tightened the belt, then pulled the shoulder straps and fastened them into the clip on my abdomen. I felt the gun barrel on my neck.

'Now pass your arms behind you.'

It was a squeeze to fit my left arm between the car seat and the door. I hoped the journey wouldn't be too long or numbness might be a problem. I would need both arms operational to try and escape. A plastic tie was used to bind my wrists. A simple escapologists trick of keeping my hand parallel, thumbs touching and pushing hard against each other, meant my wrists were as far apart as possible. If the opportunity arose a simple twisting of my hands together into the prayer position would allow enough space to remove my hands from the bindings. Difficult whilst there were two pairs of eyes looking at my hands. I would need a distraction.

We turned out of the hotel, my car was second in the line of four. We drove a short distance then pulled into a shopping mall car park. A strange destination. There were four security lanes. Each car positioned to form a line. Once released, we passed through the barriers in a different order to that in which we left the hotel.

I smiled.

'A motorised version of the shell game,' I said; 'it wouldn't work, even if we were being followed, which I know we're not.'

'Silence, Mr. Johnson. You will be given every opportunity to talk later. There are things we need to know.'

I felt the sharp scratch of the needle as it punctured the side of my neck. A vague recollection of something being pushed over my head and face.

Nothing.

CHAPTER 22

Present day
India: Location and time unknown

'Assess your surroundings,' Giacomo had instilled in me. I had been in similar situations before, though never for real. The British Special Forces were the best at this. The weeks I'd spent with them were fundamental to my ability to do what I do. Exercises in the Brecon Beacons and interrogation techniques at their training camp in Credenhill, outside Hereford. I left buoyant and feeling I could cope with anything which my work might involve me in.

Here and now, probably somewhere in the vast state of Maharashtra, it was different. I couldn't be sure how far we had travelled, or for how long. At the base in Herefordshire there would be a pint of Guinness waiting for me at the Traveller's Rest when we'd finished. A five-star meal in the Officer's Mess would not be on today's menu. I wondered if my more youthful confidence from back then was misplaced.

'Assess your surroundings,' Giacomo's voice repeated.

I kept my head bent forward, if anyone was in the room I didn't want them to know I was awake.

Step one, 'Is there anybody else around?'

Tightly fastened tape around my eyes, which had replaced the bag from the car, made this assessment tricky. I listened.

Could anyone keep as completely still as I could? Probably, but why would they? I was tied up and gagged. I heard the faint, distant boom-ba-ba-boom, boom-ba-ba-boom of drums. Another day, another festival in India.

Good, I wasn't far from some form of settlement. Then the sound of children playing, as if just let out of school. Closer to me there was an occasional scurrying sound. Rats, large ones I assumed. No audible squeaks as rats communicate at audio levels out of human range. I couldn't hear the sound of breathing; perhaps I was alone or maybe in a large room with any companion far enough away so his respiratory noises were too faint for me to pick up.

What about smell?

Body odour and perfume travel further than the soft sound of breathing. Stale urine, that could have been the rats' or my own; I had no idea how long I'd been here. The smell of smoke and garlic was in the air, but faint. Perhaps from one of the *Dalits* cooking a meal outside on an open fire.

As I concentrated I felt a bead of liquid start at my temple and run down the side of my cheek.

Blood or sweat?

I couldn't feel any pain in my head so I hoped it was just perspiration. I thought of turning my head to guide the drop into my mouth, but there was no point; that too was covered. I couldn't smell the distinctive, ferrous odour of blood but that might mean that there wasn't enough of it. I took that as a positive.

The side of my face with the droplet felt warmer than the other side. There was also a faint draught. There must be a window or opening in a wall to my right.

I was reasonably certain I was alone, so I could risk some movement. Hands first. I felt the round wooden ends of the chair arms, my wrists taped to them. I would have done it differently, arms behind my back and tied together as I had been in the car. They would have had to cut those bonds to remove me from the seat, but why not simply replace them when they put me in the chair. Unconscious, I wouldn't have been able to use the escapology trick. I was grateful, for the good fortune, that my captors were not army trained.

With the restricted movement I was allowed, I spread my fingers and could feel a spindle. This was going to be easy. I tried to move my legs; they had been similarly taped to the legs of the chair. My chest was restricted so they had obviously taped around my body and the chair.

Time to gamble.

The next few seconds would reveal if I was, indeed, alone. Everything depended on freeing my hands. I gripped the arms of the chair and started moving them from side to side. The spindles were already loose; I could feel them giving way a little more with each side-to-side movement. A faint crack on one side; nearly there. I pulled upwards. My left arm raised into the air but the right needed more work. Several more expanding arcs and that too was free.

I needed my eyes. I raised my hands. Movement was awkward and restricted by the tape around my shoulders and the chair arms attached to my wrists. I pushed my thumbs up and tried to get them into the space created by my eye sockets. My nails scratched my face. With my thumbs behind the tape I pushed up, forcing the tape onto my forehead. I took a deep breath and opened my eyes.

Timing is everything.

Just as I released my eyes, my ears took in the sound of a sliding bolt, followed by the creaking of a door. Light entered the darkened room, rats scurried away from it. It took seconds for my eyes to focus, once they had I saw a figure in the doorway, a plate in his hand and a sneer on his face. I recognized Slick immediately.

'Now Mr. Johnson, it's not polite in India for a guest to damage his host's property, this will need to be attended to.'

I could smell his expensive aftershave.

I saw his fist clench and travel towards my face.

I heard his wrist snap as the attached chair arms hit him from different directions simultaneously.

I heard his scream of pain.

I pushed myself forward and fell on him, the chair still taped to my legs and body. He couldn't be allowed to call for help. One scream could have been me; a call from him in Hindi couldn't.

The first blow ruptured his larynx, the second to his temple probably killed him but I couldn't risk it. I kept pounding the wood against his head, the hard unforgiving mud floor ensured the blows were effective.

Blood lust was something which needed to be avoided in my job. Those moments or minutes where mayhem takes over your being and death is the only aim in your life. I had studied it, I had seen it and I had, until now, avoided it.

As I pounded him again and again I told myself to stop, but my arm refused to take heed. He was dead long before I stopped hitting him.

He had to pay.

The death of Giacomo. His skull cracked.

The airport attack against Priya. His cheek collapsed

The rape of Kiki. His nose and mouth changed shape.

His ridiculous hair. A final flurry of chair-arm-assisted blows covered his greasy head with blood and brain matter.

The blood lust ended. My training was needed to calm myself. Think. Irrelevant details. Think.

Increased heart rate and shallow breathing eased as the adrenaline receded. Giacomo believed that *osteocalcin*, produced from our bones, not adrenaline, is responsible for the acute reaction that helps fight danger.

Whatever the source, the process starts in the *amygdala* section of the brain, passing information to the *hypothalamus* then through the nervous system to the *adrenal medulla*, or bones, if Giacomo is right, or perhaps both.

The system of returning to normal starts in the same way. Convince the brain there is no danger and it informs the nervous system to go to reset mode and normality is restored. I had learned techniques for decreasing this time and adopted them all now. Irrelevant facts, breathing exercises and my personal *Mantra* calmed me.

I searched Slick's pockets.

He had a knife and a gun, both useful. His smart phone was on and locked, there was also a mobile Wi-Fi connection, its battery and signal lights on the white box both flashed green. There was also a clean, folded handkerchief.

I used the knife to cut the tape around my wrists, then chest and finally the chair legs. I watched the door but there seemed to be no one coming.

I was still wearing my boots and the gun, I had concealed

in one, was still there. I couldn't believe the stupidity of my captors. They had obviously relied on the hotel security guard to check for weapons, his failure had become their potential death. I checked Slick's gun. The magazine was full, so now I was more than adequately armed to confront whatever I would find beyond the door.

I used Slick's index finger to unlock the phone.

The knife was sharp. I used it to cut through the skin at the middle knuckle between the middle and proximal phalanx. Severing the *digitorum* tendons, *profundus* and *superficialis,* the finger extremity came away relatively easily.

I wrapped the blood-stained digit in Slick's handkerchief and put it in my pocket. I might need to use it again later.

The phone's calendar indicated that little more than twenty-four hours separated meeting Slick at the hotel and him becoming a bloodied pulp on the mud floor he had taken me to. There was no telephone signal but there was the wireless connection. The map app showed me I was around one hundred and sixty kilometres from Mumbai, and thirty or so from Nasik. The wine capital of Maharashtra.

Slick could provide me with nothing else of use so I moved to the door.

CHAPTER 23

Present day
Maharashtra Tuesday Morning 11:00 a.m.

Slick's despatch hadn't taken more than a few minutes. No-one had come to his aid so I was not too surprised as I cracked open the door to find I was in a small stone hut, separated from other buildings by at least twenty metres. I didn't want to be seen, at least not yet. I closed the door and moved to the window. It was glassless; bars were covered by an old sack, presumably to keep mosquitoes out.

It hadn't worked; the little bastards must have been feasting on me all night and still were, it seemed. I flapped my hand near my ear as the high-pitched whine signalled the landing approach of one of nature's vampires.

'Go and feed on Slick, he won't fight back,' I said, but she ignored me as the piercing drone returned, greeted with a repeated useless flailing of my hand.

I want to believe that all creatures have a purpose in their lives, however I struggle to find something to entice me to like these miniscule, marauding, blood-sucking menaces. The world could do without the deadly diseases carried around nonchalantly by these winged monsters.

Malaria, dengue fever, yellow fever, filariasis and the Zika virus could be obliterated, if only we could make these insects extinct. It's unfair that the beautiful Amur leopard or the majestic mountain gorilla could soon be lost to the world but these long-legged, needle-mouthed purveyors of misery and death would continue to thrive.

I moved the sacking. Opposite me, squatting, a woman stared intently into a *degchi* cooking pot over an open fire. Her bright red and yellow *salwar kameez*, muddied at the edges, her matching *dupatta* worn over her head covering her hair. She looked about eighty years old, but this country and climate are unkind masters and she may have been decades younger. She stirred the contents of the *degchi*; the smell of spice wafted towards me. She seemed unperturbed, her life hadn't changed in the way that Slick's had and she seemed blissfully unaware of the events which had unfolded twenty metres away from her. She was no threat, unless she saw me. Darkness would have been an ally, but that was a few hours away. Someone would surely come looking for Slick well before then.

Sweat trickled into my eyes; my shirt clung to my skin as if superglued. The intenseness of the humidity opened every pore as if they were floodgates. I needed to assess my surroundings but the limited view the window gave me was inadequate.

Options were limited.

Wait for darkness? Unlikely that there would be time.

Walk out the door? The cook might raise an alarm and I couldn't be sure how many armed men there were around.

Let someone come? I was armed and would be ready. That seemed the best option, and if no-one came before dark then option one would take over.

Plans A and B in place, I turned, suddenly startled by movement on the floor where Slick's corpse lay. He was moving.

Impossible, he's dead. He couldn't have survived that. I pulled the knife from my pocket.

Sweat filled eyes and the almost total darkness, made vision difficult. He was shaking, one leg quivered, his whole body seemingly convulsing.

He lay, foetally positioned with his back towards me. I stretched my hand out towards his shoulder to turn him onto his back, knife at the ready. His body was flaccid, rigor mortis hadn't yet begun. A flurry of fur ran across my hand, a hissing rodent moved up my arm, instinctively I swung the knife and caught him on the head. He fell and ran away followed by a cascading flood of his colony.

I jumped back kicking wildly at anything which might be in reach, I struck air.

Why is a collection of rats known as a mischief?

How could anyone who had seen them gnawing as they were now on the dead flesh of a human being think of such a ubiquitous word?

A rancour of rats?

Perhaps a virulence of rats?

Or maybe a maleficence of rats?

Any of those words I could understand, but not a mischief.

A shiver rose from the base of my spine to my shoulders. I shook involuntarily as the vision which would undoubtedly return in nightmares replayed over and over. It seemed to be worse because of the almost silence in which it happened. Apart from the low hiss of the rat on my arm I heard nothing.

Rats are not silent creatures but they seem that way. Their communication squeaks, squeals and chattering shrieks all take place above our audible range. For that, at least I was grateful.

I, and professional aversion therapists, had, on many occasions, tried to cure me of the one phobia I have. Cognitive behavioural therapy in many guises, exposure therapy have all been tried with some success in the controlled environment of the treatment room. Sadly the last five minutes showed me that in practice nothing had changed; in fact probably things were worse. Now I could imagine the deafening noise as the warning cries spread through the mischief.

Part of the therapy included using a device to hear what was happening in the ultrasonic stratosphere in which rats communicated. It did not make for pleasant listening to me and now cerebral imagination was amplifying the noise by the assumed number that had disappeared further into the darkness. The knowledge that they would be back did not help.

Sweating, I moved to the wall farthest away from the corpse, the rats could have him. I needed to calm myself to be ready for what was to come. Thankfully Slick was seemingly not missed. At least there was no search party entering the rodent realm in which I had been incarcerated. The rats had a banquet awaiting them which meant they left me alone.

Day filtered towards night. I glanced through the window, the building opposite in total darkness. No evening meal being prepared, no indication of occupation. I opened the door fully and crouched out. A calculated risk, but thanks to incompetence and the benevolence of Slick's pockets I was well armed. A heavy chain rattled against the door, a lock of industrial proportions dangled from a rusted loop on the door, its key still in place.

I stepped along the wall and around to the back of my erstwhile prison. A series of low buildings surrounded a large, hardened mud area. This must have been the playground from which the sounds of children playing came earlier.

Electric light streamed from many of the windows. Outside there was no movement. The whole area seemed deserted. Sounds came out of the darkness as I approached the nearest building. Blankets lay in rows on the floor. No beds or mattresses, no signs of comfort.

The second window. A dining hall, mostly full, with children eating in total silence. Bowls of food were being mopped up with slivers of bread broken off from a larger piece on the table beside them. Only using their right hands as is the taught behaviour, none of them seemed enthusiastic enough to emulate Oliver Twist and ask for more. There seemed to be no adult supervision, no Mr. Bumble or Mrs. Corney to oversee and maintain discipline. Some other unseen force instilled silence in this room.

I moved on. A passageway led to a third room. What once might have been lace curtaining hung in shreds across the windows. The coverings offered no privacy and I had a clear view of the room and its occupants. I gagged at what I saw and turned away.

I thought I had become immune to the horror of such sights. Before, it had always been on film. Edited horror, always slightly removed, always on a screen, always with an *off* button if it became too much.

This horror was happening now, in real time, a metre or so away from me.

My heart pounded. Controlling the rampaging violence building up in my core made me shake.

'Stay calm, resist, restrain, resolve,' I repeated, steeling my being to look again. To be able to assess my next steps needed clear thinking, not adrenaline-fuelled anger.

The room was completely clear of furniture with the exception of two chairs. Seven or eight children, both boys and girls were in the room, I guessed none of them had seen more than ten birthdays. All were completely naked. All were involved in sexual activity either between themselves or with one of the seven naked adults in the room with them. One girl being raped had her mouth bound with silver duct tape. Five men and two women were cajoling, forcing and clearly enjoying the rape and depravation occurring there.

All the while a fully clothed man equipped with a camera stabilising shoulder rig and a video camera which would not look out of place on a Bollywood film set, was filming. If it was only amongst adults it could be passed off as a swingers' party or orgy of Roman proportions but here, innocence was being robbed with violence.

There were no smiles, the cameraman would ensure the adults' faces would never be shown and the crying of the boys and girls seemed to add to the pleasure of the sick bastards who would watch this video later.

Or perhaps it was live streaming, that, I couldn't know. One thing was certain, the vile video was coming to a close, more abruptly than its adult cast and crew intended.

The cameraman was lingering on a man with his hand entangled in a girl's hair as he forced her onto him; he was leaning against the wall beside the door. The cameraman was moving closer for a more detailed view.

I edged towards the door and opened it slowly. The participants were unaware of anything happening around them. The cameraman had his back towards me, crouching to be at the same level as the girl's face. I grabbed him and pulled him up, swinging him around at head height, hoping that the camera was taking in the faces of the now staring adults.

The pistol handle met his temple with as much force as I could muster. He fell in a crumpled heap. I brought the pistol into full view.

Children screamed, adults suffered intense pupil dilation as they came to terms with the new situation.

'Who speaks English?'

No reply.

'Who speaks English?' I repeated, pressing the pistol barrel an inch above the ear of the man by the door. He had let go of the girl he had been holding. All eyes focussed now on him.

Deference or fear? I wondered.

Was he the leader?

'Who speaks English? One, two…'

'We all do, sir. We're teachers,' he blurted out.

'Remove that tape. Tell the children to dress and join the others.'

A woman spoke and the children obediently picked up clothes and filed out in silence. They were used to taking orders without demur.

The woman reached for a roll of material, a sari I presumed. 'Leave it,' I said; 'I want you all to stay exactly as you are.

'You are misunderstanding the situation here, sir.' It was the one with the gun to his head.

'How so?'

'We are educating these children so they are prepared for their future lives when they leave our care.'

'What you were forcing that girl to do was education?'

'Things are different in India. Girls and boys marry very young, we are teaching them how to pleasure their husbands and wives.'

'What you were doing to that child was educational?'

'Yes, sir. She enjoyed it and it meant nothing.'

I lowered the gun and shot him in the kneecap. He screamed.

'Now, that's education,' I said. 'I enjoyed it and to me it means nothing.'

'Who is this being filmed for?'

Silence.

'I don't like repeating questions. The pistol moved slowly in an arc around them all.

'We don't know.' It was the woman who spoke.

The writhing, bloodied man spoke in a local language.

'He has a gun, Girik. You are the proof he will use it. I don't want to die today.' She turned towards me. 'We really don't know. We are paid by the cameraman. Who employs him we are not sure.'

'Not sure? So you have an idea?'

'He sometimes comes with another man, who gives him orders.'

'Who?'

'Don't know his full name. The cameraman calls him Deepak.'

'Have you seen him today?'

'He was here this morning, but he went out and we haven't seen him since. His car is still in the car park though. I think he owns a lemon and sunflower plantation not too far away.'

'Where?'

'On the road to Adgaon.' A groan came from the cameraman, he was coming round.

'Does he know where it is?'

'Certainly.'

'Okay, you two pick him up, remove the camera. I want the memory card.'

They complied without a word, sitting him down on one of the chairs.

'Tie his wrists behind his back.'

'What with? We don't have rope,' one replied

'You've got duct tape though don't you? I've seen it used in here to silence the screams of a child. Now get it.'

His head drooped, with eyelids half closed, he moved to a box in the corner. It was obviously a new box. They clearly intended to use a lot of it. Whatever the intended use, it would now serve a different purpose.

'I'm dying here. Help me,' the kneecapped Girik moaned.

'You,' I said to the woman who had spoken earlier. 'Bind his leg with duct tape. Tightly and use plenty. It won't save his life but it will delay the blood flow.'

Once done, I checked the bindings on the cameraman. He was reasonably secure, given a couple of hours and a lot of effort he could probably free himself, but he wouldn't be given that long.

'A torch,' I said.

Compliance was becoming quicker; two torches appeared.

I handed one to the woman and kept the other, a slim black LED version. I cupped the torch in my left hand and rested the pistol on it in the manner commonly seen in American TV cop shows, when the heroic NYPD enter a blacked-out building. It is beyond me why these people don't just turn on the lights.

'All of you move. Outside. Help Girik. Carry him if you have to, and bring that tape.'

They filed out, Girik was carried by two men, another carried the box of duct tape.

'If any of you try to run, I'll shoot you. This time not in the kneecap. Now, over to that outhouse.' I pointed at the low building where the rodent restaurant, with its seasonal Shitole menu, was now probably at the height of frenzy.

'Through the door and to the right,' I instructed. This would bring them towards the dining area.

The woman with the torch was first in.

'One, two...' I began counting silently.

The scream came before I reached three.

'Quiet,' I ordered, but the sound of gagging became louder as each of the erstwhile teachers saw Slick and the savage, scuttering scavengers in the light of the torch.

'Now, at least you know where he went,' I said to them.

By the time I left them, they were sitting in a circle on the ground, their backs to each other. Hands and arms bound behind and tape encircling their necks and binding them together. I used more tape to go around their waists keeping them close, limiting movement. Their mouths were covered and, finally, their legs and ankles, I was running out of ideas of how to use the tape when the final roll gave up its last few centimetres.

'Don't worry,' I said; 'I'll inform the police you're here – eventually.'

I closed the door, attached the chain to the padlock, turned the key, then threw it onto the roof. No point in making entry easy.

The thoughts that Girik would almost certainly die before release came, or that the rats would begin nibbling at the circled group gave me only one concern.

I wouldn't want those razor-sharp teeth to cut through the tape I had so lavishly used.

CHAPTER 24

Present day
Maharashtra Tuesday Evening 8:30 p.m.

Getting the cameraman into the car was easy. The pistol helped. I waved fingers in front of him and ascertained he could both see and count. His undoubted concussion wouldn't stop him driving me to Slick's farm. After that, he would be dead anyway so he didn't need to worry about his throbbing headache. He didn't know that so it didn't stop him complaining about it.

'I'm sure your headache will be gone by the time we reach the farm,' I told him repeatedly.

I didn't care if he was convinced or not. Driving along narrow lanes, the eyes of sacred cows lighting up as we passed. My thoughts momentarily returned to a conversation with Chirag, one year ago.

'The sentence for killing a cow is five, seven or fourteen years in different states. In Gujarat, Prime Minister Modi's home state, it is now life imprisonment, but the sentence for causing the death of a human being through rash or negligent driving is only two years,' he told me.

'So is the life of a man worth so much less than that of a cow?' I asked.

'Of course,' Sushma had interrupted. 'Especially if that man is a Muslim.'

'Sushma please, you are being unfair.'

'Have you not listened to what Sadhvi Saraswati has been preaching? Or Chetan Sharma? They want beef consumption to be punished by public hanging. The slaughter of cows is, according to them, responsible for global warming.'

'Don't be ridiculous,' Chirag responded.

'Ridiculous? Ridiculous? Sharma spoke recently saying, "Cow is also the reason for global warming. When she is slaughtered, something called EPW is released, which is directly responsible for global warming. It's what is called "emotional pain waves." Emotional Pain Waves? It's lunacy. Hindu vigilantes are lynching Muslims they suspect of killing cows or eating the sacred meat and the police are standing by.'

I had enjoyed the animated discussion's in Chirag's home and found them educational.

Back to the present, and the moaning driver, we stopped at some closed gates.

'Here's the farm,' the driver said; 'but I don't think Deepak is in.'

'I'm sure he isn't here. Who will be?'

A uniformed guard opened the gate, saw the number plate and waved us in, saluting as we passed. We drove along a dirt track. No sign of any dwellings.

'Not very security minded is he?' I said, 'I could be anybody, maybe even armed and dangerous.'

No reply.

'I asked you a question. Who will be here at this time?'

'I don't know, sir. I don't live here. I just come here to collect the equipment and he allows me to use one of his cars to drive to the assignment.'

'How many assignments do you have? Is it always the school?'

'Lately mostly the school, but sometimes private houses.'

'Always the same kind of films?'

'No I also do weddings, *Naamkaran* ceremonies…'

'What's *Naamkaran*?'

'A new baby's naming ceremony.'

'Always for Slick? I mean Deepak.'

'Yes. His workers. He has a joke; he calls them a school production line.'

'How many does he have working for him?'

I don't know, thirty farm workers maybe, house wallahs, cooks. Some are married to the farm workers. He is very generous. Sometimes, if there is a girl child who is not wanted, Deepak will find someone rich to take them. Often in Europe. Rich, barren European ladies like Indian children, Deepek says. They pay handsomely and Deepak gives a share to the parents.'

'Just what kind of farm is this?'

'Lemon and sunflowers, sir.' He had obviously missed the irony in my question.

The track eventually became wider. A series of low buildings were lit by lamps above the doors. We parked next to two other black 4 x 4s about fifty metres from the largest of the buildings.

'Whose are they?' I asked.

'Deepak's guys from Mumbai.'

'Two cars, how many guys?'

'Always two in each car, so four'

'Where will they be now?'

'Two on guard, two resting or eating. They work eight-hour shifts. Eight on eight off. They're here a week and then they're replaced and four more come.'

'What are they guarding? They don't seem to be looking out here.'

'That's more information than I'm allowed to know. There's a large building out back. Satellite dishes and electricity generators. Guards sit inside and *tiffinwallahs* bring them their food. The *Mumbaikers* always get plenty, more than the other workers.'

'Are they armed?'

He shook his head in a way only Indians have mastered and which confuses outsiders.

'Is that a *yes* or a *no*?'

'Yes. They're armed.'

I stepped out of the car. I walked around the front keeping my eye on him. Reaching his window, I tapped.

'I forgot to ask, how is the headache?'

'Very bad.'

'This will ease it,' I said as I shot him in the middle of his forehead.

I hoped that the shot would cause panic amongst the guards, but I anticipated it would only raise curiosity. I positioned myself behind one of the Mumbai cars with a clear view of the main house.

The rumbling of an approaching motor distracted me. Lights were coming along the dirt track form the gate. 'Shit!' My position may have been hidden from the house but I would be lit up like a beacon by the car.

Without a sign of movement from the house I ran to a row of trees on the far side of the cameraman's mortuary car. I reached an enormous tree trunk, probably seven or eight metres in diameter, out of direct line of the oncoming lights. I waited.

The front door of the house opened and a white shirted man was back lighted and a perfect target. He had no visible weapon, so obviously the gunshot hadn't aroused even curiosity. His stance was erect and he looked down the road towards the light.

Had someone informed him of guests?

I hoped it was not a replacement crew from Mumbai. Four shooters would be relatively easy to divide and dispose of; eight would be exponentially more difficult. The problem does not only double as the numbers increase, but the addition of extraneous factors including chance, danger awareness, particularly after the discovery of a kill and level of combat training, can all make the job difficult. Not impossible but certainly more challenging and risk laden.

The visitors arrived. It wasn't one car, but three. The seemingly obligatory black 4 x 4 was followed by a white Mercedes with another identical utility vehicle behind.

They didn't stop at the car park with the other cars but drove straight to the front of the house. Full light didn't reach my position, but there was enough illumination for me to feel it prudent to move back. Fortunately, there was also enough illumination to stop me from doing so.

Unlike rats, I am not phobic about snakes. I do however, have a respect for them. Especially when they are black, about three-feet-long and have twin white rings at intervals along their backs.

The slightly broadened head of a *Krait* was slowly moving across my toe cap. I recognized the species immediately. One of the most venomous in the world this nocturnal ophidian was one of what India calls its 'big four,' responsible for the most human deaths on the sub-continent.

Like most serpents, the *Krait* does not want to bite humans, its normal prey of rodents, lizards, frogs and other snakes are much more deserving of their attention, but will take a bite of *Homo Sapiens* quickly and without notice if annoyed, angered or surprised. Once its envenoming fangs get into the skin, it will hold on to ensure maximum toxin penetration. Neuromuscular paralysis rapidly follows.

This was not a snake to mess with.

Standing statuesquely immobile, I watched as its black eyes scoured and the flicking tongue brought chemical information to the Jacobson Organ in its mouth. This was a snake on the hunt. It would have slept all day, in a burrow provided for it by some rodent, or in a termite hill, perhaps even near the house in a wood pile, now it was hungry.

The sounds of voices, car doors opening and shutting, and the sound of the front door being closed were noted, but I gleaned little information. My sight was concentrated on the black cylinder slithering its way across my foot. As the car lights began to turn, the snake's tail passed over my shoe. I could risk a look. They parked up near to the dead body of the cameraman. As the drivers got out of the cars they were too busy chatting amongst themselves to notice the corpse in the car and walked off towards the house.

The passing *Krait* advised me against going further into the trees but I would need to find somewhere to hide. Daylight was not going to be my friend. The serpentine distraction had made it impossible to assess the extent of the obstacles I now faced. Some old-fashioned surveillance would be required.

I was aided by the open or curtain-less windows in the

house. The smell of spices wafted from the kitchen. A cook was preparing a meal. Presumably the Merc had brought someone important. The snippets of conversation I heard were of no value. My fifty or so Hindi or Marathi words were insufficient to follow the rapid-fire conglomeration of words that reached me. The tone seemed good humoured until a shrill male voice screeched through the air.

'I told him to be here, where is he?'

Why the switch to English? Then a woman's British accented voice replied.

'I'm sorry, Rohtakji. He left early this morning. Akshay, the photoshoot guy, came by later to collect the camera and car and said he was meeting Deepak, but nothing was said to indicate he would be late. He knew you would be arriving and it is not like him to be late. He ordered dinner to be ready on time. I've tried calling, but his phone goes straight to voicemail. This is just not like him.'

'He better have a good reason. He promised me something special. So special, I have driven all the way here to collect it. I have a 4 a.m. flight to Dubai, I cannot miss it.'

Rohtakji; I recognised the name immediately. Slick's boss and Priya's father. This was the man who wanted my death, almost as much as I wished for his. This was a chance I didn't want to let slip.

I returned to the parked cars. A 4 a.m. flight so he would need to leave no later than eleven, about an hour from now.

Should I let him go or make him stay?

To delay him would be easy, I had a knife in my pocket and cars, even 4 x 4s, struggle to move with slashed tyres. That would increase the danger however, as six cars don't have tyre deflation at the same time by coincidence. If I disabled one, it would have to be them all.

I had a little time before making that decision. Before that I needed to do some counting. The four original Mumbaikers had now been augmented by Rohtak's entourage. At least two in each of the 4 x 4s and his own driver. So there were now a minimum of nine armed men in this farm complex, maybe more. I had two guns with around fifteen rounds left. That didn't leave a great margin for error. I would need to try and increase firepower. Picking the guards off one at a time and taking their weapons had to be the primary strategy. Whether it was a feasible strategy was a completely different question.

I carried on with my check of the main house and within a short period was confident that the original guess of numbers was correct. At the back of the house across a compacted dirt yard was the building my deceased chauffeur of this evening talked about. It was well lit, both inside and out.

I couldn't walk straight across to it as I would be easily visible to anyone even glancing out of a window. I moved towards the shadows, not going as far as the tree line, I had no wish to meet up with any more nocturnal hunters. Edging my way towards the second building, a blaze of light struck my perimetric vision. A man came out of a door at the side of the main house, he was humming as he carried stainless-steel, triple-teared *tiffin tins* or *dabbas* out of the house and walked towards the outbuilding. There were three of them. But the cameraman had said there were only two guards. He did say they ate well so perhaps the third was a dessert to be shared.

I had been fascinated in Mumbai seeing the 130-year-old tradition of the *dabbawallahs* bringing home cooked food to the workers of the city. A fast-food system that is the envy of many new App based companies. Thousands of men collect food, sealed inside the steel tins, from a worker's home midmorning, and take it to a train station, coded to mark its destination and recipient. It is received in Mumbai and office delivery is made on foot, with a cart, or by bicycle before one o'clock. 200,000 meals a day or eighty million lunches a year. A remarkable feat.

Here, the *tiffin wallah* had just a short journey to make by foot. The *dabba* was probably not necessary to keep the food hot on such a short journey, but tradition must be observed and it is a very convenient system.

He knocked on the door. A few moments passed before it was opened and another white shirted man opened the door taking the tins without a word and closing the door abruptly. As the *wallah* arrived back at the house, I ventured nearer the outbuilding. Keeping low and in the shadows, as much as possible, I peered through the window where voices were coming from.

Two guards, the deceased driver had said, but there were three men in the room. The faces of two I could see clearly and both were dressed identically to the guards I had seen before. The third man had his back to me.

Dressed in a white smock, his long, lank, grey hair reached his shoulders, glimpses of a long beard showed with the movement of his head. He immediately reminded me of the pictures Chiara and Giacomo had shown me of *Maharishi Mahesh Yogi*, the guru who introduced the Beatles to transcendental meditation.

Why did he need armed guards? The two of them chatted incessantly but Yogi didn't join in. Perhaps speech was something he no longer participated in.

Silently rising from his seat, the old man made his way to the door, the guards' eyes followed him as he left and laughed once he was longer in sight.

CHAPTER 25

Present day
Maharashtra Tuesday Evening 9:45 p.m.

The clock above the guards' heads showed I had about an hour left to make my decision and act upon it. Remove Rohtak and take on the larger number of guards or let him go and deal with the four who were left, along with the household staff and, presumably, the recently widowed Mrs. Slick.

I returned to the front of the house and made my way to the car bloodied by the exsanguination of the cameraman. I didn't want to risk, Rohtak's drivers coming across him as they were leaving, if that is what I decided to let them do.

As I opened the car door, the corpse fell towards me. I grabbed him under the armpits and dragged him out. I laid him on the ground and rolled him into the tree line. I wasn't going to risk stepping into that undergrowth again.

I closed the door and walked to the open window. There was angry shouting but all in Marathi or Hindi – no more snippets in English, so I was completely ignorant of what was happening. Then a word I recognised. It was Rohtak. '*Challo*,' he said. It was an order for them all to leave.

'Tell your husband, this will be the last time he disobeys an instruction. When you speak to him, tell him to meet me at the airport before 2 a.m. or he will have to bring what I need to Dubai in the morning. He's a dead man if he doesn't. Understand?'

I smiled.

'Where will you be?' she asked.

'I will be sitting in the First-Class check in area beside door one. He should call when he arrives as he won't be able to enter the terminal. If he comes to Dubai, I'll be in the *Burj al Arab* as usual.'

'I'll tell him,' she said; 'If he ever answers his phone.'

'He'd better.'

They had made the decision for me, I would have to let them go, but, at least I knew where I could find him after tomorrow. He certainly enjoyed opulence. The *Burj al Arab*, the symbol of decadence and reputed global icon of Arabian luxury, as the owners like to boast.

I had to wait for them to leave. I worked my way through the shadows to the back of the outbuilding. There was less chance of being stumbled upon. Someone had kindly left an old plastic garden chair so I could sit whilst I waited. I heard the engines start beyond the house and caught occasional sight of red lights as they made their way down the dirt road. My plan formulated, I decided to relax for an hour or so.

Eight hours on and eight hours off the cameraman had said. So I anticipated that the times would be eight in the morning, four in the afternoon and then midnight. Assuming the changeover would take place at the outbuilding, all four would be in close proximity, away from the main house and at their most relaxed. Various scenarios played out in my head. I would be ready for all eventualities. I inhaled deeply, sat back and began to unwind.

Then the scream.

Shrill, loud and sustained from the front of the house. I jumped up and jogged in the shadows to the side of the main house. I reached the corner and saw several people near to the parked cars. Someone had found the body.

Mrs. Slick was shouting. 'Who is it? Is it Deepak?'

'No, it's Akshay. The killer must still be here somewhere,' one of the guards shouted.

'Or he's fled,' said the other.

'Only if he's stupid. It would take a special kind of fool to venture through there at night.'

'Shall we call Rohtakji and ask him to come back? His men could help us look.'

'Are you crazy? Tell Rohtak that Akshay was murdered whilst he was here in the house?'

'We don't know when he was killed.'

'Precisely, but the car wasn't here when I came back earlier so it must have arrived around the same time as Rohtak.'

'It's only the cameraman. Rohtak doesn't even know him I suppose.'

'We'll deal with it.'

They picked up the body and carried it towards the house, laying it down in the light beside the front door.

'I thought it was Deepak,' his widow said; 'Why isn't he answering his phone.'

'He'll be back soon, maybe his battery died.'

'He would have been here if he could. He wouldn't disrespect his boss in this way. Something's happened, I know it has.'

'You're right,' I said, as I moved into the light, Deepak's pistol in my left hand, my own in the right. 'He's dead. Just like the perverted cameraman by your feet.'

One of the guards went to move inside the house. They had been careless, they were unarmed. He had been slightly in front of Mrs. Slick but as he edged toward the door, I had a clear shot without the danger of collateral damage. I took it. The second shot took out the other guard.

'Now Mrs. Shitole, we need to talk. What I do next will depend on what you tell me. Inside, and call all your staff into the same room.'

'It's not pronounced that way. It's Shee-toe-lay,' she said trying to disguise the shaking. I took her by the arm, guiding her through the door.

'It's what I say it is. The staff, here now. Tell them to bring their phones.'

'There's only the cook and one house girl,' she lied in a loud voice. Not a good start.

'Ok let's go into the kitchen.' I pushed her gently. She opened the kitchen door. There were two women cowering in a corner. They could have been mother and daughter, the younger one being about twenty years old.

'What's in there?' I said pointing to a door which was slightly ajar.

'It's just the pantry where we store the food.'

'Mrs. Shitole, I told you outside what you tell me now, will determine what I do next. It is not sensible to lie to me. There are three dead bodies outside your front doorstep, do you want more inside?'

'I told you the truth, it's just storage.'

'OK, next question. Who's inside there?'

'No…'

I slammed the gun on the kitchen table.

'Tell the fucking *tiffin wallah*, to get out here... now.'

'Gupte, please come out. He knows you're in there.'

A wiry frame appeared at the door.

'Come and join us,' I said. 'Put your hands where I can see them, you're hiding something what is it?'

The flickering of his eyes was enough for me. Another head shot. He fell; a large kitchen knife clattered from his hand as his body thudded onto the floor. The three women screamed.

A call for help?

'Silence.' They obeyed.

I moved to the back door. Had the guards in the outbuilding heard? The lighted area was clear. No sign of movement.

'Get this door locked. One of the women did so and removed the key.

'Leave the key in the lock and place some pans behind it.

It was more difficult to open a locked door from the outside if the inside key was left in the lock, especially if it had a slight turn off vertical. More difficult but not impossible. The pans would at least give me some warning if someone came in in the next few minutes.

'Now the front door the same. All of you, out.'

They trooped out, closed and locked the door and placed some pans behind it.

'The three of you, in that room.' I pointed to a room which I assessed faced out the back. I would need the external light. It was a sitting room with several large settees. 'The three of you, move that to face the window and sit down.'

I switched the light off in the room; the light filtering in was enough to see my way. Grabbing a cushion, I threw it on the floor under the window and sat down, making sure my head was well below the glass and therefore not visible from outside. I sat cross legged, not a position I found comfortable, but it reduced my visibility from anyone looking in through the window.

CHAPTER 26

'Mrs. Shitole. I need to know how much you know about your husband's interests. In particular, what does... sorry, what did he do for Mr. Rohtak?'

'He's his right-hand man. He does whatever he's told.'

'And what might that include?'

'I don't know, a lot of different things.'

'I haven't got much time, Mrs. Shitole. Please do not waste what little is available to you. I'll start by shooting one of these two. You can choose which one will be first. Now the next few minutes are important and you can save your life and also theirs. What exactly does your husband do for Rohtak?'

'I don't know the details. Deepak never tells me. He tells me when he is, or is not going to be home. I've tried asking him, but I learned years ago that I should keep quiet. He gets very angry.'

'Violent?' I asked, ignoring the fact she spoke in the present.

The movement of her gaze to the floor was answer enough.

'OK, let's say for now I believe you. What does the dead man outside, I think you called him Akshay, what does he do for your husband?'

'He's an IT guy and does social filming for Mr. Rohtak.'

'Social filming, what does that include?'

'Family events, weddings, engagement parties, that kind of thing.'

'What's his involvement at the school? He was there today.'

''Which school? Do me mean the Rohtak Academy?'

'If that's what it's called.'

'Nothing, as far as I know. Deepak goes there occasionally, but I think that's to check on the condition of the children. I'm not sure; he doesn't even tell me that.'

'I'll come back to that. But first, tell me about the outbuilding. Why all the security?'

'There's some old man that Rohtakji wants to keep safe. There are people out looking for him and Rohtakji wants to make sure he stays safe.'

'Why is he important?'

'I don't know. I just have to organise food for him and the guards.'

'What about child pornography? Do you enjoy watching that?'

'How dare you? What has child pornography got to do with me or with the old man out there?'

'That's what I was hoping you'd tell me. I was at the school today and your friend Akshay was there, filming teachers raping and abusing the children.'

'That's not possible. Deepak would never have allowed anything like that.'

'Do you really not know your husband? He was there, he organised it.'

'I don't believe you. That can't be true. Deepak would never do anything like that.'

'What about kidnap? Or torture? Would he do that?'

'Don't be ridiculous. He's a businessman, not some grotesque, Italian Mafioso.'

'Why do the Italians always get the blame? Do you think that organised crime only exists in Sicily? In Italy? Perhaps you need to learn a little more about your husband and his paedophile employer.'

'You can't throw words around like that. It's disgusting. What do you mean paedophile?'

She caught the memory card I threw at her. If you don't believe me watch what's on there. You'll need a very strong stomach. That's the reason the cameraman is lying out there with a bullet in his head.'

Disbelief was etched on her face.

'It's not true, it can't be true. Lila here went to that school. Tell him Lila, tell him he's wrong.'

Tears flowed down the girl's cheeks.

'Lila, Lila, what is it?'

'I swore I would not tell you.'

'Shut up Lila, you've said enough already.' It was the older of the two who spoke.

'*Mammii*, he knows, it's no longer a secret. He knows.'

'Kali? What is Lila saying?' Mrs Shitole asked. 'Are you saying this man is right? Are you saying you knew? That Lila was abused, and you knew? Am I the only one in ignorance here?'

'You are happy to live in luxury here in this house. You don't care where the money comes from. You want to be like some *Maharani* waited on hand and foot. Your imperious tone, more suited to a British Raj *Memsahib*, always demanding, never asking. Kali do this, Lila bring me that, make my tea, the coffee is late.'

'Don't speak to me like that.'

'Why not, what are you going to do? Sack me? This man might kill me. I don't care, your life here, in this house, has been brought to an end by this messenger of *Yama*, the god of death. Lila's life has been ruined by your husband and he used our poverty to buy our silence. But no more. Do you hear me *Memsahib*? No more.'

'Sit down,' I said. 'I'm not finished with any of you. Give the memory card to Lila. This is your chance to try and put right some of the wrong done to you. The teachers are all tied up in the outbuilding in the school. One of them might be dead by now. Mr. Shitole certainly is.'

'What did you do to him? Why?' She paced around in a small circle, her hands banging the sides of her head. 'No, no, no. You bastard, what have you done?'

'Your husband was an evil man, Mrs Shitole. He was keeping me prisoner in the outbuilding in which he is lying now beside the teachers who abused Lila and countless other children in their care.

'He died because he was a facilitator for Rohtak and his associates to film the rape and often horrific murders of children and babies, some of them only months old. He died because he tried to kill me, and Rohtak's former wife, because I prevented Rohtak's daughter from being sold to a paedophile in Dubai to settle a debt. He died because he deserved to die. Justice would never have been found in India, he had access to too much money. Countless children's' lives have been saved today.'

'It's not true. It can't be true. I don't believe you.'

'If you don't believe me, believe Lila and Kali. He was an

237

evil, paedophilic bastard and you are better off without him. The world can breathe easier now he's gone. Enough talking about garbage, tell me more about that outbuilding. Why all the satellite equipment?'

'I already told you. I don't know. I haven't been inside there for years. It was Deepak's domain, his office.'

'Until the man moved in it was used as a kind of studio,' Lila said. They didn't stop using me when I left school.'

'Who's they?'

Mr Shitole and others. They would come and film themselves raping me. Sometimes there would be as many as five of them taking it in turns. They would wear masks, usually of animals.'

'And all of this stopped when the old man arrived?'

'No. It would have been a month or so before. I heard one of the men complain that I was too old for him and refused to take part in the film. I was scared of what they would do to me if they had no use for me, but *mammii* spoke to Mr. Shitole and he let me become a housekeeper.'

'Kali, why didn't you report this to me, or the Police.'

'What good would that have done? You would not have believed me and as for the police… She turned her head and spat on the ground. 'They are in his pay. Some of them raped my daughter and laughed about it in my face afterwards.'

'How do you know they were police officers?' I asked.

'They came here in uniform. It's all part of the intimidation. Letting me know, that it was useless to complain to the police.'

'How many of them? What rank?'

'Three or four, all three stars or above.'

'Do you know their names?'

238

'No, but she will,' she said, pointing to the woman with the glazed-over eyes and suddenly pallid skin beside her. There was no response.

'So do you?' I asked.

No reply.

'I asked a question, do you know their names.'

She shook her head.

'Yes you do,' Kali shouted. 'They were sitting at your table two days ago. Did you not see the smiles and sneers whenever I, or Lila, served them and your husband?'

'What are you talking about Kali?' She had clearly not been following the conversation, her eyes were water filled but no tears fell. She seemed to have stopped blinking, staring at the window.'

'I'm talking about the police officers you entertained the other evening with your husband. What are their names?'

'Why do you want their names?'

'They raped Lila, in that outbuilding, and you fed them. They ate *Kosha Mangsho, Murgh Chettinad* and *Gongura Mamsam* here at your table. You drank imported wine with them and plied them with whisky. You made Lila and I serve them.'

'They raped Lila? On Saturday? When they were here in my house?'

'Not on Saturday, before.'

'It doesn't matter when they did it, they did it,' I said; 'Lila needs to go to the police but she can't go to these men. Give me their names.'

'They'll be in the diary, over there,' she said pointing to a small table in the corner.

'Lila, can you go and get it for me, please?' I asked.

She handed it to me and sat back down next to her mother, who took her hand. 'I'm sorry Lila. I should have been braver. I should have protected you.'

'Then you and I would both be dead *mammii*. You know what they said.'

Her mother bit her quivering lip.

Mrs Shitole turned towards her young housekeeper. 'I'm so sorry, I really am so sorry. I didn't know, I didn't know, I didn't know.'

I flicked through the diary until I found the entry for Saturday.

'There are five names here,' I said. 'Four of them have police ranks but who is this other person? Durvish Deshmukh. You have an asterisk by his name. Who is he?'

'Mr. Deshmukh is an old school friend of Mr. Rohtak. He now lives in Dubai. It's who Mr. Rohtak visits there.'

'Why the asterisk?'

'He insisted that Lila be available to serve him as she had done the last time he came here. The asterisk was to remind me. The meal was organised a month ago. I might have forgotten.'

Lila was shaking.

'He raped me the last time he was here. It was three years ago, I was sixteen. He told the others to handcuff me to themselves, wrists and ankles and to pull hard as he raped me. I was in pain for days. Then, when he was finished, he spat in my face.'

'Did they film you?'

'Yes, and this time there were no masks. He said he wanted to enjoy it and keep it as part of his own special collection. He didn't need to hurt me like that. I would have let him do what he wanted. I was lucky. At the school, one girl died during a session with him. He was angry. "The bitch died too soon" he kept shouting. I was in the room next door. I heard everything including her screams. He liked the screams, that's why he hurt me so much. I would have screamed for him if he had asked me to, but no, he wanted to cause real physical pain.'

'Did he touch you this time?'

'No, but he whispered "ugly old bitch" whenever I leaned over to serve his food.'

'OK. I need to go and find out what is going on in the film studio. What time do the guards normally change over?'

'Midnight,' replied Kali.

'They must have heard the shooting over here, why didn't they come to investigate.'

'Gunshots are not unusual around here at night. Deepak likes to shoot vermin.'

'So do I,' I replied.

'He also sets traps which go off and scare the monkeys away. There... like that one.'

The single crack of exploding gunpowder was faint but unmistakeable.

'Now, I need to make sure you three don't do anything stupid whilst I'm over there. What shall I do?'

'Please don't hurt my daughter,' Kali pleaded.

They would be expecting someone to either knock on the door, if it was kept locked, or walk in, if not, around midnight. A door, heavily bolted from the inside and a coded knock would aid security. My experience of Slick's operation so far indicated these were untrained thugs with a brawn to brain ratio grossly weighted in favour of steroid-enhanced body mass.

They were relaxed, safe in this hideout *nel bel mezzo del nulla*, as Giacomo would have called the middle of nowhere. Now I needed to prove their theory of being safe, wrong.

I skirted the building looking to see where the protection detail was and what they were doing. The old man was sitting at a desk, his back to the window, looking at a computer displaying multiple pictures. His head blocked my view of most of the screen. Was this CCTV? Was he a part of his own security? Did he know about the carnage out front? Had he seen my approach? Would I have to deal with him too?

So many questions, the answers to which would have to wait. First, deal with the two guards. They didn't seem to be anywhere in the building. The television was still on in the room where I expected to see them. There was no sign, or sound, of them being in the bathroom, the only room with opaque glass. I moved further around, they had to be inside. But they weren't.

They must have gone. Were they seeking help? How much time did I have? I needed access to that computer, even if I had to kill the old man to get it. Act quickly and try to escape seemed my only option. There were two exterior doors. One near to where I was standing and the other, the main entrance, at the front. I tried the back; it was firmly locked. I moved around towards the front. The old man hadn't moved.

The door gave way easily and noiselessly but stopped suddenly. I pushed hard but only moved it slightly. There was a heavy weight behind it. I managed to get enough purchase to open a gap, sufficient to squeeze through. His lifeless body lay, face down, blood oozing from a head wound.

I pressed against the wall. Who had done this? His partner?

The old man? Either way there was someone in here prepared to kill and perhaps ready for me.

The short corridor led to the room with the television. I saw the flashing lights before I saw the second body. Rope still around his neck. Eyes open and bulging, he looked surprised. Not suicide then, I thought. His body sat upright, cross legged, mimicking the position I had adopted in the house, talking to the women. Was I being mocked?

Only the old man left to deal with, unless, he too, was dead. Reflecting back to when I saw him through the window he didn't appear to have moved. Was he still alive or not? Was there another killer in here somewhere? But where? From the outside it seemed there was no one else in the place. But if all three were dead, murder-suicide did not appear to be realistic. I moved towards the old man's room. He hadn't moved, whereas, from the window, his head obstructed the computer screen, now, that same black monitor blocked my view of his face.

I moved to the side. His hands were under the desk.

'Don't worry, Mr Johnson, I'm alive and I've been expecting you. I didn't think I'd have to wait so long.'

I froze.

Of everything I had imagined, it was not this. Not that voice. The voice I'd grown up hearing. The voice that had taught me so many things.

'*Papa*? Is that really you?'

Giacomo rose and held his arms out to me.

'Yes, my son. It's me. What kept you?'

CHAPTER 27

Present day
Maharashtra Wednesday 01:00 a.m.

'So many questions. There's no time now to answer them all. I was the tethered goat to entice the lion. They wanted us both dead, particularly you. Especially after you got Priya out of the country. Deshmukh wanted her so badly, even though she had become too old for his taste. Rohtak was becoming too independent. Deshmukh was afraid he would get out of control. Being married to Rohtak's daughter, and him knowing what Deshmukh is capable of, would have given Deshmukh the upper hand.'

'Why didn't they let me know you were alive? I would have been straight here.'

'They were afraid that you might have brought an army with you to rescue me.'

'I couldn't have done that.'

'I know that, you know that, but they didn't. I might have dropped the occasional false information bomb about the strength of our group and the nature of our relationship with certain government departments. I needed you here to rescue me. They desperately wanted you on their soil so your death could be for their pleasure and at their leisure. They planned to kill us both together and film the executions. Disposal of our bodies would not be an issue. We'd be dead and no-one would ever find us. Killing you in Europe would not have given them that security.'

'If you have access to the computer, why didn't you let me or Chiara know that you're alive?'

'I tried. I couldn't send any direct message as everything going out from here is monitored by Deshmukh and his network of underground IT guys – the sort who can do almost anything, and will, for enough bitcoins or hard cash. I had to do everything to stay alive. I tampered with my crime scene photos. The ones I had Pinky and Perky deliver to your boathouse.'

'What? You sent them? What about London. You sent them there too?'

'One thing at once. I thought that Chiara would have picked up on the message. Perhaps like me she's getting older.'

'She never saw the photos. I burned them.'

'Why the hell did you do that?'

'The guys had me a bit spooked. The photos looked the same as the other ones to me. I didn't want to upset Chiara.'

'Blood and gore would never upset your mother, you should have known that. She would have seen beyond the obvious and found out where I was, and still am.'

'But London? How did you do that? How did you know where I was?'

He pressed a few keys and turned the computer screen towards me. A red dot flashed on a map. 'There you are. I can get to within fifty metres of you twenty-four hours a day. It's how Chiara and I keep an eye on you.'

'How?'

'You remember when you went into hospital for the removal of the growth on your neck?'

'Yes. It's left a subcutaneous lump. I can feel it if I press it.'

'That lump is a GPS tracker.'

'What? You had me chipped like a dog?'

He laughed. 'I never thought of you as a dog. Just someone precious who needed your mother and me to keep an eye on you. Also don't forget, we only knew where you were, not what you were doing.'

'So, London?'

'That was easy. Find your location, check out Google Earth and find the most likely spot. Tell Pinky and Perky to go nearby in the hope you'd see them. In many ways you are a man of habits. Favourite pub, favourite coffee shop. You need to think more carefully. They didn't know what you looked like and were told to go and stand in certain places for half an hour. They were told to deliver the letter to your house, but didn't know it was your house. They thought it was a contact of Rohtak and the message was about the murder of Kiki Jachenholz.'

'You know about that?'

'Of course, though not until after she was killed. But it was all part of Deshmukh's plan to bring you in. Let's leave full explanations until later. We must act quickly. Go outside, telephone Chiara, use this phone, which I've borrowed from the corpse in the hall. Keep the call at less than a minute so it won't cause anyone to monitor it. Tell her I'm safe and you're with me. Say that we need to get to Dubai, immediately. Rooms at the *Burj* and we'll need the team. She'll know what to do.'

'What team?'

'Please, just do it, we don't have time for debate. I've had a year to plan this.'

The call to Chiara was short. '*Statevi bene*, keep safe,' she said as the call ended; 'Both of you.'

'We need to act before news of what's happened here reaches Dubai. This is a vast network of very rich, very powerful people. I have a lot of information from Rohtak's computer system but to deal with this thing properly, we need access to Deshmukh and his computer in Dubai. That's the heart of this.'

'I think *heart* is not a word I'd use for these people,' I replied.

'Deshmukh lives in a highly fortified house in Jumeirah Islands, he also has a large house on The Palm, but that is mostly for entertaining. It's the island house we need to get to but the security is extremely high.'

'Rohtak is staying at the *Burj*.'

'He always does. Deshmukh keeps several suites there for visitors. That is their weakest point. Rohtak will be relaxed and that is where we'll take him. Deshmukh will need some work, but we'll have help.

'From whom?' I asked.

'You'll see.'

CHAPTER 28

Present day
Dubai Friday 5:30 p.m.

Chiara was waiting for us at the airport as we arrived on the Emirates afternoon flight from Mumbai. She and Giacomo had talked by video-call at great length last night.

Our extraction from the farmhouse had been as dramatic as it had been swift. Chiara had obviously been tracking me and when she saw no movement for the extended period I had been locked in the school outbuilding, she contacted Arjun.

Within hours he had organised a CoBRA unit to be on standby. Formed in 2008 to act as a rapid reaction force, particularly against the *Maoist Naxalist* movement, it is one of the best equipped paramilitary forces in India. Before being seconded to close protection duties, Arjun had been a senior officer in this specialised unit of the Central Reserve Police Force and he hadn't found any obstacle in organising a, so called, training exercise.

A convoy of Merlin light support vehicles, bullet, land-mine, and blast-proof Vipers plus several capsule-based Marksman light armoured vehicles pulled up in front of the house. Arjun was with them.

'I heard you couldn't manage without me,' he said, as he jumped from the front vehicle.

'We weren't doing too badly,' I replied looking at the dead bodies lying by the door. 'We need to get to Dubai.'

'I know. Chiara has been quite specific in her instructions and said no expense was to be spared. She has already transferred substantial sums to more than cover the costs. You will travel on the Emirates flight tomorrow afternoon, first class and with Diplomatic papers. The equipment requested by Chiara is going by specialist courier on a separate military flight in the morning and will be delivered to your rooms at the Hotel.'

'What about our passports?'

'I still have mine,' said Giacomo.

'And yours is presumably in the luggage you left at Ganesh's apartment. I'll bring you there tonight. You can rest and take a flight tomorrow after midday.'

'Please look after Lila, she's a bit fragile. She has the memory card showing the filming in the school earlier today. Has someone been sent to the school?'

'That's all taken care of. A unit has arrested the teachers, at least those still alive. I assume that the body in the suit is Mr. Shitole; the crew there said there wasn't much of his face or hands left to identify. We'll have to use dental records.'

'It's Shitole,' I said. 'Guaranteed.'

In Dubai, a hotel supplied helicopter was waiting to take us from the airport. The pilot insisted on flying us on a scenic tour of Dubai, the opulent city on the edge of the desert.

The high-density, high-quality and high-priced housing, situated on artificial islands shaped like a palm tree and encircled by an effective circular harbour, could only be appreciated from the air. At ground level it looked just like rows of houses. Still, many who could afford to live there could also afford the helicopter rides to see it, if not their own helicopter. Chiara and Giacomo remained silent, holding hands and seemingly ignoring the view. There was work to be done.

We were greeted in style and the butler showed us to our high floor three bedroomed suite.

'A Campari soda, I think,' Chiara said as she sat on a stool and placed her handbag on the walnut topped bar inside the room.

'I'll get that for you madam,' the butler said.

'No thank you, that's very kind of you, but my husband knows exactly how I like it and it's been so long since he prepared one for me.'

'Shall I call someone to unpack your suitcases?'

'That won't be necessary,' Giacomo said, his tone read immediately by the butler who half bowed and left.

'Please call if there is anything I can do for you,' he said from the doorway.

Chiara's phone rang.

'Wonderful,' she said. 'I'll come down and meet you in reception.'

She took a key from the bar counter and made her way to the door. 'Help has arrived. You'd better start mixing those Camparis, Giacomo.'

She returned ten minutes later. I had taken the first sip of my gin and tonic made with Giacomo's generous alcoholic measures. Three glasses of ruby red cocktail stood on the bar next to a more orange coloured drink where the Campari had been mixed with orange juice. As the door opened familiar voices entered the room.

'This hotel has one of the biggest collections of *Statuario*

250

Marble in the world,' a woman's voice said.

'Never mind that. The luxurious down for the duvets is harvested from abandoned eider duck nests in Iceland and there are seventeen different types of pillow available. I'm going to try them all,' an equally well recognised male voice replied.

I was stunned to silence as Chiara and her two new companions entered the room. That silence was quickly broken.

'*Häschen*, aren't you going to kiss me?' Christiana asked.

'You can kiss me too, if you'd like,' Freddy added.

A thousand questions and no answers came rushing at me. I looked at the grinning faces of my parents and best friends, dumbfounded.

'We needed everyone together,' Chiara said. 'This wouldn't work from a distance.'

'Meet some other Atenisti,' Giacomo said.

'I think he already knows us, well enough,' said Christiana, 'Now, which is our bedroom? I need a shower. *Häschen*, close your mouth and show me the way.'

'Yours is the gold room,' Chiara said to try and ease at least some of my confusion.

I took her bag and walked towards the room. As we entered, she pulled my arm, jumped up and kissed me.

'Thank God, you're safe. I hated you leaving Düsseldorf this time. I thought I may never see you again.'

'What are you doing here? I don't understand?'

'Did you really think that your world is so secret from me, or from Freddy or Johann?'

'What has Johann got to do with this? Is he here?'

'Not yet, but he will be soon. He's getting into character.'

'What?'

251

'All in good time, *Häschen*. First I need a shower. Are you going to join me?'

When we returned to the giant blue and gold sitting room, Chiara, Giacomo and Freddy had almost finished their cocktails.

'Time for another drink, I think,' said Giacomo. 'The ice has melted in yours and our glasses are as good as empty.'

'Can someone please explain what is going on?'

'I'm pleased we can still surprise you son,' Giacomo replied.

'Christiana and Freddy have worked with us since University,' Chiara continued. 'We thought it safer if they knew about you, but you didn't know about them. Christiana's eye for precision and art has made her invaluable for preparing your additional ID documents and passports. Freddy's talent at finding his way through multi layered firewalls is legendary.'

'I can hack into any computer system. That is what Her Majesty's Government have been paying me for. NASA were particularly annoyed at me. Especially as I had a five hundred dollar bet with their IT head that I couldn't get in within three days. He hated paying me that money. But we did design special DPI packages together, which are now used throughout ours and the US network.'

'You did more than that together, if the photos from Aspen are a guide,' Christiana said.

'Bitch,' replied Freddy and everyone joined in the laughter.

A knock came on the door. Christiana got up to answer it. Before she reached the door a second knock and a call of 'Butler Service' was audible.

The impeccable Butler's Uniform suited the tall man now entering the room.

'You always look good in uniform,' Freddy said.

'Drink?' asked Giacomo from the bar.

'Not when I'm on duty,' replied Johann.

'Good, just checking,' replied my father. 'Is everything sorted?'

'Yes, I've been assigned to Rohtak's room.'

'Of course you have,' said Freddy. 'That one was easy.'

'I've introduced myself to Rohtak. He seemed a little upset his usual Butler had been taken ill so suddenly, I think they had some sort of arrangement. But he accepts the situation, I told him it would only be for a day or so.'

'That should be more than enough time,' I said.

'Leave Rohtak to me.' Giacomo's instruction was clearly and immediately understood by everyone in the room.

'He stole a year of my life. Twelve months away from Chiara, my home. Everything I hold dear was forbidden to me. Now he'll pay. Johann, let's deal with it tonight. Where is he dining?'

'In *Al Mahara* at nine, he has a table beside the aquarium.'

'Freddy, get me a table next to him, somewhere I can watch him.'

'Consider it done.' Freddy picked up his laptop, and within minutes he shut it. 'Eight forty-five,' he said. 'I recommend the langoustine followed by the salt baked sea bass.'

'How do you know what to recommend?' asked Johann. 'You've never eaten there.'

'I can read a menu though, and dream,' Freddy replied.

'We'd better get ready,' Chiara said. 'I'm pleased it's the *Al Mahara*. I'm looking forward to the John Dory followed by Wagyu striploin.'

'It seems I'm not the only one who likes to look at menus,' chuckled Freddy.

'Freddy, we'll need to deal with Deshmukh early tomorrow. Can you sort out the security details?'

'Once I've eaten,' he said. 'All this talk of food, I'm starving. Pass me the room service menu. Johann, you'd better leave before our real Butler comes back.'

It was gone midnight when Giacomo and Chiara returned.

'The meal was superb,' Chiara said. 'We decided on the Culinary Flight menu. Six courses and perfectly matching non-alcoholic beverages.'

'I found the post-dessert dessert, particularly satisfying,' Giacomo said.

'He looked peaceful and asleep,' Chiara said.

'Better than he deserved then,' I replied.

'Essential we don't arouse suspicion,' Giacomo added. 'He's dead and that's what's important. Now for Deshmukh. Is everything ready?'

'We have an appointment at eight-thirty tomorrow morning. He thinks we are a like-minded, cocaine-rich group from Medellin. I think he pissed his pants with excitement, it must have been Christiana's Spanish accent,' said Freddy.

'I thought it was more Argentinian than Columbian, but I'm sure he can't tell the difference.' The punch on my arm from Christiana hurt.

Johann was the last to arrive. Now dressed in his usual sharp suit and tie.

'We all need a good night's sleep. Johann you can use the guest room down those stairs. Ready to go by eight o'clock everyone. Now goodnight.'

Throughout my entire life, Chiara's nocturnal dismissal had never allowed for debate.

CHAPTER 29

Present day
Dubai Saturday 8:00 a.m.

The rental Mercedes seven-seater was waiting for us as Christiana, Freddy, Giacomo, Johann and I walked from the hotel. Chiara was staying at the *Burj* to arrange our departure.

Giacomo took the keys from the delivery driver and got in behind the wheel, Johann beside him. Freddy joined Christiana in the rear seats as I finished loading everyone's briefcases into the luggage compartment. Johann punched Deshmukh's address into his phone. No point in leaving a trace on the car's own GPS.

'Twenty-eight minutes,' he said.

'More than enough time,' replied Freddy, opening up his laptop. 'His security system is so basic; I haven't had to deal with such simplicity in fifteen years. Still, I'm sure he feels it's value for money.'

I still had not fully recovered from the shock of discovering my three greatest friends had been working with me in secret. Going on our first job together was exhilarating. I knew that I could trust them.

'Can you check for any secret rooms, Freddy? Somewhere he might hide a private collection?'

'Consider yourself already inside,' he replied. 'Nothing can escape me.'

In precisely twenty-eight minutes we pulled up outside a glass and marble villa set amongst palm trees. A guard was waiting for us.

'You are expected. The master is in the dining room, please follow me.'

We entered a hallway, dominated by glass. Panoramic views from every angle. Even the stairs were made from this transparent fusion of sand, soda and lime. A full-sized snooker table and a smaller pool table flanked the staircase. We were guided into a room which contained not one, but two dining tables. One was big enough to seat twenty around its carved mahogany sides. The second was smaller and obviously for daily use.

Sitting at one end, rising and wiping his mouth with a napkin, was our host.

'Beautiful lady, and gentlemen, welcome to my humble abode,' he said with the practiced air of a man who liked to display his wealth and play at self-deprecation.

Christiana replied in her best Columbian accent. 'It is kind of you to meet with us at such short notice. Our time here in the Emirates is so limited, and we would like so much to conclude some special business with you here.'

'It will be my pleasure,' he replied. 'Mutual benefit is my main aim in life, and when this can be combined with dealing with a beautiful woman like yourself, then there is enhanced pleasure.'

Cameras were clearly visible in every corner, Freddy said that there were over one hundred of them in the house, many would be well hidden from view. It didn't matter as they were all now sightless thanks to Freddy's wizardry. A fact that must have been on the mind of the young man who rushed into the room.

'Master can I speak with you?' he said, sweat pouring from every pore.

'Not now, you imbecile. Can't you see, I have guests?'

'Yes but, Master…'

'If you want to stay in my employ, don't ever say *but* to me, get out of my sight. Now you half-witted moron.'

His ire turned to charm. 'Please forgive the intrusion, senorita. He is an ignorant fool.'

'Not the only one in this house then,' Freddy whispered.

'Your home is wonderful, can I see some more?' Christiana asked.

'Of course, my dear. Please, follow me.'

'Darling,' she said, turning to me; 'please come too. We might want to use some of these ideas in our new villa. You others, wait here.'

'Gentlemen, make yourselves comfortable, either in here or out by the pool.'

We walked through reception rooms, with seating for thirty people, a kitchen any Michelin star restaurant would be jealous of, a fifty-seater cinema, a gymnasium and sauna.

'Can we see upstairs? Christiana said, 'Bedrooms are my favourite places.'

I walked obediently, two paces behind, and saw Johann and Giacomo move from the dining area. Freddy remained seated, now with his laptop open. Once he had found his way into the camera system last night he made detailed notes of the layout of the house and had a clear idea of where the staff would be. It was Johann and Giacomo's job to round them up, not too

257

difficult as both were well armed.

'I have eleven bedrooms here in total. Two of them are for me. I get so bored in just one all the time. All the bathrooms are Carrara marble and here, in my special room I have a Swarovski ceiling, similar to the *Burj*, but not as big you understand.'

'That's wonderful,' Christiana gushed and I love that mirror over your bed. I've always wanted to have one just like it.'

'It can provide a very different view on certain aspects of life,' he said. 'I like to use this room to watch television, I love home movies. Maybe we can make some together in the future, if your husband agrees.'

'Don't ask me,' I replied. 'I do as I'm told. Is your television big enough?'

'Aah, you noticed my two-hundred-and-nineteen-inch, wall TV. I was one of the first in Dubai to get one. Everything is seen in such magnified detail. Let me show you.'

The distraction worked. He didn't see Christiana remove the syringe from her pocket, remove the protective cover and plunge the needle deep into his neck.

'Sweet perverted dreams, you monster,' she said, losing her South American accent with ease and letting his body fall onto the bed.

'OK, leave him to me,' I said. Check the others have everything covered and have found what I was looking for. Be ready to leave in thirty minutes. I want him to be awake when I do this.'

She kissed me on the cheek and walked out.

I removed the plastic tags and tape from my briefcase, rolled him over, and joined his wrists behind his back.

'That'll hurt, when you wake up,' I told his unhearing ears.

Lint stuffed hard into his mouth and silver tape to hold it in place, as I had seen at the school in India. I positioned him so he was lying straight on the bed and on his back.

I replaced the tape, scissors and tags in my bag and removed the thin box.

I now had a choice to make. I wanted him to be awake when I made that choice.

He began to rouse after about ten minutes. I waited a few more as his disorientation passed into panic, before speaking.

'Mr. Deshmukh, welcome back to the world even though temporarily. I've been waiting a long time to meet you. Ever since I had to rescue Priya from your clutches.'

He appeared to sink into the grey flowered bed cover as realisation hit him.

'Yes that's right,' I told him; 'Now you realise who I am. You should not have got Rohtak to kidnap my father, making my mother and I believe he was dead. You shouldn't have paid for the rape and murder of so many innocent young people, just so you could gratify yourself with your two-hundred-and-nine-teen-inch television and equal-sized ceiling mirror. I am going to kill you, and the implement of your death is in this box. But which shall I pick? Should I use the *santoku* or the chef's knife?'

I sat beside him on the bed. He didn't smell as sweetly as before. I placed the box beside him, knowing he could see it clearly through the mirror above. I picked up the chef's knife first.

The black handle rested comfortably in my palm. Its broad, gently curved blade, perfectly designed for rocking motion chopping, spoke of the finest German quality. Forged from a single piece of *chromium-molybdenum-vanadium* steel, it had the slim sharpness of a razor.

I placed the knife back into its box. The fearful, inquisitiveness of Deshmukh's gaze met my eyes each time I looked at him.

I smiled as I turned my attention to the *santoku*, the Japanese cousin of the classic chef's knife.

'Very apt,' I said, out loud.

At about six inches, the blade was shorter than the other. The handle, similarly of African Blackwood, was equally comfortable. The blade, lined with elliptical indents, was flatter and not designed for rocking.

The manufacturer included all sorts of useful information on its bright, shiny surface. I thought it was time to share some of this with Deshmukh.

'Both these knives were manufactured in Solingen, Germany,' I said. ' Over two hundred years of tradition and skill have gone into their making. They're so proud of what they do, they give all kinds of very interesting information, right here.'

I pointed to the black writing on the blade. Deshmukh couldn't read it but I wanted him to know all about the implement which would end his paedophilic life. His eyes flickered.

'Do you know anything about stainless steel production Deshmukh?' I asked. 'Your blank expression is answer enough. It's a pity because now you won't understand the irony, at least not yet. I'll have to explain it to you. There is so much I could tell you about what makes this steel *stainless* and could talk for hours about chrome-depleted layers, passivation and oxidation processes, it's fascinating stuff, but that might be a bit too much for you to take in right now.'

It must have been ten seconds before he blinked, he had no

clue where I was going with this.

'It's enough for you to know that there are four main group-ings for Stainless Steel, all based on the mix of metals alloyed together in the production process. Scientists would talk about metallurgical phases and microscopic structures, but that's not really relevant. I hear that you are the owner of a water desal-ination plant, is that correct?'

He couldn't say anything, other than with his eyes and they were extremely informative. Confusion they shouted. Almost all of the water in Dubai comes from the desalination of sea water, it was a lucrative business.

'No, Deshmukh, I'm not changing the subject. I'm trying to explain. It's important to learn something new every day. Today the lesson is about steel. In your water treatment factory you undoubtedly use stainless steel vessels; these will certainly be austenitic stainless steel, a mixture of chromium, nickel and iron. Similar to the handrails on your very expensive glass stair-case. That's stainless-steel family member number one. Take out the nickel, add a little more chromium and you'll end up with family member number two, ferritic steel. You understand, I am over-simplifying things, to make it easier for you. I don't want to tax your brain too much. Are you following, so far?'

His eyes closed momentarily.

'Yes, Deshmukh, this is relevant to you. Your professionally designed shiny kitchen you were so proud to show us, will be predominantly ferritic stainless steel. So you see how relevant all of this is to your own world. Now, let's go back to your desali-nation plant. You now know that the vessels you use there are austenite, however the pipework connecting them is probably a third family member. I can't be certain as I've never been there but, your pipes are likely to be a marriage of austenitic and ferritic and known as Duplex Stainless Steel. So now you know how three of the four stainless steels impact on your life.'

Decision made, I put down the santoku and picked up the chef's knife.

'Let's move on to the potential impact of the last family member,' I said, moving further up the bed.

His eyes flicked between the knife and my face, a grunt emanated from behind the gagging tape.

'You see here on the blade? No, that un-desalinated water in your eyes is probably preventing you from focussing.'

Tap, tap, tap. A knock on the door. Without waiting for an answer, Johann walked in.

'We found them,' he said. 'A display cabinet in a hidden room behind the Cinema screen. Exactly where Freddy anticipated.'

'How many?'

'Sixty-five. All in individual containers, labelled with first names only. They're in a box outside, shall I bring them in?'

'Yes, and place them around the room, I want him to see them, as I do this.'

'Now to continue your education about stainless steel,' I said, returning my attention to the man lying on the now urine-soaked duvet.

His eyes were moving rapidly between me and watching Johann place small clear plastic containers around the room. Several he put on the wide wooden rail at the foot of the bed.

'I was about to tell you about the writing on the blade and how it's relevant to you, here today. There are some numbers and letters, X 50 Cr Mo V 15, to be exact. This is where irony enters your life. Those letters mean nothing to you, but they mean a lot to me. I have come a long way since you and Rohtak decided to take me on. Shitole is dead, along with a random teacher enrolled in your sick game. Superintendent Pawar Bhatt is also no longer with us, Rohtak is gone as have several of his bodyguards. Such a high body count, but this chapter in my life started in Bellagio. A small hotel room with your little Belgian child recruiter. Do you remember his name?'

Neither comprehension nor interest entered his eyes.

'His name was Martens, Peter Martens.'

Johann chuckled. 'Now I understand the conversation,' he said. 'That's the last of them, shall I leave you to be alone?'

'Yes, I won't be long.'

As Johann closed the door, I leaned over and pressed the blade just below Deshmukh's sternum. The angle needed to be correct. Too vertical, I might miss his heart. Thirty degrees I decided was about right.

'We are now, just about closing the circle,' I told him. 'Martens was the start and here we have, X 50 Cr Mo V 15 on a blade. Chromium, molybdenum and vanadium. Numbers twenty-four, forty-two and twenty-three in the periodic table. All smelted together to create the fourth member of the stainless-steel family. And here is the irony, Deshmukh, this knife is made of Martens-itic Stainless Steel, so Martens was the first to die, but his name is here on this blade, which is going to end yours. I don't normally like an audience but today is an exception.'

I pushed the blade firmly and deliberately into his heart. His struggle was limited, death virtually instantaneous.

'And so it ends. Almost,' I said, as I got up from the bed and joined the others downstairs.

'It's done,' I said; 'let's go.'

We had all been careful not to touch any surfaces with un-gloved hands, so there would be no fingerprint or other evidence that we had ever been here. The staff would only be able to give general descriptions and in any case, the evidence which Freddy was now displaying, on continuous loop, on every television in the house, would be enough to ensure very little publicity would attach to this particular death scene.

The last of us to board their plane would send a text message, from a once-only-use burner telephone, to a specific senior police officer. Freddy had discovered the name and personal telephone number, of this policeman, to be a *friend* of Deshmukh and a regular at his film showing parties. No time to stop flights or cause us to be detained.

With all of the staff, bound and secured in the wine cellar, we drove back to the hotel. Chiara had seen to the packing of the suitcases and check out. We needed to get to the airport and board several different flights to differing destinations.

Chiara, Freddy and Christiana took a flight to Milan. Johann flew to Rome. We would all meet up in Bellagio in a couple of days, but Giacomo and I had some unfinished business to attend to first.

EPILOGUE

FRANKFURTER ALLGEMEINE ZEITUNG :
ELTERN VON KIKI TOT AUFGEFUNDEN

(Kiki's parents found dead)

Yesterday, Police were called to the home of well-known children's lawyers Thomas Jachenholz and his wife where two bodies were found in an apparent murder suicide.

Frau Schneider died from asphyxiation and was discovered in a hidden room behind a wardrobe, her husband was hanging from a cord attached to a door.

Police sources say that a detailed suicide note was found, implicating the lawyers in the heavily publicised death of their adopted daughter, Kiki.

No other persons are being sought in relation to these deaths.'

As he finished reading aloud, Johann put the newspaper down on the table beside him.

'It's made the Times of India online,' said Freddy.

'What? About Kiki?'

'No.'

He began reading the report to us.

'Prominent Indian businessman found dead in gruesome scene, is the headline. It continues:

Durvish Deshmukh, philanthropist and leading member of the Dubai based Indian community, has been found murdered

265

*in his home in a scene which police have described as macabre.
Displayed around his deathbed were dozens of plastic receptacles,
each containing what appeared to be eyes and names of people
on them. Police are trying to discover to whom these belong. It is
thought that the killer or killers brought them with them...'*

'Enough,' I said. 'They obviously want to hide as much of
the truth as possible. At least Kiki and the others now have
justice.'

'Your guest has arrived,' Miguel, the house caretaker and
chef, said, appearing from the house.

A smiling Arjun walked from behind him. 'What a spectac-
ularly beautiful place this is.'

'Welcome to your new home, Arjun,' I said rising and giving
him a hug. 'Releasing Giacomo would not have been possible without your help. Please, come and put names to faces.
Giacomo, you know.'

'And this must be Chiara,' he replied. 'You are a very persuasive lady.'

'I do what I need to do, to continue our work. As Ricci
says, it would not have been possible without you. You have
demonstrated all the skills we need in our team. I'm thrilled
you agreed to join us.'

'I assume, Ricci, is your real name,' he laughed.

'Yes, I said 'and this is Christiana, Freddy and Johann – real
names!'

Arjun joined us. Chiara poured him a coffee and pushed a
plate of pastries towards him.'

'Have we really made any difference?' Freddy asked. 'Here's
another report in the Times of India.

10-YEAR-OLD RAPED BY EMPLOYER IN PUNE.

Raped repeatedly and traumatised a 10-year-old victim was unable to coherently tell police officers the details of the horror she had been submitted to and no headway could be made in the investigation.

She could not even remember her proper name. Concerned for her welfare, police admitted her to hospital. Doctors reported her condition was serious and stated her injuries were consistent with her being raped repeatedly and assaulted with extreme brutality.

Breakthrough finally came when a 45-year-old man walked into the police station to lodge a missing person complaint about a runaway employee. His description of the missing girl fitted the complainant exactly and police were soon able to put two and two together and the accused was arrested.'"

'Ten years old and working?' Chiara asked.

'That's India for you,' Arjun replied. 'The problem is too big to be solved in less than a generation. India must come to terms with the reality of its treatment of women and children.

'People like Chirag, Sushma and her friends are starting to try and bring about political change, but it needs more than just a willingness to change. It needs better education and the change will come through the young, like Priya, Ganesh and the others. As their generation and their children come to rule India, things will improve. I doubt dramatic change will happen in my lifetime.

'I love my country and it has many positive aspects, but its problems are deep rooted and complex.'

The sun was high in the cloudless azure sky. The azaleas and rhododendron were in full bloom and their scent filled the air.

My family and dearest friends were gathered together, around the large table, in Bellagio, for the first time since my University days. We hadn't known of secret organisations then, we were just young students bound together by love and companionship. Now, joined by Arjun, we were The Atenisti.

'Time for Chiara and me to take a break,' Giacomo said, pouring more *Lugana* white wine into our glasses. 'We're going to the villa in Luxor for a while.'

'How long?' I asked.

'Six months, a year? Who knows? We have no plans. The organisation is safe in your hands, the four musketeers you used to call yourselves. Now you can continue the good fight, together with the help of our newest recruit.'

'*Alle für einen,*' said Freddy

'*Und einer für Alle,*' we responded in unison.

'We'll have to teach Arjun to speak German,' I said.

'Only if you learn to speak Hindi,' he replied. 'Anyway, I always preferred the Scarlet Pimpernel to the Musketeers.'

Christiana squeezed my hand. We were home.

The phone rang in the office. Giacomo went to answer.

'Diamond Insurance Services,' he said, then listened.

THE END

AUTHOR'S NOTES

This novel has not been easy to write. I don't mean the putting of words onto paper, which is always difficult, but researching the subject matter has been harrowing.

When I was living in India, I was horrified by the almost daily reports in the *Times of India* and *The Hindustan Times*, of offences of rape and murder committed throughout India against boys, girls and women. In the 21st Century, it seems that some communities still believe that rape is a justifiable punishment for women who may, or may not, have committed even minor transgressions against local norms or traditions. Even the relationship between a Hindu girl and a Muslim boy can lead to this.

In January 2022 newspapers throughout the world reported the story of a young wife and mother, in Delhi, who rejected the sexual advances of a teenage boy. He subsequently committed suicide, for which her rejection was blamed. This led to her rape by 4 of his relatives as a punishment. She was then dragged around the community for several hours, with her hair cut and covered in soot. This event was read by millions around the world.

How can this happen in today's India?

Yet it, and many similar stories, occur every day. In 2019 the Supreme Court in India in a suo moto action noted that between January 1 and June 30 that year, 24,212 First Information Reports (FIRs) were registered by police across

India on incidents of child rape. That amounts to over 120 reported cases per day or 5 PER HOUR! As in most, if not all, countries the number of reported crimes is perhaps just the tip of the iceberg and in reality the true number is probably much higher.

Of course, atrocities against women and children take place everywhere in the world, but in India the numbers are extraordinary.

Also in 2022, a politician, in India, stated in a Council meeting '...If rape is inevitable, you should lie back and enjoy it...' This was greeted with laughter in the Council Chamber. This kind of attitude should not be permitted in a civilised society.

ACKNOWLEDGEMENTS

Novel writing is often described as being a lonely profession. It's true that many hours are spent poring over books, newspapers and a computer, locked away from loved ones and friends. But no book is ever published without enormous support from fellow writers and friends.

The same is true of this novel and there are many people I wish to thank:

James Essinger and Zoe Verner from The Conrad Press. Your help has been invaluable.

The KBOers, which little group includes a number of terrific writers both published and not, for their encouragement, constructive (and other!) criticism and support. Remember what doesn't kill us makes us stronger.

Crime author Adam Peacock and all at the South Shields Fiction Writers' Group.

British Airways for taking me to the places I needed to go to complete my research, and providing a comfortable seat on long haul flights where many a scene or chapter was drafted.

My old school friends from St. Mary's, Lugwardine, Hereford. Fifty years have not diminished the friendship and humour of this fabulous group.

Friends from my days at Leicester University, still drinking and laughing together.

Finally, and above all, my wife, Alison, proof reader par excellence, patient editor and tough critic. Without her this book would not have been possible. Any errors which remain are entirely my own and will be where I have ignored her advice.

Aidan K. Morrissey June 2022